W9-CLX-403

# ANABASIS

A NOVEL BY

# Ellen Gilchrist

# ANABASIS

## A JOURNEY TO THE INTERIOR

UNIVERSITY PRESS OF MISSISSIPPI JACKSON

By Ellen Gilchrist

*In the Land of Dreamy Dreams*

*The Annunciation*

*Victory Over Japan*

*Drunk With Love*

*Falling Through Space*

*The Anna Papers*

*Light Can Be Both Wave and Particle*

*I Cannot Get You Close Enough*

*Net of Jewels*

*Star Carbon*

*Anabasis*



Manufactured in the United States of America

97 96 95 94 4 3 2 1

CIP data appear on page 298.

FOR RITA

This is not a book of history. It is an attempt to tell a story I made up when I was a child. My mother was a student of the classics and filled my head with tales of Ancient Greece, a world where babies were sometimes thrown away and where only some of the people learned to read. This bothered me greatly, as I was already much in love with books, and I began to make up a story about a girl who was raised by a wise man who taught her how to read. Later, the girl would grow up and save one of the babies.

This book begins where my childhood fantasy always began. The girl is sitting beside a marble column copying out a lesson on a wax tablet. The brilliant Greek light is shining over the shoulder of her short white garment. She is very intent on her work.

# PART I

# Auria

*Of Auria, and of Philokrates, who had known Anaxagoras of Clazomenae, who had known Anaximander, who had mapped the world*

# Chapter I

Four hundred and thirty-one years before the birth of Christ a girl named Auria was bending over a wax tablet copying out a lesson. She was in a sunny courtyard, in a villa near Thisbe on the road to Delphi.

The villa was on a bluff overlooking the Gulf of Corinth and was a famous trading post known all over the Aegean for its honey cakes and dyes of periwinkle and scarlet and the brilliant obsidian that came from its nearby quarries. Its hospitality was famous and traders went out of their way to take the road from Athens to Delphi or tie up their ships in the small uncertain harbor, dreaming of the fine meals and clear wines of the villa of Meldrus Helonai.

There was even a healer there, an old man who had been at Epidaurus. His name was Philokrates and he had knowledge of herbs and could repair broken bones by binding them in linen casts and in clay. The jealous whispered that the distinction of Meldrus's blue dyes was due to the old man's knowledge of alchemy for no one could duplicate them although they picked indigo from the same fields.

On this sunny morning, late in the winter of 431 B.C., Philokrates was in the courtyard watching Auria copy out her lessons. She was his apprentice, a slave who had been purchased in Thrace and given to him to live in his rooms and wait upon him.

They had been together nine years now. He had taught her his knowledge of herbs and he had done a more dangerous thing. He had taught her to read and write and what he knew of astronomy and mathematics. This morning's lesson was geometry. It was difficult for her and she bent over the tablet with a fierceness that pleased the old man although he pretended to scold her for it. He watched her from a sort of dream for he was very old now and was tired, even in the mornings. It was taking all his skill to keep himself alive but he was managing it for there was much more to teach her if she was to be safe when he was gone.



He had grown meticulously careful with his diet, and at night, when she imagined he slept, he practiced the breathing techniques he had learned when he traveled in the east.

Auria put the wax tablet aside, took up one made of clay, dipped it into a crater of water and began copying her work, not waiting for the clay to soften properly.

"Geometry is not a bowl of dough to be kneaded," the old man said. "Be patient."

"But this afternoon we are going to the woods for herbs and then the traders will be here from Macedon and by the time I start again I'll forget the theorems and have to start all over." She straightened her back and lifted the stylus from the clay. "I'm tired of triangles. I want to copy some more of the book of Solon."

"Don't make enemies of things you don't understand," he said. "The triangles won't dig through the walls at night and rob you. All they want is a little time. Well, come along, finish your lesson and I'll show you the new parchment."

She bent over the tablet again. He could smell the fresh smell of her body in the warm sun. Since winter he had noticed her breasts beginning and her hips widening which had been as thin as a boy's in the fall. The chiton barely came to her knees.

Soon they would come for her. Sooner or later. Still, for now Meldrus was busy with preparations for the caravan bringing goods from across the gulf. He would be too busy to notice a young girl for a while. Philokrates watched her as she worked, the long muscles of her back moving like a bird's wing. He had been a chief votary at the temple of Asclepius and he knew the connections of the muscles, had seen the human body dissected and traced the muscles with his hands, had felt the heart and spine and examined the brain.



"There is a man on Kos who holds we came from the sea like fish," he said. "I have been thinking a good deal of that lately."

"Is that the new book you have to show me? I saw you hiding it in your room. I thought it must be about the stars."

"It is a drawing of the world. It came from Corinth yesterday with the messenger. When you finish your lesson I will let you examine it."

"I want to see it now. Phoebe might eat it before I finish. Remember last year when she ate the letter from Diokou. . . ." But she was not allowed to finish the sentence. The old man had hurried into his rooms. Auria followed him and there was the little nanny goat backed into a corner with a piece of parchment moving up and down in her mouth. Philokrates stood by the bed shaking out what was left.

"She's eaten half of Persia," he said. "Oh, damn it all to the gates of Laurium. Why does this goat plague my old age. Well, damn it all, let's see about this drawing." He stood up, very straight and tall. From the back he hardly seemed to be an old man at all. He held the parchment up to the light from the window. "Oh, see here, this island isn't in the right place. It's beside Zacynthos. And look where he has put Zacynthos! This won't do at all. Not at all. See here, Auria, look what this madman in Corinth calls a drawing of the world. No wonder the caravan is late getting here. With such drawings being made it's a wonder anyone gets anywhere at all. I must take this to Meldrus at once. I could draw a better world out of my dreams!"



"I want to look at it anyway," she said. "Please let me look at it."

He laid the parchment down on the bed and began to show her the places he had traveled when he was young. "And all of this is water, so vast you can not imagine it. There is a man on Miletus who says all things are made of water." He looked up from the map with the crazed look he wore when he was entertaining an idea. "Mist, clouds, rain, oceans, rivers, springs. 'But what of the mountains?' I asked him. They are concentrated water, he told me. I was young then. So all one winter I pounded stones with a pestle trying to make them give up their water. Not one drop could I unleash. Well, enough of this drawing with the islands in the wrong places. Fetch our morning bread if Kefallinia has finished the baking. We will eat, then I will take this to Meldrus. I told him to send for one of Karia's, from Tegea, who does them right." Philokrates was rolling the parchment between his hands. "There was another man, also of Kos, who said all things are made of fire. I could not tell you all I have thought of that. Well, go on. Fetch our bread while I milk this cursed map-eating goat. I do not know what power has entangled my life with this creature's, or for what oracular ungodly purpose." He reached down and took Phoebe's hard white skull between his hands, muttering curses to the gods he disavowed, looking into the goat's soft blue eyes for the lost secrets of his destiny.

~

It was a measure of Philokrates' power that he was allowed to keep the goat in his rooms and not tethered in the byre or loose in the fields. A boy brought fresh hay for it each morning, and if anyone complained of the smell, Philokrates pretended he was divining omens from its feces. The truth was he loved goats and always kept them near him. He was especially fond of this one and was given to reading aloud to it whenever he came upon something he thought might be useful to a goat's mind. He had read it Solon's laws and a funeral oration from Homer and some poems of Mimnermus and some he had written himself when he was young.



The other inhabitant of the rooms was a dog Philokrates had bred from a sheep dog and one of the thin intense dogs of the Persians. His name was Metis and he went along for protection when Auria and Philokrates went to the woods for herbs. Wild boar and wolves still roamed the plane forests that lay between the villa and the mountains.

It had been more than a year since they had gone to the forest. Two festivals of winter and three full moons had passed since they had gone to the deep woods searching for lionsroot and the small white mushrooms whose crowns are said to relieve pain.

On the last trip they had slept in one of the high caves, whose entrance could be seen from the woods below, and there, in the back, on an altar of stones, Auria had found the remains of the baby. It was a baby that had been taken from the villa a week before. It had been born to a slave girl named Doris. The wailing of the girl had gone on for days. Everyone had known of it.

Auria found the little bones and she was sick at the sight of it. Nothing Philokrates said could make it better for her.

"It is not our doing," he said. "It has nothing to do with us."

"It has to do with me," she said. "For I have seen it." When they returned from the trip she was pensive and withdrawn for days. Since then they had ventured no further than the stream which bordered Meldrus's land, for Philokrates' back ached when he slept on the ground and his bowels would not move in the morning without warm milk and much coaxing.

# Chapter II

In the kitchen Kefallinia gave Auria the loaves. The big room where the food was prepared was full of activity and the smell of fresh bread. In the villa it was said that the smell of Kefallinia's bread could raise the dead. The caravan from Macedon would be the first of the season and pots and clay boards that hadn't been used all winter were being searched for and found and inspected for leaks and dusted off and put into service. Kefallinia's arms were covered with flour. She was bustling about with an ecstatic expression on her face, tying new aprons on the kitchen slaves, pulling the long clay pans of travel cakes in and out of the oven. Kefallinia's travel cakes were famous all over the Aegean, thick and rich with dark honey from the bottom of the comb, chewy with linen leaves and nuts and raisins and wild cherry bark fermented in wine.

The long flat loaves of morning bread were stacked up on a tray. Auria put two of them under her arm and filled a cylix with honey. "When are they coming?" she asked. "When will they arrive?"

"Sometime today. The mistress is in bed, of course, as always when we need her. And Meldrus sent Thisson to meet them so it's all left to me. Tell Philokrates to come speak to me about the customs of these Persians. I could be serving their sacred animals for all anyone has told me. Don't forget, Auria. Tell him to stop by this morning. I can't run things around here all alone although you'd never know it to watch me." She looked into the cylix. "How much honey can an old man eat? It's enough he can't come to meals on time like everyone else. . . ." Auria gave her a quick kiss on the floury cheek and attempted an escape, backing through a door licking honey from her fingers.

There were eighteen slaves at the villa and five free metics who were supposed to oversee them, but only Kefallinia and Philokrates and Thisson were capable of giving an order and seeing that it was carried out. Meldrus ran the business, making deals, spending hours at his books, going off on trips for supplies. His wife, Eleuria, stayed in her rooms drinking wine, even in the morning, and giving birth every few years to another of the small, unhappy girls who played in the courtyard waiting for someone to love or notice them. There had been four of them. Another was on the way and the slaves whispered among themselves about the blonde lute player from Samos who had spent the summer in Eleuria's quarters, then disappeared as mysteriously as he had come.

Kefallinia caught up with Auria at the door to the courtyard. "Don't forget you're expected to serve at the banquet tonight. You be on time, Auria. And wash and tie down that hair. We don't want these strangers thinking we're barbarians."

"I'll be here," Auria said. "But now I must get back. We're going for indigo this afternoon. For the blue dyes. Is it true the traders are bringing silk? Arditos said they are bringing silk."

"So I have heard. And a machine for measuring time. But that's all Thisson's talk. He'll say anything."

"I really must go," Auria said. "He's in a bad mood. The goat ate his new book."

~

"A backache, the sun at dawn, a song, a backache song at dawn," Philokrates was singing to himself as he milked, singing and milking and chewing the last of the lionsroot.



"What were you singing?" Auria said, coming in, laying out the things on a small triangular table called a trapeza. "What was your song?"

"About a heron I saw on the shore, or a singing bird I dreamed of in a winter tree. No, perhaps it was about this bread. I'll say one thing for Meldrus. He feeds us well. This bread is half-wheaten. Where has Kefallinia been hiding this flour all winter?" He broke off a piece of the round flat loaf, dipped it in honey, then took it into his mouth, watching her.

Shining, he thought. She is a shining thing. "To tell the truth I was singing about a gold flower that grows so high up in the mountains only a few men have ever seen it. It grows in the rocks with roots like a hundred spiders. If you pick it, it withers in a moment and loses its color. I have forgotten its name. It's sacred to Artemis, for those who believe such things."

Auria went over and put her hands on his shoulders, which were wide and straight and as heavily muscled as a young man's. She drew strength from him with her fingers, then slid her hands down his arms until they met his hands in a circle. It was a ceremony he had taught her. A ceremony for power and for healing. "When I am gone you will pass this on to another," he said.

"You will never be gone," she said. "You will live forever, like the old shepherds they sing of. Besides, I would not let you go. I, Auria, forbid it."

"Well, in case your powers should not be equal to the ignorance of nature, do as I say." He pulled his hands away and went back to his bread. But she was thinking of it now and would not leave it.

"How will I know who it should be?" she said. "How would I recognize him?"

"You will know. It will come to you like a memory, like all true knowledge comes, all at once, in light, without question. We look up one day and there it is. What we needed to know. Well, enough of this talk. Pour the milk. I wish to be in the woods before the sun rises higher. If that dog can be found. If he hasn't run off without us."

They took an old path down into the north pasture where some years before Philokrates had coaxed a patch of lionsroot to grow in a stand of linden trees. He was always hoping it might have come back up. Lionsroot grew in several places on the northern scarp of the mountain, a day's walk to the west, but he trusted no one at the villa enough to send them for it and he refused to let Auria go alone.

"In Asia it is worth more than gold," he said. "If they knew how it springs up in our mountains, they would come in their ships to plunder us. So I try to keep it a secret. Look at this, Auria. What is that, there in that root? Bring it here. It might be potentilla. Oh, yes, gather all of that. Be careful. Don't bruise the plant. Oh, I am very fond of potentilla. I think it's much underrated as a treatment for coughs. Not as dramatic as some others, but it does less damage to the throat. Well, let's see what the earth has thrown up around here. Then we'll go for eupatoria.

I meant to send Thisson out for it last week. It's quite plentiful now, but not for long."

Auria walked along beside him, daydreaming about the silk that was coming, dreaming of herself in a silk cloak dyed scarlet or purple or blue with a purple lining.

It was a beautiful day, the light reflecting the sea below the cliffs, the air so clear it was like something you could touch or drink or gather. Auria reached up her hand to touch the light, imagining it was a cloak she would wear to meet a great warrior.



"Pay attention," Philokrates said. "It's the best time of year to learn the lichens. Later the other plants will hide them. This little beauty here, also found in the roots of oaks, induces sleep. Always be careful to keep the doses small or your patient will begin to crave it. Candermoss, the old ones called it. Sometimes a spotted mushroom grows on it in late spring. A mushroom that produces visions. Well, never mind about that.

"See how green this is on the underside. That's how you recognize it. Take bearings of this, Auria, in case I need to send for it."

"What sort of visions?"

"Never mind about that. I'm sorry I brought that up. Now, examine this lichen. See how the parts mesh and form a network. I want you to be able to draw that for me tomorrow. See how the pores hook into each other. Ah, it's a beauty, isn't it?"

"It induces sleep?"

"And cures bronchitis. I wish I'd known where to find this when Alcathous was so bad a while ago. I could have used this. Well, I've gotten lazy. I don't get out enough."

"Shall I cross the bridge and pick white vine for you? You don't have any left in the jars. I know where it is."

"Take Metis then. And don't stay long. I'll rest here while you're gone and study these lichens. Be watching out for valerian. I need valerian for Clio." As soon as she left he sat down in a bank of ivy and fell promptly to sleep. I never used to sleep, he thought as he drowsed off. Who would believe I would sleep in the afternoon?

Auria left him and with Metis beside her went over the creek and into the woods to a place where wild grapes and white vine grew tangled together on a rise. White vine, "three leaves," as the ancients called it, a poison so deadly to sheep that men dig it out wherever it grows. Philokrates boiled it and used it as an expectorant for coughs and pneumonia. "There is nothing a wise man fears," he had told her. "Although some plants and animals require more care than others."

The caravan arrived while they were coming home from the fields. As they came up over the hill they saw the robes of the drivers blowing in the wind. The animals looked sorefooted and thin. The gate was open and a shaggy white mule was being dragged through it by a lead boy. From the courtyard they could hear the sounds of the traders beginning to unpack, laying out their wares to dry in the sun.

Meldrus's villa was built in two parts. Two rectangular courtyards with covered walkways connected a labyrinth of rooms. The courtyards were divided by a wall of sundried brick with an arched doorway and a heavy wooden door. The whole compound was surrounded on three sides by a stone wall and on the fourth by a bluff overlooking the sea.

Meldrus was given to hysterical fits of raising the outer walls. Rumors of war and rebellion came in with every caravan and each new report threw him deeper into gloom. The richer he became the more certain he was that at any moment it would all be snatched away. In his dreams hordes of wild bearded men appeared and danced through his rooms breaking storage pots with their swords. He would wake from such dreams choking with fear and Philokrates would be called to come with elaia leaves to brew him a tea of tranquility.



Of all his metics Meldrus trusted only Philokrates. As for the rest of his staff he was always hiring and firing them, always buying and selling his slaves, even some of Greek birth, although the practice had been unlawful for years.

The caravan that was arriving now was led by an old associate of Meldrus's from the days when he was engaged in the slave trade in Thrace. The visitor's name was Polymion. Meldrus had been looking forward all winter to trading with him, knowing that Polymion was off somewhere doing the same, buying this and that with an eye for what he would find irresistible.

It would be a good week. Meldrus planned to soften up his old partner with a lavish feast, leaving him hung over and vulnerable. He had customers waiting for Polymion's silk, in Thisbe and Doris and as far away as Delphi. Even Philokrates was interested in silk and had asked to be granted an audience to ask about its manufacture and inquire whether healers in the east had tried using it to sew up wounds in surgery.

Auria and Philokrates were greeted as they came up the hill by the Thracians who were working on the wall that year, a pair of slaves so alike they were taken for twins. They wore tatoos on their faces and down the sides of their arms. They were hard workers and worked from sunup to sundown even on the coldest days, moving stones from the neighboring hills or the creek bed, adding them to the wall with a mortar of sand and limestone. They laughed and joked with each other as they worked, singing the deep staccato work songs of their land. Auria loved to listen to them talk. It was a language with so many vowels that the men seemed to be voicing endearments even when they asked each other to move a stone. The one who talked the most had a sun tatooed on the side of his face. The quieter one had a snake going up his neck, with its tongue ending beside his eye.

"Why do they carve and paint on themselves?" she asked Philokrates.

"They believe it makes them beautiful," he said. "Whatever a man can be led to believe he will act upon."

"How will I know if what I believe is true?"

"Some say you can not know. I say it is like the smell of Kefallinia's bread. Or the air above the sea on a bright day. Or, perhaps, more like an order, a command. So I believe, but there are many who argue with me. There are men who make good argument that we are here by chance and have no cause or purpose. Others believe we are moved by a hundred jealous gods for their amusement. I have held all these beliefs and more. Now I think we are here to listen. To see what each day brings."

The Thracians greeted them from the wall with news of the caravan. "Polymion came in a cart pulled by horses," they said. "And they have brought a machine for measuring time. It is made of sand and you can see through it but we have not seen it with our own eyes yet."

"Come with us," Auria said. "Let's go and look. Can't you stop your work?"

"The master says Corinth has allied with Sparta against Athens. We will be caught in the middle of three lions. The wall must keep growing. Tomorrow we are to have helpers. This Polymion brings news that makes work for everyone."

"Couldn't you stop for a while?"

"Oh, no, he would be angry."



Auria turned her back on them. It bothered her to be reminded that they were slaves. It bothered her to remember that she was a slave, that in Meldrus's desk was a parchment saying where she had been purchased and for how much and what she had been named. It was a different name from the one Philokrates had given her, that she was called by. Tissapher, the parchment said. It meant uncouth, uncivilized, untamed. Even my name is not my own, she thought, wishing she never had to look at the Thracians and their tatoos. Wishing her hair was blonde and her eyes blue.

Philokrates went off to see about the silk and Auria went to the cistern behind the women's quarters to wash herself. On this side of the villa the rooms were covered by pitched roofs that allowed rainwater to be collected in cisterns for washing and bathing. The walls there were brick, covered with a plaster of colored lime, pale pink and very pretty. There was even a painted mural on one wall, from a time when Eleuria had been interested in making the villa beautiful. It was a procession of boys and girls in long chitons carrying gifts to a feast.

On a second story were the women's quarters, reached by a flight of wooden stairs. Eleuria leaned out the window, watching Auria as she bathed. "Are you feeling better?" Auria called up. "Kefallinia said you were confined to bed."

"I'm better than I was yesterday. Although the size of two cows. My time will be here soon, thanks to Athena."

"This time it will be a son," Auria said. "This time you will have joy."

"We'll see," Eleuria said. She smiled down at the girl, taking a long drink of the cup she was holding. She had only been drinking for an hour and was still in a good mood. "They're having the feast tonight? Are you serving?"

"Oh, yes," Auria said. "I promised Kefallinia. I'll go over as soon as I dress. They haven't started, have they?"

"Then come up here and let us give you a better chiton. You can't go around dressed like a goatboy with company here. Come along. Let's see what we can find for you." Auria went up the stairs and Eleuria opened some trunks and pulled out several garments, then settled on a long white chiton with yellow bands around the hem. It was a soft new wool, very clean and light, and Eleuria fastened it at the shoulder with a pin made in the likeness of two butterflies. She was just drunk enough to be expansive and was having a good time bestowing gifts on the little bright-eyed slave.

Later she mentioned the girl to Meldrus. "Philokrates would be angry if I did that without speaking to him first," Meldrus said. "He thinks she belongs to him. You know how irritable he gets lately."

"What a coward you are. You even fear that old magician. He looks down on you because you are of mixed blood. Anyone can see him sneer at you. And he's not the only one around here that can make potions. Alcamena makes them twice as good. I wouldn't drink those nasty things he cooks up. Besides, the girl belongs to you. It would be a good move with Polymion to give him a virgin. The gods know there aren't many to be found anymore, in the hills or the cities. Well, do as you will. I have other worries."

"Do you think it will come this week?"

"Who knows? My back's been aching for days. It's a big one. I don't look forward to bringing it out. Still, I hope it waits until the caravan leaves."



Meldrus turned away. He did not like to think about the baby that was coming. Which everyone knew could not be his. But he was a practical man. He had seen no sense in killing her. Her dowry was land that bordered his land. He stared at her fat, nervous hands, caught between disinterest and a kind of pity. "Your cousin, Clarius, has been seen in Corinth and in Athens. Polymion says he has heard it everywhere."

"Nonsense. Clarius is dead. Why do you plague me with these rumors?"

"I thought you would be glad to hear it. You always defended him."

"Anyone that knew him would defend him. He is, he was an unusual man. Even as a boy he was, so bright, so much stronger and more beautiful than the rest. If you had known him you would have defended him. I don't know how anyone could take his life no matter what he did."

"I would not defend anyone that started a riot anywhere, much less in their own father's household. It's ideas like that which are weakening the Greek spirit everywhere. Only the Spartans seem to have ideals anymore. I heard that in Athens the impious laugh on the streets. . . ."

"Where is he said to have been seen?"

"They say he was in hiding in the mountains. And now is in the cities seeking followers. Many are former slaves. Some say he is on Cithaeron with the wildwoman Penelaiaa, and the followers of Leucippius. I can't believe the authorities just let insurrection go on and on."

"Imathei went to the burial. She saw him go up in flames."

"Have it your way. I am only telling what I heard." He turned away



and made as if to leave. They were speaking of Eleuria's cousin, Clarius, who had led a rebellion of his father's slaves some six years before. When he was caught his father was supposed to have had him put to death. Now the father was dead and they were saying it had all been a ruse to save him from justice.

"What about the girl, Auria?" Eleuria said. "Will you take my advice on that or not?"

"I'll see," he answered. *The little black-haired Thracian,* he was thinking as he left. *The one with the sharp tongue. Well, I have no use for that myself. It's not the sort of thing that could excite me.*

The next afternoon he went for her. She was alone in the rooms. Philokrates was off talking to a yellow-skinned woman who had come with the caravan. She had come from the land of silk and he was questioning her concerning the silkworms, how the thread was gathered and spun. He had been taking a piece apart all day, examining the threads, thinking he might import some of the worms and grow them in his rooms.

When Meldrus came to the door Auria was trying on the new chiton, fastening and unfastening the pin. She was parading around the room, talking to Metis, telling him what a hit she had been at the feast the night before. "Alcamena said the women paint their hair for feasts in Athens now. I might do that. What do you think I should look like with painted hair?" She picked up Philokrates' steel-bladed knife and cut a few pieces from the front of her hair, wishing she had a mirror of polished brass, like the one in Eleuria's rooms.

Then Meldrus was there. He had spent the morning trading her to Polymion. He had traded her for three clay coins from Tenedos, stamped with the head of a goat and said to leach poisons from the blood. Also, a bolt of woolen cloth from Cyllene, very coarse and heavy. 
"Three antidotes and a whole bolt of cloth for one night," Polymion said. "You Greeks deserve your names."

"She can read and write. Her hands are quick and clever."

"Then bring her on. If she pleases me I will keep her several days."

"And if not?"

"Then you give back half the wool." They drank wine to the bargain and Meldrus went off to fetch the girl.

"I wish you to entertain Polymion for me," he said, taking Auria's arm. "I may be able to use you as an interpreter. They say you are clever with languages." Metis followed them to the door. His ears were standing up. He was making a sound in his throat. Auria reached down and petted him.

"You should wait on Philokrates for that," she said. "I will disgrace you with my small knowledge. Last night I couldn't understand half of what was spoken."

"Polymion wishes to talk with you. Well, come along. And tell that dog to stay there. What a nasty-looking creature. I don't know why Philokrates keeps it in his rooms."

Auria shut the dog into the room and went along with Meldrus. She barely knew him although she belonged to him. She had worked in the women's quarters when they were short-handed but if she thought of Meldrus at all she thought of him bending over a ledger, looking irritable and worried. Now she went along with him, moving her shoulders from side to side as she did when she was excited. It was a walk that made Philokrates think of her in his mind as "a little bear."

In the walkway they passed the Thracians, who were on their way to supper in the kitchen. Auria waved. They watched as she went with Meldrus through the gate between the courtyards. They looked into each other's eyes. Then sighed and looked away. There was nothing they could do. And they loved the little girl with her bright wild eyes.



She was taken to a chamber with painted walls and rugs covering the floor. She stood in the doorway looking around. In a corner incense burned in a bronze crater. The shutters were closed although it was a warm evening. The incense filled the room with its acrid smell. A guard wearing a cloak of chamois stood by the door. Polymion sat in the middle of the rugs eating from a platter of cakes. He seemed smaller than he had the night before. Darker and more foreign. Auria shivered. This is the wrong place, she thought. I should not have come here. Her mind filled with a memory. Another room. Strange men. And a face she had not thought of in many years. It was her mother's face.

She drew in her breath, letting it out in long slow exhalations as Philokrates had taught her to do. She looked down at Polymion. His face was loose and soft, coarse and wide. Like an old woman's, Auria thought. He is only an old woman. She looked at Meldrus but he would not meet her eye. "Do as Polymion says," Meldrus was saying, "and no harm will come to you. He has decided to favor you with his love. What a fortunate girl you are that he has noticed you. If you please him perhaps he will take you to see the world." Meldrus was backing out of the room as he spoke. The guard let him out through the door, then closed it and stood before it. He was a tall man with a face so impassive it hardly seemed to be a face at all.

Auria let her breath go in and out very slowly. I am a slave, she was thinking. Now I will be treated like a slave.

She looked at the guard, then down at Polymion. The smell of incense was everywhere, acrid, bitter, unclean. "What do you want of me?" she said. "Why am I brought here?"



Outside in the courtyard she could hear the voices of the drivers talking among themselves. Then the guard knelt behind her and tied her hands together and she began to scream. She screamed as loud as she could scream, sound coming from deep inside, a wild screaming such as Auria had never heard, much less known she was capable of making. From the other courtyard Metis began to answer her, his keening rising to the skies like a lute with a hundred strings. Then Polymion undid the pin and took the yellow-bordered chiton from her shoulders and it began.

She learned from him then that what men give to a woman is blood and the taste of blood and of terror. A man comes into a woman like fire in a dry field, taking and burning. A man takes pleasure of a woman's body and returns darkness and sorrow, pain and fear, bitterness and burning.

When he was through with her he ate and drank again, tearing the meat apart with his hands, offering pieces to her as though she were his companion. As if violating and terrifying were no different from the offering of meat and bread, as if one act were no different or more important than another.

Philokrates heard Metis howling from the room where he was attempting a conversation with the yellow-skinned woman, who had turned out to know nothing of silk and kept trying to sell him the boots she was wearing. When he heard the dog wailing he excused himself and hurried to his rooms but by the time he understood what had happened it was too late to intervene.



At dawn the guard opened the door and allowed her to leave. Polymion was asleep, rolled up in his rugs. The memory was all over her, and the smell of incense burning and the smell of his body and the guard's blank eyes. The taste and smell of the things that had been done to her covered her like a caul. She hurried out of the rooms and down the cloister, taking the fresh air in and out in quick furious gasps. Rage was beginning to replace the cold unconsciousness of fear. I will have revenge for that night, she swore to herself. I will return that evil. Before my life is out I will cut his body into a hundred pieces and those eyes that watched will lie in my hand like grapes for the press.

Philokrates was waiting for her in the second courtyard, sitting with his shoulders slumped over by the round outdoor hearth. Metis was beside him. They leaped up when they saw her come through the gate. Philokrates took her into his arms and Metis jumped all around, licking her legs and feet.

"My hands will fall off," she said. "If I can not kill him I will lose my fingers. My fingers will not stay on my hands, or my arms on my body. And Meldrus too. Why did he allow that to be done to me? What have I done but be a good servant all my life? How will I live after this? I will not live. Now I can not live. . . ."

"Do not speak their names. Come, Kefallinia and Aeo are waiting for you. We have waited all night for you." Then he took her into his rooms and Kefallinia was there and Little Aeo and they bathed her with warm water and massaged her body with oil. Kefallinia's strong hands rubbed the sweet-smelling oil of valerian into her hands and arms and feet, and Philokrates' own hands followed the cruel ones into the soft places between her legs and onto her stomach and breasts and when he saw the bite marks his hands shook and he could feel his old heart tighten within his chest, clenching and unclenching like a fist. "Sleep," he said out loud. "Sleep, little song. Nothing will happen to you again. It will not happen again." She closed her eyes. All around her and above her in the room she could hear them breathing, Kefallinia's long smooth breaths and the quick determined ones of the old man, and Little Aeo sighing as he came in and out bringing pans of warm water and poultices made of the bruised leaves of the yellow lutea.



When she slept Philokrates left her with Kefallinia and went to Meldrus in a rage. "She is my apprentice," he began quietly, thinking he could contain it, reminding himself that the only important thing was her safety. "She was given to me for that purpose. I have spent nine years training her to take my place, when I am gone. I will not always be here, Meldrus. Who will keep you alive when I am gone? When your breath stops who will know where to find the white vine or how to mix it so that it does not poison?" He paused.

"I will not have her used as a woman. I thought we had discussed that. I thought you understood. I can not believe you did this without consulting me. That barbarian, Polymion, has beaten and terrified her as if she were a common slave. I tell you, Meldrus, you have lost your mind to treat me this way. Am I not your ally ever since we came across that gulf together and have I ever in any way betrayed you. . . ." He was standing up and pacing around now, his voice and presence filling the room. Meldrus had not seen him put on such a show in years.

"It was poorly conceived. I had no idea he would use her harshly. I couldn't find you. You were off somewhere."

"What if I die?" Philokrates was saying. "Who will heal you then of



your tremors? Do you think skills such as mine are to be had for the asking? Do you think anyone will come and live in this outpost to treat your snivels? I tell you, Meldrus, I can't forgive this. . . ."

"It won't hurt the girl to know what life is. Well, I'm sorry if it upsets you so. There is trouble from one end of the Aegean to the other. It will upset trade for years. We must have allies. Polymion can get through. He'll be coming through when the rest of them are dead. I've known him. . . ."

"She is my eyes and ears. She is my hands. How dare you use her so! When you weaken her you weaken me. I am not well, Meldrus. I have pain many nights."

"Calm down, old friend. I can't believe you're going on like this over that insolent little creature. Polymion was displeased with her. He made me give back half the wool."

"Half the wool!!! Half the god-cursed wool!!! You speak to me of wool!"

"All right. All right. What do you wish? What reparation shall I make you?"

"Your promise that she will not be violated again. Not touched. I want everyone in the villa to understand she is inviolate. Perhaps a ceremony. Yes, a ceremony. I will think of how."

"As you wish. Now, will you drink with me and hear the reports from Sicili? I tell you we are in for hard times. We will remember these years as a golden age. I told you a year ago I smelled a boil across the water and you said I talked like a Messenian, always fearing the worst . . . well, now it has come. . . ."

"I could not drink with you today," he said. "But I will take your promise." He gathered his cloak around his shoulders and left the room without looking back.



At the end of the week Polymion's caravan left, taking their goods to a fair at Tanagra. They left the villa in a state of disarray. The courtyard had to be scoured and the rooms aired and cleaned and the kitchen restocked with supplies.

Eleuria was confined to her bed. She was so large people were saying it might be twins, the worst luck a woman could have. Meldrus kept to himself, brooding over the disruption of trade routes to Sicili, spending his mornings overseeing work on the outer walls.

Philokrates was not well. Ever since he had sat up all night waiting for Auria, the pain in his side had grown stronger, coming and going like waves in the sea, cresting and subsiding, but always returning. One afternoon Auria was sitting with him, watching him play with some threads of silk he had unwoven from a square of cloth. He was comparing them to the inside of a spider's eggcase. Auria was writing on her tablet. She held it up to show what she had written. He spoke to the tablet politely, thinking it was a pilgrim arriving at the temple, when he was a boy, sweeping the temple courtyard with a broom of bay leaves. "May you fare well while you are with us," he said in a sweet young voice. "It is a good day for kind omens." Auria put her hands on his shoulders and shook him, but his head had slipped down on his shoulder and he dozed off. In a moment he woke. "It is time for milking," he said, and made as if to get up and cross the room to Phoebe. But instead of rising to his feet he lay down on the couch and curled up in a ball, talking in a soft voice to someone named Ikokous. "All things are opposites," he was saying. "Good and bad, male and female, limited and unlimited, light and darkness, crooked and straight, birth and death. If you do not care for one, wait and it will pass over into its opposite. Ikokous, you know these things better than I. You must teach me to set my feet upon that day. . . ."



"Father," Auria said. "It's me. Auria. Can't you see me? Look at me. Oh, please, please look at me." She took hold of his face and pulled it toward her own. Then for a moment he looked at her with recognition. "Little flower," he said. "Solace. It is so light today. Here, little song, take this burden of light from my hands."

She took his hands, holding them in her own. The strong, wide, gentle hands. She put her face to them as if to drink of their touch. But he was gone now. She flew out into the courtyard calling for help but there was no help.

"The wisest man I knew no longer walks in time," Kefallinia said, taking Auria into her floury arms. "It was a kind death. The death of a good man is not a cause for sorrow. And yet we must sorrow."

Little Aeo and Palemon began preparing the body for burial. The people of the villa began coming one by one into the room to view the magician, who had turned out to be mortal after all.

The afternoon wore on into the evening, then into night. Sometime during the night a midwife's assistant came to the mourning room to call Auria to Eleuria's quarters. "Bring *aristolochia* and valerian and anything else you can think of. It's a difficult birth. A breech. And coming fast. They're trying to turn it now. Hurry. She is calling for you and Lanis needs the herbs."

"I can not leave here," Auria said. "I must stay with him."

"Go," Kefallinia said. "He went when he was called. He would wish you to go." Auria gathered the powdered herbs from the jars, ran her hands once more over the old man's smooth fine head, tied a cloak around her shoulders and followed the woman out the door and across the courtyard and up to Eleuria's rooms. It was cold again. A wind was blowing off the gulf. Winter had not left the villa yet.

# Chapter III

It was dark in Eleuria's rooms, lit only by torches in high sconces. The light flickered across her struggling face. Childbirth was hard for her. This time was worse than the others. She fought against herself, calling for wine, prolonging the struggle. The midwife had managed to turn the child with her hands. The pain of that had undone Eleuria so that now she was of no help at all. Perhaps she does not want it to end, Auria thought, watching her beat herself upon the chest and head. Perhaps she does not want to know what it is.

There had been four daughters in a row. Two of them stood at the foot of the bed. They were small dark girls, younger than Auria, quiet and well-mannered and shy. What do they wish? she wondered. Do they wish a brother, a boy to keep them in favor? Or do they want the bad luck to continue?

"Auria, get over here," the midwife called. People in the villa were in the habit of calling on Auria for assistance if she was around. She obeyed orders quickly and never had to be told things twice. Also, she did not become clumsy when she was yelled at, like most slaves. "Here by me," the midwife directed. "Give the herbs to Prezo. I need you here. The head's coming, blessed be Artemis. Move back, everyone. Auria, get your hands down here while I push on the stomach. That's it. Be gentle. Get your fingers under the head. Be careful of the neck. That's it. Guide it on out as it comes." Auria positioned herself between Eleuria's legs and did as she was told. The head of the baby slid out into her hands. As it came spiraling slowly out she felt the plates of the skull pull apart, stretching loose from their last constriction. The soft wet hair was slippery beneath her fingers. She moved her fingers down to support the neck. As she did the face turned up to meet her own. It was shining, covered with mucus, the mouth still closed. Dark blue eyes as big as her own looked up at her, so huge and clear and new they took her breath away.



Eleuria stopped her moaning. "Push it on out," the midwife said. "Push again. End your travail. Let it be over." Eleuria gave a last long cry and the constriction moved the baby out into Auria's hands. "What is it?" Eleuria said, raising up on her elbows. "What have I had?"

"A girl," the midwife said. A sigh went around the room and Eleuria turned her face to the wall and was of no more use to them.

The midwife cut the cord and busied herself delivering the after-birth. Auria took the child to one side of the room and began washing off the blood in a bowl of warm water. She lowered the small body into the water, holding it with one hand, running her hand down the arms and legs and across the stomach and down the spinal cord. The little girl was screaming her head off, filling her lungs with air, filling the room with sound, a wild determined screaming that made Auria want to laugh out loud. Her hand found the warm places under the little girl's arms. Her fingers ran warm water across the buttocks and into the soft crease of the vagina. When Auria's fingers touched her there the child stopped crying for a moment and smiled up at her out of beautiful clear eyes.

She washed the mucus from the hair. The child screamed again at that and fought against her. "A little more," she said to the tiny face.

“Just a little more. Let me see this hair you have grown.” Under the blood and mucus the hair was bright golden blonde, as thick as Auria’s own. “So much hair,” the midwife said. “Well, she stayed in there long enough to grow a mane.”



Auria lifted the child from the water. An old slave named Baikleides handed her a cloth of soft wool and she dried the tiny head and wrapped the baby in a shawl and started walking toward Eleuria’s bed. “No,” the midwife said, stepping in front of her. “Not there. Give her to Simiondes.” Auria turned. The two little girls had retreated to a corner of the room and were looking in a chest of garments. Auria pressed the baby close against her chest, then carried it over and gently let it down into the hands of the wet nurse, Simiondes, who opened her chlamys and took out a breast.

A flower, Auria thought, watching the little head settle into Simiondes’ bosom. A gold flower.

“Go on now,” the midwife said. “You have much to do. At noon they pay high honors to Philokrates. They have put off the burial until midday so that men might come from the village. Very unorthodox, almost sacrilegious, but what can be done. I heard they will put him into the new crypt Meldrus had built for himself. An exhumation in the grave with every honor, a goat and a ewe lamb for company. You must get some sleep now and prepare yourself for the ceremony. There will be a large crowd from the town for he was of service to many there.”

“I suppose,” Auria said. She walked back over to Simiondes and looked down at the little girl, sucking greedily away at the breast. She touched the child’s head, feeling the soft place at the top pulsating like a heart. Then she touched its hand where it lay spread out on Simiondes’ breast.

She left then and went out and down the stairs and along the cloister and took her cloak and made a pallet outside the room where Philokrates' body was laid out waiting for morning. It was still very dark, the middle of the night.

Somehow she slept. And all night she dreamed. All night her mind raced this way and that looking for a place to rest. She dreamed of Philokrates speaking to her in his strange young voice. In the dream he was lying in the crypt and he spoke to her and told her to take him someplace else. Then she picked up the body as if it were weightless and carried it away and laid it in a pasture and took the body of a wolf and put it in the crypt in his place. When she returned to the pasture many people were standing around the body of Philokrates. They were in a circle, singing. She joined them and the song rose higher and higher, a beautiful song without words.



Then she dreamed of Eleuria's chambers full of torchlight and the smell of birth and the little girls standing forlornly by the chests fondling their mother's garments and the baby's slick wet hair beneath her fingers and the plates of the skull pulling apart in her hands and the child's beautiful clear eyes turned up to her own.

~

As soon as the sun woke her she washed at the cistern and dressed in a clean tunic and wrapped her legs against the cold and put on her sandals. She was just tying down her hair when she saw the slave Bachydes hurry down the stairs from the women's quarters carrying a bundle. He was a sour-faced unpleasant man who ran Meldrus's errands and was distrusted by the other slaves.

Now he hurried across the courtyard as if he were half-awake. Auria put down her comb and walked to the edge of the building so she could watch him without being seen. When he reached the gate he shifted the bundle to undo the latch. The baby let out a scream. And it went on screaming as Bachydes carried it across the terrace and down the hill. Auria followed him to the gate and watched as he hurried down the path and across the field leading to the lionsroot patch.



She stared after him, seeing the bones of the child she had found in the cave. Then she thought of the live baby, of the hand on Simiondes' breast and the soft line of the tiny vagina, and she imagined a wild creature eating into that flesh, a bird or a bat or a dog.

She was breathing very freely now. Purpose was upon her like a dream of order, like a song. All her decisions were over in a moment's time. After that, all she had to do was act.

She turned and walked back into the villa. She went into the room where Philokrates lay and opened his trunk and took out his heaviest wool traveling cloak and a wooden box with herbs and the bronze knife with the steel blade. "I have to deliver these things," she said to the guard sitting by the door.

"The ceremony is at noon," he said.

"I know," she answered. "So I must hurry. I will take the dog with me now." She untied Metis and he got up and followed her.

She went into the kitchen and spoke with Kefallinia. "I was sent for things," she said, and took figs and dried meat and travel cakes, wrapping them in a cloth. She put the things she had gathered on a bench outside the gate and tied Metis beside them. "I'll be back," she said. "I'll be right back."

She went to the byre and spoke to the goatboy. "I was sent for the old man's nanny," she said. "They put it here for the night." The goatboy untethered Phoebe, and Auria led her away. She walked across the compound and out through the gate and picked up the bundles and set off down the hill to the woods.

When she reached the bottom she turned and looked back up at the villa. It seemed to sleep in the sun. "We are the only ones awake," she said to Metis. "And now we must hurry."



She tied the bundles on her back and took the halter off Phoebe and quickened her pace, trying to figure how long it would take Bachydes to reach the cave, and how to avoid meeting him on the way back. Half a morning had passed since he left and he would travel faster than she had ever traveled with Philokrates. I might be too late, she thought. He might strangle it. Sometimes they strangle them.

She held her hands out in front of her, asking her body for what she needed, asking gently and courteously as he had taught her to do when she ran races against the other children. Take me like a crow, she prayed to her hands and feet and legs. Take me like a hawk, take me like the wind.

She entered the woods with the animals beside her. Several times she stopped and wrapped the leggings more tightly around her legs to protect her from brambles. Once she stopped and ate some of the honey cakes. She was worrying constantly about Bachydes, listening for sounds of him returning along the path.

At a cleared place she left the main path and took a parallel one that she had traveled once with Philokrates. She was heading straight for the mountain. Already she could see the bluff and the black holes of the caves. She will be there, Auria said over and over to herself. And she will not be dead. His spirit has entered her. She is waiting for me. All will be well. He has willed it so. He has left me this to do.

And all this time it was as though she were being led. One step leading to the next step leading to the next. Even the progression through the woods seemed easy, for spring had just begun and the



underbrush was still dry and easy to break through. Phoebe and Metis followed her without straying. Philokrates had trained them well. They were content to be led.

She hurried on. Once she heard a crashing in the distance. Metis growled and she signaled him to be still, certain it was Bachydes going down the other path. Then she was more determined than ever and quickened her pace. In front of her the bluffs rose in the morning light. They were closer with every step. She could see the cave clearly now and the path that led to it along the ledge.

She stopped and felt of Phoebe's milk sacs. The little goat had been milked early that morning and seemed all right for now. Auria looked up at the cave. Everything was so still. There was no wind. Even the clouds were not moving. A hawk drifted down from the cliff and came to rest in a fir tree. It was all as she had remembered it from the last time she was there.

She put the pack down and rested a few minutes. Now the real climb began. And she did not want to tire Phoebe. If the little goat's milk dried up there would be no point in finding the baby. So she moved steadily up the path, being careful of the goat, trying to remember how the women made wild orchid salep for the small children, wishing she had paid more attention to the things that went on in the kitchen.

She stopped at a stream coming out of the rocks and let the animals drink. She felt of the milk sacs again. Phoebe rubbed her chin across Auria's hand, returning her touch. Metis moved beside her like a shadow. Whatever power Auria had tapped into, the animals were sharing.

And so they climbed, pulling themselves up the flat rocks. Auria pulled herself over the last rock and was onto the ledge. She was running now, jumping over the jagged rocks, hurrying around the corners. She could hear the crying. A long soft crying, rising, then falling, then rising again.



Alive, Auria thought. She is alive. "Kleis," she called out. For so she had named the little girl in her mind. "Little one. I am coming. I am coming as fast as I can." The child cried again, louder, more insistent. Auria was running as fast as she dared along the ledge. She sprinted the rest of the way and turned into the cave and the baby was there, wrapped in a cloth on a bed of rushes, for even Bachydes had had that much humanity.

Auria grabbed up the little girl and held her to her breast. The little body was fat and strong in her arms. Auria thought of the fat on her own body, which Kefallinia was always teasing her about. "I will need it now," she thought. "If I am to keep us all alive."

Phoebe followed her into the cave. Auria spread out Philokrates' cloak as best she could with one hand and motioned the goat over beside her. The baby was sobbing against her chest. "It's all right," she crooned. "It's all right now." She pulled Phoebe nearer and made her lie down. Then, holding the baby with one hand and rubbing the goat's stomach with the other, she put the baby to the goat's teat. Phoebe was a mountain goat, from the high country to the west, and was small all over. Still, the teat was much larger than a human mother's. But hunger was the architect now and as soon as the smell of milk reached its nose the baby opened her mouth and closed it down on the long pink teat and began to suck. Sweet rich milk began to flow down the little throat, warm sweet rich milk, life itself, and the little girl sighed and patted the teat and closed her big eyes and drank.



Milk was pouring out the opposite teat. "Oh, well," Auria said, and bent her head and put her own mouth down on that side. Metis came in and stood watching them, looking very haughty and aloof, standing guard between them and the cave's entrance. Now he'll want to be a goat, Auria thought. Now he'll get jealous and wish he was a goat. Then Phoebe will be a mother and Metis will be a goat and what will I be?

I am free, she thought. Clear and perfect the thought was all around her like the air. I am free. I am not a slave. A slave does what it is told to do. A slave thinks what it is told to think. A slave is afraid. I am not afraid. I am Auria, the fearless, who knew Philokrates, who knew Anaxagoras of Clazomenae, who knew Anaximander, who mapped the world.

## Chapter IV

Then, with Kleis curled up at her breast and her head on Phoebe's stomach and Metis guarding the entrance to the cave, she slept, the first real sleep she had had in days. She slept for many hours, hardly moving on the bed of stones, dreaming of rivers rising in the mountains, falling down over stone ledges, on down to the fields behind the villa. Philokrates came into her dream, sitting on a stone bench in the field where they had sung to him. He was sitting on the bench with his old cloak around his shoulders, his hands resting on his knees. In the dream Auria walked towards him carrying the child. All around her were soldiers and women with their faces painted white so she could not tell what they were thinking. They paid no attention to her as she walked between them. They were talking among themselves, holding out pieces of cloth or baskets of fruit. She kept on walking toward her old teacher, the grass soft and wet beneath her feet, cool and soothing.

She woke in the morning full of resolve. Outside the cave the sky was a brilliant clear blue. It would be a good day, sunny and warm, and Auria meant to be deep into the mountains by sundown. She fed the animals part of the stores, ate several honey cakes herself, strapped Kleis across her chest as she had seen the Boetian women do their babies, packed up their possessions on Phoebe's back and started off down the extreme northern scarp of the mountain, heading north and west toward the snow-covered peaks in the distance.

"They will never find us," she told the animals. "Nothing can harm us. I, Auria, the fearless, lead us. Besides, they only think I'm off somewhere mourning. They won't look for us for days, maybe weeks." She  climbed a tree to check her directions. Between them and the next mountains was a stand of trees with leaves she did not recognize. She decided to cut right through it. "Surely there's a path," she said. "Someone's left a path. And there will be food there. We must start to watch for food."

She tied the baby down tighter across her chest and started down the hill. The little girl seemed content. She cuddled up against Auria's breasts, sighing and sleeping. I will search for thistle, Auria thought. I will chew it and milk will come in my breasts in case Phoebe dries up. Yes, the minute I have time I must find thistle. I wonder what part you chew, the roots or leaves? Well, I'll just eat them both. "Don't look that way," she said to Phoebe. "Anyone can give milk if they want to. Philokrates saw men giving milk once, in a famine. Among a tribe in Epirus. You are not the only one that can feed a baby, you know."

The path became steeper. She shifted the child to her back so her hands would be free in case she should fall. Several times she stopped and tied her sandals tighter. It is spring, she thought. We won't go hungry. And I will find fish. I must remember to stay near water. Always stay near water. She walked along, beginning to daydream about the strings of silver fish the Thracians brought back from the gulf. I must make a net, she decided, trying to remember what Philokrates had shown her about net-making. He had allowed spiders to build in the corners of their rooms so he could study their webs as designs for nets. Or I could make wicker traps. I know how to do that. I've helped Aeo do it. All you have to do is find the proper vines. No, we will not be hungry. Nothing will go wrong. I am Auria, a free person. I find my own food. I obey my own orders.

All morning she walked along telling herself such things. Everything Philokrates had taught her about the woods she called to mind, playing the teachings over and over in her mind like a string of beads. All morning her good mood carried her along. The animals were caught up in it and the little band moved along, moving down the mountain and across a field and into the trees. Several times she stopped and fed Kleis and crooned to her, hardly daring to believe that the little girl was still alive, putting her ear to its chest to hear the tiny heart beat.



Finally the way came steeper again, the underbrush thicker and harder to break through. Auria let Phoebe lead the way now. "Find the mountains," she told her. "Lead us to water."

At noon they came to a river. For some time they had been going along beside it so close she could hear its rushing. Now the trees opened up onto a bank. Before them was a line of fast-moving white water, so cold the surface was covered with a cloud of mist. It was rushing down out of the hills, at least twenty feet across, too fast and cold and deep to ford.

Auria stood on the bank surveying the problem. A cloud passed over the sun, turning the mist gray. Auria stuck her hand in the pack and found a honey cake and ate it. Then she ate another. Then another until there were only two left. A crow called from a tree, then glided down and sat near them on a fallen log.

It is too deep, she thought. There isn't any way. She sat there, holding the baby, wishing she hadn't eaten all the cakes at once. She was wondering if she should wash the clothes the baby had soiled. She picked up one of its hands and held it. The tiny fingers clamped around her own. How strong, she thought. It has hardly been born and already it is so strong. How does this happen? Where does all this come from?



"Their power is hidden from them," she heard Philokrates saying. It was an argument he was always having with visitors. "They can only reach it by magic. Or by wine. They have to believe that magic lifts the stones. When they come upon the buildings of their ancestors they gape in wonder, thinking giants walked the earth.

"I tell you," he would continue, getting up and striding around a room, "if a wall was falling on someone you loved you could push it away with the strength of ten. Why must you believe a god visits you at such times? I tell you, that power is here, every minute that we live. Only we can not reach it. *Because we do not know it's there. We have lost sight of it. We can no longer see it!*

"How are your teeth faring?" he would say, returning his attention to whomever he had been haranguing. "If I had another life I would spend it finding a way to repair teeth. Look at these teeth of mine. What a mutiny they are against me."

Auria was looking out across the river, thinking of him. I must remember to clean the honey from my teeth, she thought. Then she stood up and started picking her way along the tree-crowded bank, moving upstream. She walked for awhile, aimlessly, moving the baby from arm to arm. The river was wider upstream, the banks narrower, the mist on top thicker and whiter.

"I should have gone downstream," she said to Metis. "I should have tried the other way." She walked on, thinking she would catch up with Phoebe, who had run ahead, then start back in the other direction. She turned a bend and there was a tree fallen across the water, a great white oak with a smaller tree lodged against it as if they had fallen together. The root system was still attached to the bank and on the far side the crown had fallen across boulders. Auria put the baby down on the bank and climbed up the roots and sat down on the trunk of the biggest tree, looking it over. Behind her Kleis started crying. The cry turned quickly into a scream. Every time I put her down she starts crying, Auria thought, and heaved a sigh. Will I have to carry her for the rest of my life? "I'll be right back," she yelled at the baby. "First I have to figure out a way to get us across this cursed god-cursed frozen fishless river." The little girl screamed louder than ever. With that sound pounding in her ear and the sound of the water beating against the tree trunk beneath her feet Auria stood up and began to walk gingerly across the tree. "I, Auria, of Boetia, and of Thrace. I, Auria, the surefooted, the beloved of Artemis. I, Auria, now walk across this tree." Then, holding her sandals in her hand, balancing with both hands out, she walked all the way across to the other side and let herself down through the branches. The baby's screaming was growing worse every minute. She hurried back across and picked her up and tied her down and carried her across. Then she went back for the supplies.



When she was across for the last time she called out to Metis and Phoebe and they trotted across the tree as if it were not a great feat of daring but only a perfectly natural way to cross a river. Auria ate the last two honey cakes, and then, without looking back, she struck off into the real woods. We will be in the mountains by dark, she promised herself. We will build a fire. *Every act is sacred,* she could hear his voice saying. *Every moment is holy. Every step a destination.*

They moved into the deep woods now, a forest of shaggy-barked plane trees, rising above them in long straight lines, all bare and waiting for spring. Auria looked ahead, north and east to the snow-covered peaks. The baby was still content, settling against Auria's breasts, sighing and sleeping, lulled by the motion. The path was worn here; perhaps a woodcutter had used it, or a hunter looking for pelts. A fear took her, at the thought of wolves.



"I will loose your pack if they come," she said to Phoebe. "Well, let them come. I will kill them with the knife. And Metis will tear them apart. Besides, Philokrates is with us. He is in the baby. Well, he might be. There was this man he knew that said no one ever dies. They just get new bodies. He said there isn't any Hades, or spirit rivers. I mean, where is this Hades? No one ever sees it. In the lands to the east they believe you just get a new body.

"They don't have any wolves there either. They killed them all a long time ago. They all went out together, all the people in the whole land and killed all the wolves and then they had this great sacrifice. . . ." Auria was walking along, chattering away, making up the story as she went along. Phoebe had run ahead. "They have these temples there," Auria was saying. "With towers, many towers like horns. . . ." Up ahead, where Phoebe had stopped to graze, there was a tree fallen across boulders. The top branches were shaking like a storm was in them.

As Auria got closer, a creature about three feet high emerged from under the tree, took one look at Phoebe and fled into the woods. A fur-covered pig, Auria thought, for she had never seen a bear.

She moved closer. Then she saw what he had been about. A piece of honeycomb the size of her hand lay on the ground where the creature had dropped it. Several cold-looking bees still buzzed around the honey. Auria picked up the comb and put it in her mouth. "I will come back later and rob this tree," she said to Phoebe. "I will mark a path so I can come back to this place." She licked the honey from the comb, thinking of the huge old tree packed with honey from limbs to roots. Somehow it seemed a friendly thing, something that made the woods and the river and the journey less frightening. For they were frightening. No matter how fast she thought or how much she talked, Auria knew what she was really doing. She was walking along carrying a baby without the slightest idea where she was heading. "I will wrap my legs and arms and head and come back and get this honey. The bees can't sting you if you hold your breath. Kefallinia said you can rob them all day long if they don't hear you breathing. Well, Aeo said that wasn't the truth, but, after all, Kefallinia is from Arcadia and their honey is famous all over the world. I guess she knows more than Aeo, who has never even been to Thisbe."

Auria walked along the path, talking away, chewing the comb, feeling lucky, thinking of how she would come in the winter when the bees slept and rob the tree of its treasure.

## Chapter V

That night they made camp beneath a bluff. And all night, with a huge fire blazing away, Auria slept and dreamed. Every now and then she would get up and see to the baby and put wood on the fire and dream and sleep and dream again.

She dreamed of Kleis's birth. Over and over she stepped between Eleuria's legs and the crown appeared and the head came twisting out, spiraling out into her hands until the face turned up to her those huge clear eyes.

In the middle of the night Phoebe was petulant about being awakened and did not want to let the baby suck, but Auria petted her and rubbed her stomach and in the end she relented and allowed it. I must find thistle, Auria reminded herself as she fell back to sleep. I must make milk come in me.

She slept again, dreaming of vines spiraling up trees, of vines that turned into snakes, then into the child, then into the veins of her arm, all turning and spiraling upwards, turning and turning, searching for light.

In the morning they started back up the south face of the mountain. At one point the path leveled off and went in two directions. Which shall I take, she wondered, staring up the mountain, waiting for a sign. *I am the sign,* she decided. *I am the one who chooses.* She threw back her head and started up the more traveled way. She climbed steadily, making note of everything, every plant, every tree. I am alone, she reminded herself. I must know the way back.

Philokrates had taught her well about the woods, making her draw the leaves and flowers of plants from memory, making her name the colors with six different names for green, so she would never make a mistake and poison someone.



She was climbing higher now. In the flat places were plants she recognized as ones that could be used for food, wild orchids for salep, iris, laurel, *araceae,* lobelia, castor beans, potato roots, viburnum, ilex, rhododendron.

I know a hundred things a man can eat, she thought proudly. We will not go hungry. *Iris in meadow, orchids in March, bay on the plane, nuts in the forest.* It was a song the children in Boetia sang.

So the morning passed and part of the afternoon. They had moved out of the foothills and were traveling straight up. Kleis would sleep for a while, then struggle against her, beating her tiny fists against Auria's tunic, searching for food. Little piglet, Auria thought. So tiny and so strong. Oh, be strong. Live and be strong as the sea.

She was following Phoebe now. They were making their way up a line of washed-out rocks that seemed to be a creek bed. Auria could hear the water but it was nowhere to be seen. The sun was high, hot and dry. She was getting thirsty. The only thing she had forgotten to bring from the villa was a waterskin.

Metis had run ahead. In the distance he looked thin and tired, hardly a match for a wolf. I am not afraid of anything, Auria said to herself without much enthusiasm. *We should have stayed near water.* Why was

I stupid enough to leave the river? Well, I can hear water. It must be near here. I'll watch the birds. I'll see where they go.

Several small birds were circling a ridge a hundred feet above her. She climbed in that direction hoping to find the spring that fed the creek bed. The baby was fretting now, tired of the sun. She climbed for a while longer and reached the ledge but there was no sign of a spring. She stamped her foot in disappointment. We'll have to go back to the river, she decided. We will go back and I'll trap an animal and make a waterskin. It was foolish to travel without water. She turned and looked back the way they had come. *If they don't come looking for us.* If they don't find us by then. She looked back across the stand of plane trees, imagining a band of pursuers. Then she turned her attention to the ledge on which she was standing. Phoebe had begun to walk along it, picking up her heels in an excited manner. Metis passed her and disappeared around a corner. The ledge was wide and flat. Now that Auria examined it she saw that it had been widened here and there with stones and caulked with a paste, some clay of a blue-gray color. "Someone made this," Auria said out loud. "Someone has been here. It leads somewhere."

She walked carefully along the ledge, catching hold of the vines for support. It was wide enough for comfortable walking, but below the ledge was a sheer drop of several hundred feet. The baby was quiet as Auria edged her way along the path. Already the tiny thing had begun to reflect her moods, waking when she woke, sleeping when she slept, fussing when she worried.

She made her way carefully along the ledge for twenty yards. Then she turned a corner and there before her was a sight she would remember all her life: a series of wide stone steps leading down into a valley, a beautiful little sanctuary no larger than Meldrus's compound. The valley seemed to be surrounded by the mountain. At one end a waterspring poured out of the granite, forming a stream that disappeared into a cave. It was the source of the sound Auria had been hearing all morning.

Beside the spring, all overgrown now with vines and weeds, and with a tree growing up in the middle of it, was a house, or, more correctly, a hut, like a woodsman's hut, with a stone bench in front and ring of stones beside it for a hearth.



A line of fruit trees grew beside the hut, forming a border for a terraced garden, all overgrown now with vines. Auria walked down the steps, hardly daring to believe her eyes. Phoebe was at the spring, drinking greedily. Metis was beside her. "Someone built this for us," Auria said, looking down at the baby, pressing it close to her heart. "Someone left us a place to be."

The first thing she did was inspect the garden. It was a series of terraced beds, bordered by stones and overgrown with weeds, but here and there iris was coming up and the shoots of potatoes and onions. Auria knelt and ran her finger along the bright green shoot of an onion plant, then down into the earth beside it. Already the bulb was forming.

She walked over to the hut, circling it, half afraid to look inside. It was a solid structure, on a foundation of stone, surrounded by a footing of rough brick. The brick seemed at first to have been fashioned by some sort of serrated blade. Looking closer Auria saw that the design was different on each one. It's writing, she thought suddenly. It tells a story.

Kleis was beginning to fret. Auria cuddled her for awhile, sitting on the bench looking at the hut as if it would go away if she stopped looking.

Coriander was growing by the door and blackberry bushes. The door was of wood, still firmly on its hinges, and there was a window, shuttered and closed. "I'm going in," Auria announced, and taking Kleis  in her arms she pushed open the door and stepped into a room with benches along either side. Half the roof was rotted away and a persimmon tree was growing up in the middle of the room. "I'll fix that," she said. "It's nothing to fix a roof." She laid Kleis down on the bench and walked over to inspect the oven. It was beautifully made, of sun-dried brick plastered with clay. There was even a door that opened sideways on hinges held together with staves of wood. Auria opened the door. Inside, on a clay grill was a copper pot. Auria took it from the oven and turned it around in her hands. There was a top, with a ring for lifting it. Auria lifted it off, then put it back on, then lifted it again.

Beside the oven were storage jars, large jars in the Cretan style with scenes painted on them: a journey with two men on donkeys, a meeting of five people beneath a tree, something that looked like the valley itself, with the hut and stone bench. A cat was sitting on the bench, very large and wild-looking. Beside it was a creature like a small donkey.

The jars were widenecked with wooden tops. Auria opened one. Inside were wooden axones the size of her hand. She took one out. It was carved of wood with three flat surfaces, each covered with small precise handwriting. On one side the writing was in Greek, close enough to the Greek she knew so that she could decipher part of the words. On the second side were figures, numbers and figures like the figures in geometry. On the third side was the same writing that was on the bricks along the side of the hut—letters that looked like buildings, or labyrinths, each one a little maze.

Kleis began to cry. "I've got to wash those clothes," Auria said, picking up the little girl, cuddling her against her. "You've soiled every piece of cloth we own, little golden pisser, little dung machine. Little angel. You're my baby, aren't you, Kleis. My own little baby girl. Say you belong to Auria. Say Auuurrriaaaaaaaa. Say Auriaaaaaaaaaa." The baby smiled up at her and she covered its tiny face with kisses.



Later, when she had cleaned up the hut and made them a bed of *araceae* and built a fire and cooked some roots flavored with onions and washed all their things and hung them up to dry and had finally gotten Kleis to sleep for the night, she took the axones out of the jars and lined them up on the bench. There were nine in all. She picked up the first one and read the Greek out loud. THE NAME OF MY PACK IS BIRTH AND DEATH, it said.

HERE IS A PLACE WHERE THEY WILL NOT KILL A MAN FOR ASKING QUESTIONS, said another.

THE UNION OF OPPOSITES GIVES RISE TO THE SUN, said a third. I'm too tired for this now, Auria thought. This is worse than talking to Philokrates. She took one of the axones and set it beside the bed. Then she cuddled down next to the baby, putting her face close to its neck and hair, smelling the soft sweet smell of its skin. We are safe, she told herself. I must make new boots. I must make boots for her. I must set traps. I must learn to fish. I must remember everything.

Far away in Athens the man who had built the hut got up from the table where he was discussing plans with his lieutenants. He was tired of them. He was tired of their arguments and their fears and their jealousies. He was tired of the long time it took their speeches to arrive at the truth.

He excused himself and walked out on the balcony to look out over the city. He leaned on the balustrade thinking of the mountains, of the sanctuary he had built for himself, of the six years he had worked and studied and planned. He thought of the oven, and of the copper pot he had left there.



Then he thought of the other camp, further up in the hills, and of Penelaiaa. Well, he desired her still and she had chosen to stay with Leucippius. He must send word to them. It was drawing near: the day when they would set Attica on fire.

He wrung his hands, hating his wrath, hating his anger. I was a lover of wisdom once, he remembered. Once I held women in my arms and knew children and built an oven with my own hands for baking bread. How am I come to this, that my days are filled with inventories of weapons, my nights with dreams of revenge?

The man standing on the balcony was named Clarius Arasistratus. He was a kinsman, through Eleuria, of the child Auria held in her arms. He had been born into a wealthy family in Athens. When he was a young man he had fallen under the spell of philosophers and had disavowed his citizenship and led a rebellion of his own father's slaves. Now he was the leader of a movement that numbered more than a thousand men, with outposts on three islands and two camps in the mountains. The purpose of the movement was to free every slave in Attica. This was four hundred and thirty-one years before the birth of Christ and men still believed in miracles.

# Chapter VI

In the morning Auria set to work rebuilding the roof. She laid small trees upon the walls for beams, then covered them with a latticework of branches. She worked very hard and by sundown she had made a barrier against the rain.

"When the vines thicken I will weave a real roof for this house," she said to Metis. "And pitch it so the snow will fall off." She was standing off to one side surveying her work. The baby was sleeping. A supper of vegetables was cooking on the outdoor hearth. "Well, it will do for now. It will keep out the rain."

Metis came and stood beside her, rubbing his head against her leg. She reached down and massaged his back and legs. "I remember the day that you were born," she said. "And Philokrates pointed you out to me. That one, he said. That is the one we must have. I wanted to take you that night, you were so soft and funny, but he would not let me. We left you with your mother three months before we took you to our rooms. He got you to be with me now. I know he did. Everything he did was done with knowledge of where it would lead. Well, come along, let's eat before Kleis wakes up and drives us crazy. We are alone now, old friend. Every day we will do what we can. Any night that finds us safe will be a victory."

The weeks that followed were filled with work. She made a cradle for the baby so she could swing it from the persimmon tree, which she had left growing through the roof to support the new beams. She cleaned out the gardens, nourishing the root plants, pulling the vines away from the bushes and fruit trees. The valley, which had seemed impenetrable at first, opened into a meadow, with a stream running along one side. She found turtle eggs in its sandy banks and caught small fish in traps she wove from vines.



She dug iris roots and mashed them into cereal and attempted to feed them to Kleis but the little girl only pursed her lips and spit it out. Auria had a constant fear that Phoebe's milk would stop. Her own attempts to lactate failed although she chewed thistle until she was sick at her stomach and pulled and twisted her nipples until they were red and sore.

Sometimes at night she would take down her chlamys and offer her breasts to the baby but Kleis would only pat them with her hands, or put her mouth down on one of the small nipples, then pull it away, laughing as though at a good joke. She was a funny little girl, full of laughter. At night she would burrow into Auria's arms, singing a little song. Happy, happy, happy, the song meant. Warm and safe and full of milk.

So the weeks went by and then the months of summer and the baby grew and flourished and they were safe. Auria was growing taller. I must make a mark on a tree, she thought. Else I might grow as tall as Kefallinia and never even notice.

Philokrates had known only one fact about her parents, that her father had been a runner, a courier for a Boetian king. "That means you will be tall and strong," he had said. "Only the strongest ones are trained as runners. Only the ones with strong hearts."

• • •

When Auria grew lonely she would get out the axones and try to decipher them, trying to match the Greek to the picture writing to see if they said the same things on each side or were different. One interested her in particular. KEEP YOUR SOUL IN HARMONY, it said. NOT BY YOUR WILL IS THE HOUSE CARRIED THROUGH THE NIGHT. On the picture-writing side was a set of scales and a house and something that looked like a well. I wish he was here so I could ask about these things, she thought. I wish he would come back to get his kettle. 

There were blank sides on some of the axones. Auria added her own words to these, scratching them into the wood with the blade of a knife. I, AURIA, THE FEARLESS, LIVED HERE WITH MY SMALL SISTER, KLEIS OF THE GOLDEN CURLS, WITH PHOEBE, GODDESS OF GOATS, AND METIS, WOLF-DESTROYER, SNAKEBANE, CHIEF OF DOGS.

On rainy days she would set the axones out on a bench and talk to them. "What carries it through the night if not my will? The will of the gods? There are no gods. Philokrates said only fools believe in gods. He said men are worse slaves to superstition than to armies.

"Well, tomorrow I have to work on that roof again. That god-cursed soulless roof. Nothing stays where I put it. Every storm moves it all around. Some night it will fall right on us. Every day the roof god conspires against me."

She put her chin in her hand and stared wildly at the place where a steady drip of rainwater was falling down through the latticework onto the storage jars.

# Chapter VII

It was some time before Auria discovered the pottery. One day, when she was filling a water jar at the spring she noticed a square of blue off to one side. At first she thought it was a hyacinth. Then she saw it was a piece of tile. She walked around the spring and began clearing the leaves and brush away. Beneath the debris was a mosaic pool, made of glazed tiles fitted together with the same mortar as the stones on the ledge. The pool was a circle with a design in the center, a donkey, or perhaps a young deer, with some sort of long singular horn growing from its snout. The end of the horn formed a ball, as if the artist had meant the whole thing to be a joke.

There were clay pipes beside the pool, broken now, but Auria pieced them together and found they could be used to divert water from the spring. She filled the pool. By noon the sun had warmed the water and she took it into her head to use it for a bath for Kleis. The little girl went crazy with excitement when Auria set her down in the warm water and began throwing handfuls of it up into the air. It became a daily routine for them on warm days. Auria would take off her chlamys and get into the pool with Kleis and they would slide around on the tiles laughing at each other. "This time I'll get you clean," Auria said. "This time I'll make you shine. Little woodsprite. Little wildthing. This time I'll get the shit off your legs. Holy Zeus, I'll be glad when you go to the wood like a person. Well, first you have to walk. That won't be long, not as smart as you are. You're the smartest baby I've ever seen. Yes, you are. The smartest and quickest and strongest of all the babies in Attica and Boetia and all the islands of all the seas."

Then Auria would press the baby onto her stomach, pretending the baby was her own, pretending it had grown there and she was giving it birth. "Ohhhhhhhhhhhhhhhh," she would say. "Once more. One more push and she's here. Oh, see, everyone, Auria, the great mother, has given birth to the strongest, bravest, quickest baby in the whole world. Quick, hide her lest the goddesses be filled with envy."



Later she discovered the pottery. A series of clay pipes led away from the pool, sealed off with a brick at the pool's edge, broken and covered with leaves.

One afternoon Auria began cleaning the leaves away, following the pipes to see where they led. She followed them down an incline to an opening in the face of the mountain, hidden from view by a boulder. She walked around the boulder and into a large cave that was not really a cave at all, for sunlight poured in through a crevice at the top not fifty yards from the entrance. It was noon, a bright hot day, and the cave was filled with light, long beams of light falling on the granite walls and onto the benches and tables.

Auria turned in a circle, looking at everything. Near the place where she was standing words had been chiseled into a flat place on the rock wall. The lettering was very formal and precise, like the chiseled letters of a temple entrance.

IN THIS PLACE I STUDY ALL THOSE THINGS WHICH ARE MADE OF CLAY AND HARDENED BY FIRE, it said. Below that, in smaller letters, was a name, Clarius.

"Clarius," Auria said out loud. "Clarius." He might be on his way right now. He might be coming any day now.

She turned back to the room. There were several worktables. One held woodworking tools and carvings of birds. A half-finished piece, which might have been on its way to becoming a dove, lay on its half-finished wing.



The main work of the room, however, was pottery. Covered storage jars stood in a row holding different kinds of powdered clay, white kaolin and campane, and the dark red clay of the hills called caria. On the table were tools of wood and bone, tied together with leather strips according to their uses. There was even a wheel, attached to a pedal which turned a disc of stone. There had been potters at the villa and Auria had seen such wheels but she had no idea how to use it. She turned it with her hand. It creaked and moved half a revolution. She took a rag from the table and cleared the dust from the gears. She turned it again. This time it moved more smoothly.

I will learn to use this, she thought. I will make bowls for us. I will make Kleis a bowl with a face in the bottom like the one Philokrates had Aeo's woman make for me.

She picked up the tools, marveling at how beautifully they were made. Who was this Clarius, who could build a place like this and walk off without even taking his tools? I will study the axones again tonight, she decided. I will know more of him.

She was turning to leave, thinking Kleis might be waking from her nap, when she noticed a shelf at the back of the room. She walked back to examine it. It was more than a foot wide and held an assortment of small clay figures, men and women and children, all brightly painted, all bending and twisting in different postures as though in a dance.

Auria had never seen such lifelike things. The dolls at the villa had been made of straw or rudely carved from wood. These figures were like real men and women, with hands and feet and expressions on their faces. Some wore sandals or carried things in their hands, flowers and cups and bowls. One held a loaf of flat round bread. Another had a pig on a lead.



Auria marveled at the figures. She reached out her hand and touched them, tracing the lines of their arms and faces. Then, suddenly, she was filled with a sense of how alone she was, how far away from the world where men and women ate together in the evenings and played music and danced in a circle and told each other their dreams.

She thought of the men and women of the villa dancing together on feast days, of lyres and citharas playing, of wine and mead and wheaten cakes rich with raisins. Of Kefallinia and Little Aeo and Euporia, of Nedde and Leusistra dancing and holding out their hands to her. How the moon shone on such nights. She thought of the smell of meat cooking for the feast, and the music of human voices.

"I do not care," she said, holding her hands out in front of her, clenching her fists. "Curses on loneliness and feeling like this. A slave obeys his feelings. A free man rules himself. I am Auria, Freewoman, Treewalker, I fear nothing. Not even loneliness. I am hardened by loneliness, by the wolves waiting in the mountains, by the rain that comes in the roof spoiling the grain. I will be hard as a river, hard as the mountains. I will kill wolves. I will kill loneliness. I will never go back. They will never take her. They will never make her a slave."

She was crying then, not sure whether it was Kleis she wanted to save or herself. Tears poured down her cheeks and she let them pour. She put the little figure she was holding back on the shelf and walked out to the spring. Metis got up from where he was sleeping and came and put his head against her leg. She knelt beside him and began massaging his big body with her hands, rubbing and kneading his legs and back and shoulders. "I remember the day you were born," she said through her tears, "and Philokrates pointed you out to me with his long old finger. That one, he said, look at his head, how he holds it. That is the one that will leave no tracks, that is the one we must have.

"Well, come along. What use is it to sit here crying like a puppy? I will wake Kleis and play with her. We must make a larger cradle. And tomorrow we set squirrel traps. She will need leggings and boots when winter comes. Oh, I wish I had a bow and could take a deer. A deer would provide us with everything. Well, we must find more eggs. We must fatten her up. Winter takes the thin ones, that's what the old women say. Well, it won't take her. Tomorrow we start fattening her. And you too. Look at your ribs. I have smelled winter already. We must make use of our time. And now that I have the pottery I must make clay tablets. I must leave records. A philosopher always leaves records. It doesn't matter what it says as long as it's accurate. Well, that's not as simple as it sounds. You don't always have all the words you need . . . well, first I'll make the tablets. . . ." Metis had lost interest and gotten up and walked away, so Auria went into the hut and picked up the sleeping baby, still talking away about her plans. "Wait till you see what I found," she said. The baby came drowsily to consciousness, then began to cry, irritated at being jerked from sleep.

"Oh, I love you," Auria said, hugging her fiercely. "It's good here, isn't it? Isn't it? There is food and shelter and the roof only leaks half the time. We can stay here forever if we have to. There will be food for the winter. I will make the cellar so big it could feed twenty. And there's the cave. Oh, stop crying now. Please stop crying. I know I shouldn't have waked you when you were sleeping. Oh, Kleis." The baby was screaming now. "Oh, come on, don't scream. I'll sing for you. I'll sing 'The Dance of Letters.'" And holding the little girl in her arms she began to dance around the cleared place before the hut, singing a song Philokrates had made up to teach her the letters of the alphabet. He had made up the words but he had stolen the tune from a song the Asclepiads sang when they harvested grapes. Some of that was still mixed in with the alphabet. "Alpha, beta, gamma, delta," Auria sang, "leading on to epsilon. Zeta, eta, theta, leading on to golden wine. Iota, kappa, come and help us. Lambda's hiding, so is mu. . . ." The song went on and on. Auria started adding words of her own. "Purple gowns, flying chariots, incense, myrrh, and cassia . . . for none of these would I trade you, little flower of my heart. . . ." Auria held the baby out in the air, then pulled her back down into her arms, turning and swooping and dancing. Finally she stopped, exhausted, and sat down on the bench with the child in her lap. The little girl reached up and put her hands into Auria's mouth, as if to find the source of music. A stream of warm urine ran down Auria's legs and onto her sandals.



"Oh, damn it all to the gates of Laurium, will I never learn not to pick you up when you've been sleeping. Now I have to wash again. I tell you, Kleis, I'm glad I'm all alone if I am to go around smelling like a byre. Well, come along, let's wash off and get something going for dinner. I'm starving and Phoebe needs milking. You won't believe what I found. A pottery. A real pottery with a wheel. And these figures. Oh, you've never seen anything like them. So real, they can almost talk. I'm going to make us dishes. Bowls and cups and a cylix for you with two handles like the one Philokrates had Little Aeo's woman make for me.

With a face at the bottom. And a bowl with a ram. And tablets for me to write on. Oh, I have to begin keeping a record. He said every man must leave a record as we do not know who might need it. . . ." Auria carried the baby over to the spring chattering away as if Kleis understood every word she was saying.

# Chapter VIII

Auria worried about the winter. What will we do when it comes, she wondered, when the rabbits have gone underground and the squirrels have fallen from the trees and the wolves are hungry enough to come past Metis. Then she worked even harder on the roof and brought stones into the hut to pile against the door and gave Metis extra helpings of everything she cooked, although he fed himself quite well in the woods.

So she worked while summer lasted. Every day the gardens and woods yielded new surprises; black and blue and red berries were all around the meadow and she found a stand of nut trees near the creek and harvested them as they fell.

She enlarged the storage cellar and filled it with roots and nuts and the small hard apples that grew by the hut. She even emptied the fine clay from the jars in the pottery and filled them with grain and set them in the back of the cave to stay cool.

Then it was fall and Kleis had been alive nine new moons and had begun to walk, pulling herself up on the bench, taking small careful steps, watching to see if Auria was watching, expecting to be applauded for every move. She would take a few steps along the bench, then fall back on the floor and pretend to be interested in something else. In a few minutes she would be back at the bench, trying again. She was quick on her feet, and one day, in her ninth month, she simply let go and went walking off in the direction of the hearth, waving her hands in the air and babbling away as she walked. "Is that how I look to you?" Auria said. "Is that how I look, walking around all the time talking to myself like an idiot? Is that what I've taught you to do?"



Kleis had begun to feed herself with a fork made of birchwood. Auria would sit her on the floor with a bowl of cooked vegetables before her and she would beat on the food with the fork, then carefully pick up a piece and guide it to her mouth. If Phoebe were near she would hold out pieces trying to coax her near.

Auria was milking Phoebe and feeding the milk to Kleis in a cup but the baby still longed for the teat and when Phoebe would give in and allow her to nurse she would lay her little golden head on the goat's stomach with her eyelids half-closed and a dreamy expression on her face.

"What a little hetaera you are," Auria would say. "What a bacchante. I will make you a thyrsus. Like that luteplayer who left you that hair. Well, suck on your teat. What harm can there be in being happy?" Then Auria would wonder if the world held any such things for her, thinking of the strange uneasiness she felt when the moon was full and when the blood came out of her as it did with women.

In the afternoons, when her work was done and Kleis was asleep for a nap, she practised writing, copying things from the axones or writing down things from memory. Finally, she began to write her own creations, little stories and poems, pieces of her history turned into songs.

I have had my fill of loneliness
Like a roof of blue hyacinths
It lets the rain through

. . .

By the creek anise fills the air
With memory
If he returns I will wear a spray of dill
In my hair and embroidered sandals

. . .



Today the wind howls like the day I found you
Kleis of the golden curls
When you sleep your lips move in the language
Of milk

. . .

Now leaves turn the color of blood
We must have leggings and fur collars
Sing, wind, of Auria,
Who suffers winter before it happens

She wrote other things. Meditations she called them. *What is a slave?* she wrote at the top of a list. A slave adores its master. A slave will do anything for praise. A slave believes it is a slave. A slave forgets how it became a slave.

While she was writing this Kleis woke up and began to cry. "I'm a slave to you," Auria said, picking her up. "A slave obeys its master. A slave does what it is told to do." The baby smiled seductively up into her eyes and Auria began to laugh.

# CHAPTER IX

She made lists on her tablets. THINGS I KNOW, she wrote at the top of one. She had been sitting a long time trying to decide where to begin when Phoebe came in from grazing, her mouth still half full of galega leaves.

"Did I ever tell you how you got your name," Auria said, taking the goat's chin in her hand, looking down into its watery blue eyes. "He named you for a very small goddess of the mountain herdsmen. A goddess who travels the skies in a cart pulled by tiny goats with silver hooves and silver harness. Once this goddess was married to Vulcan but he grew angry because she was always giving his inventions away to mortals. So . . ." Auria paused and straightened her back, getting caught up in the story, which was half something Philokrates had told her and half something she was making up. "So to punish her, Vulcan went to Zeus and Zeus made her so small she was ashamed to be seen among the gods. She came down to earth to live on a mountain with a herd of goats. That's where she is right now and on the winter solstice she rides the sky in her cart looking for mortals who have done brave deeds and rewards them with gifts. Well, she is a whimsical and undependable goddess, but he named you for her, nonetheless."

Phoebe nudged Auria's knee, wanting to be petted more. "What a lucky creature you are," Auria said. "As long as you have food and company you don't complain. I would like to be a goat, with the sun to shine on my bones and a patch of sweet root growing up all around me." She rubbed her hand down Phoebe's bony skull and whiskered chin. "I might as well gather some walnuts. I know the winter's coming. I hear it at night in the mountains, waiting its time. Well, come with me, let's bring walnuts into the cellar. Let's do what we can."



She was building a second room onto the cellar, lining it with stones and pieces of broken clay from the pottery. Filling it with everything she could find in the woods and gardens. In the old cellar she had found jars of spices, thyme and valerian and some bitter black oil, like the sap of a tree. She kept meaning to collect herbs while she could still recognize the leaves but there never seemed to be time for everything she thought up to do. Kleis was always there, distracting her, slowing her down, having to be carried and fed and cleaned up and talked to.

So the days passed and early fall became late fall and the meadows were rich with berries and the woods with nuts. She trapped small game and made a cape for Kleis and leggings and boots and even a little hat. It was growing colder every day. She chinked the holes in the hut and piled straw on the floor. Her dreams were changing now. She dreamed of the honey tree. The small brown creature came up to her in the dream and it was one of the Thracians, the one with the snake going up his face. He smiled and held out his hands to her and they were full of honeycomb. Honey dripped from his fingers and fell to the ground and Auria knelt before him and caught the honey in her mouth. "Come home with us now," the Thracian said. "Come home and have some honey."

She dreamed of the food of the villa. And she longed for the sound of human voices. She would lean over the baby and look deep into her eyes. "Talk," she would say. "I want to hear you talk. Say Auria. Say, Auriaa, Auriaaa, say, hello, Auria. Hello, hello, hello. Please talk. Come on. I'll teach you. Say Auria, Auria, Auria. When you get bigger we'll go rob that honey tree. Yes we will. We'll sit on the ground in a sea of honey and eat it all day and all night. We'll eat every bit of it. Come on, say Auria. Say Momma, Momma, Momma, Momma, Momma, au, au, Auria, hello, hello, hello. All right, if you don't want to talk I won't take you to get the honey. I'll eat all the honey myself." But Kleis only laughed and held her hands up in the air, waving them in time to the words.

Then winter was there, coming over the mountains so fast and suddenly Auria didn't even have time to seal the cellars. The first storm of winter blew in from the east, coming from the sea, cold air and freezing rain followed by snow. For three days it blew without ceasing.

Auria worked furiously, keeping the fire in the hut blazing away, making thick stews, forcing the little girl to eat. Phoebe's milk had stopped. Just like that. One morning there was milk. The next day there was a thin watery substance. Then nothing.

And the snow continued to fall, filling the valley, icing the steps, turning the spring to a trickle. By the third day Kleis had begun to cough. By the sixth day she was coughing all night, barely able to swallow the food Auria prepared for her.

"This is the underworld," she said to Metis. "This is Hades. Freezing to death in this god-cursed snow while she coughs her little chest out. What am I supposed to do? Will you just tell me that? What am I supposed to do now? Well, maybe it will let up tomorrow. Maybe tomorrow the sun will shine."

But the bad weather continued and the baby's cough grew worse. The mucus in her nose was so thick Auria had taken to sucking it out with her mouth as she had seen Philokrates do once when a child at the villa was dying of pneumonia.



The little girl was burning with fever and eating nothing. She seemed half the size she had been the week before. Finally, she slept the whole day one day and would eat nothing. She would barely drink water. Auria was frantic. I must make a tonic, she thought. I must leave her here and go find white vine. I must have white vine and amaranth and *cnicus*. I have to have *cnicus*. And honey. If I could only get that honey I could heat it and drip it into her mouth. Then I must go for it. I must go right now. No, not now. In the morning. She is better in the morning. I can find the way. I know I can. If the snow hasn't covered all my marks. Well, I will find it. I'll bind my legs so tightly and I'll run all the way. Yes, in the morning I go for white vine and *cnicus* and the honey. I will run like the wind. Now, it is settled. So be it.

Then Auria dropped to the floor and drew a picture of the honey tree in the dirt of the floor. And she prayed to all the gods whose names she could remember. You must grant it that I find the honey tree and white vine and *cnicus*. Where does it grow? I can't remember. I can't remember what he told me. Where shall I look under all this snow? I don't know. I can't remember.

She took her drawing stick and drew the *cnicus* plant, with its sticky leaves and podlike flowers. As she drew, the lesson came back to her. *Cnicus grows in the roots of elm, along the streams, at the edge of mead-*

*ows. Look where the bushes shade its flowers. Sometimes it lives in the house of oak.*

I'll eat now, she thought. I'll eat all I can hold and sleep through the night and in the morning I'll bind my feet and legs and leave her with Phoebe. I will run all the way. She will not die while I am gone. I will  not allow her death to come.

And what of Philokrates, a voice howled in her head. Remember when you would not let him die? Remember when you swore he could not leave you, Auria, the Fearless, beloved of Polymion, Slave, Runaway Thracian Slave?

She turned, letting the firelight throw her shadow onto the wall beside the door. She held her hands high up into the air, making the shadow taller and taller, making it fall across the roofbeams. "I am Auria, the Free, of Thisbe and Boetia, beloved of Philokrates, who walked across the Tree of Danger, Auria, child of Runner, First Born of my own mind. I have come this far in safety. I will live and all I love shall live. So be it by all the gods who choose to help me. I go now into the house of sleep. I go to prepare for morning."

So saying she curled up in bed beside the hot sleeping child. "Tomorrow you will be well," she said, touching the burning little forehead, feeling the heat in the fragile beautiful little neck. "Tomorrow you will drink my tonic and look up and laugh at me. Tomorrow you will eat. Tomorrow you will breathe."

In the morning Kleis seemed better and even smiled when Auria pushed salep into her mouth, even managed to swallow some of it. Outside the snow continued to fall, but it had abated somewhat. Auria tied the little girl into her cradle, built up the fire as high as she dared, and, with Metis at her heels, struck off across the clearing to the steps.

The snow gave them some footing but by the time they were to the top they were soaking wet. Auria walked around the ledge and found a protected place and took off all her things and wrung them out and tied them back on tighter than ever. She tied the leggings around her legs with strips of a cloak Methania had made her, so long ago that seemed. A million moons ago, in another land.



"Are you ready, good friend?" she said to the dog. "Are you ready to come with the daughter of a runner?" Then she began to run, moving with a lightness and sureness she had not felt since the day she left the villa. That same feeling was upon her now, as if she were a beam of light, as if there were nothing in the world that could prevent her from arriving at her destination. Energy and light were all around her and she ran down the slippery path as if it were nothing at all, as if it were not even cold.

She ran as fast as she dared, letting her breath in and out in long deep exhalations as Philokrates had taught her to do. A vision was before her of the huge tree full of honey, a sea of honey, dark and rich and sweet. Now it was not only Kleis's need that drove her but her own hunger. As she ran she dreamed she dipped her hands into the rich golden stuff and raised it to her mouth.

She ran on and on, along the path and into the woods. An hour passed, then another. She passed a mark high on a branch where two trees grew together. She was certain that was where she had marked the path in the spring. She ran even faster. Metis was at her heels. She made a last turn and went along a narrow path and came out at the grove where the tree had been.

It was gone. Someone had chopped it open and taken the contents. The honey was gone.

She ran around and around the broken tree. She stopped and picked up a piece of broken comb and brushed the snow from it and sucked at it greedily. Then she threw it down on the ground. She circled the tree over and over. She was so cold and angry she could not reason. She pulled at her hair and shook her fists at the skies. She thought of Kleis, alone in the hut. It seemed a million hours away. I must go back, she thought. Why did I come here? What have I done? How will I ever get back?



Above her, sitting on a ledge in a cloak made of sheepskin, a boy was watching her wild strange dance. Who was this, he wondered, this half-dressed girl screaming and pulling at her hair like she was possessed?

The boy's name was Meion, Meion Doryphorus, he called himself. The Javelin Hurler, the Spear Thrower. He had gone out scouting from Penelaiaa's camp high in the mountains and had been stopped by the snowstorm and taken refuge in a cave. At first he was amused at the sight of this wild girl in her rage, then he began to feel sorry for her. There was a quality about her anger that was more than rage, more like hunger. Besides, he liked the wild black curls she kept flinging from side to side. There had been a woman at Laurium with hair like that who had been kind to him.

Now he watched as Auria slowed down and tried to compose herself. She held her hands straight up in the air, then brought them down to her chest with her hands pressed together, as though in prayer. Then she spread them out as if she were balancing on a beam.

She stayed that way for a few moments, very still, then started walking back the way she had come, stopping every now and then to search the roots of oak trees, as if looking for something she had lost. She favored one foot. She was limping.

He pulled his cloak around his shoulders and decided to follow her. He went into the cave and took the shepherd's bread Penelaiaa had made for him and a container of honey. He strapped them to his belt and began to descend the bluff, watching the way that she had gone.



Auria found a patch of *cnicus* in the roots of the third tree she searched. It was in the roots of a birch, not at all where it was supposed to grow. She tore off pieces of the leaves, then pulled up half the plant and stuffed it into her girdle. She turned to go back up the path. Her foot was aching; she had sprained it in her furious dance around the tree. Who cares, she thought. Let it hurt all it wants. Let it bleed all over the god-cursed snow. She called Metis and began to run on the foot. She is dead, Auria thought. There will be nothing I can do. So thinking she dragged her foot along, going as fast as she could. The snow had abated but it was still bitterly cold. The sky was gray and overcast, gray from horizon to horizon.

She had gone almost a mile when he caught up with her, coming up behind her, calling out in a kind voice, holding out his hands in a gesture of friendliness. She turned to him in the snow, holding onto Metis, who was growling beside her. "Who are you?" she asked, standing up as tall as she could, turning to the boy.

"I am Meion, Meion Doryphorus, the Javelin Hurler, the Spear Thrower. Here, I have brought you food. Eat. It will warm you." He held out a lecythus to her, of the sort used to carry oil. "Take it, it is honey with mead. And there is bread. I saw you from the cliff. I followed you. You've hurt your foot."

“She is dying,” Auria said. “Kleis is dying. Help me go there.” She pointed up the mountain. “Please, we must hurry. She will die.”

“Let me bind up your foot,” he said. “Then we will go as fast as the snow allows us.” He knelt before her and took the bindings from her leg and wrapped them around and under her foot, over and over, doing a good job. “Now,” he said, “show me the way. We will go to your friend.”



The last hour he carried her, stopping every now and then to catch his breath. It was late afternoon when they began the climb to the ledge. “You must leave me and go on,” she said. “There, it is easy to see the way. Go around the edge and down to the hut. The goat is with her. Give her water and warm the honey. Build up the fire. If she lives. If she is dead come back and put the spear through my chest for I do not wish to live. Go, please, I will make my way behind you.”

He did as he was told and gained the ledge and let himself down the stairs and into the hut and the baby was there, asleep in the cradle, with Phoebe standing guard beside her. She was wrapped in so many layers of covers, so tied and bundled into the cradle that Meion could barely see the little face. He put his ear to her mouth. She was breathing.

He built up the fire, listened to the baby one more time, and went back for Auria. She was almost to the ledge and was pulling herself up the rocks. “She is asleep,” he called out. “She seems to be sleeping. She is only sleeping.” Then he carried Auria up the rocks and down the icy stairs and across the yard. She pushed open the door to the hut and went over to the cradle and started untying the strips that held the covers. “Put water on to boil,” she said. “We must boil the *cnicus*. No, first we'll feed her. Maybe we won't have to use the plant. It's a dangerous plant. Perhaps the gods have healed her. Oh, most holy and precious of all things in the world. Oh, I thank the earth that did not take her from me." She was untying the wrappings one by one and found the little girl in them and took her out and held her in her arms, crooning to the baby and giving orders to Meion all at the same time. But she was fading now, the pain in her foot and the terror of the day and the cold were overcoming her. She lay down on the bed with Kleis still in her arms. "Now you must care for her awhile. Feed her. Put honey into the water and drip it into her mouth and take the cereal, no, there is bread. Give her bread. Give her water each time she will take it. There are clean clothes on the bench. You must dry her clothes. Do not put her down. Do not let her fall. . . ." Then Meion took the child from Auria's arms and covered her and stood in the middle of the hut holding the little girl, shaking his head from side to side, wondering how in the name of all that grows and waters he had come to be in Clarius's old sanctuary holding a baby girl.

# PART II

# Meion

*"The slaves, however," Polymion was saying, "the ones that are fit neither for the household nor for the shop, perhaps one in four or five, are sent of course to the mines. They feel no loyalty to their work, nor to the hands that feed them, and they are always trying to escape. There are bands of them in the mountains now, raiding and stealing down into the farmlands. Athens is too busy arguing with Corinth and Sparta to do anything about it."*

# Chapter X

Who was he, this Meion Doryphorus, as he called himself? Doryphorus, a name he had taken from stories of his father, who had fallen trying to save the city of Megalis while Meion was still in his mother's womb. The city had been lost to the Athenian invaders, the women and children put on the block, the men slaughtered. So Meion had been born into slavery, on a ship from Megalis bound for the mines of Laurium.

His mother's fortunes went well there for a while. She was a beautiful woman, tall with lidded eyes, and soon was a favorite of the mine overseer. She had a house of her own and robes of cotton and silk and other slaves to wait upon her. It was not until Meion was twelve years old that she lost favor and they put a lamp on his head and sent him into the mines.

It was four hundred and thirty-one years before the birth of Christ and metals were being dug from the ground all over the world, copper and tin and silver and gold. Legends grew up around the metals, of a king who turned his own daughter into gold, of a princess who killed her own brothers to deliver a golden fleece to her lover, fatal conception as a shower of gold, discord as a golden fruit, yarn spun into gold, golden cloaks with poison linings, treasures, ransoms, dragons, bribes.

The stories were warnings but the hearers ignored the warnings, dreaming of the strange shining beauty which meant power, power over the earth and the lives of other men, power stored in ingots and medals and coins and bars.

Copper and tin, silver and gold. In the mines of Laurium twenty thousand slaves labored to take silver from the ground. "What is this stuff that does not even shine until it is polished?" Meion said to his mother. "Of its inertia no bread is baked, no stanchion filled, no trees felled to make masts or roofbeams. For this we should breathe dirt and die?" He asked such questions of his companions as they tied candles to their foreheads and water jugs to their waists and crawled into the shafts with picks in their hands.

The root of evil, wise men were calling the metals, the root, that which goes deep, which waits, feeds, spreads, evil and discord spreading out to cover the earth, a vast network passed from hand to hand in the form of drachmas and staters and shekels and tetradrachms.

Southern Attica, the silver mines of Laurium. At Sounion, a mile away on the seashore, beautiful seaside villas bloomed with iris and anemones and orchids. At Laurium the earth was a honeycomb of pits and shafts and holes and galleries. A deed to a mine in Laurium reads, "The ground, the installations and the andropoda, the human cattle."

The richest and most dangerous shafts were on the western face. It was to these that Meion was sent for being rude to Eutorian when he came in to his mother. The day the western quarries caved in Meion was the lead boy in his section, stretched out in a narrow shaft with three smaller boys behind him. "Put the candles out," he said in a low voice, as soon as the dust settled and the noise subsided. "Extinguish them."

"I won't die in the dark," Eleckamenes said. "No, I won't do it."

"Don't talk," Meion said. "Do as I say and you won't die at all. Methos, turn, begin to turn. You must dig us out. *Do as I say.* Eleckamenes, put the light out or I will strangle you. I mean it." His voice was having to do it all. "If you wish to live, obey me without question. Turn, Methos, begin to dig, breathe as softly as you can. I am going to work  my way back there over the others. Eleckamenes, make yourself small, I am going to pass over you. You know I can do whatever I say. You know my powers. Be quiet. Do as I say." He crooned to them, hypnotizing them with his voice as he moved his body over Eleckamenes and then over Pelly and past Methos and began to work on the rocks with his pick. "The god speaks in me. He tells me where to touch the rock. Breathe softly. Do not speak. Trust me. The god will save us. He speaks with my tongue. Obey me." While he whispered to them, he was cutting a line between the rocks, feeling it give. It was possible. It was moving. "Breathe like a moth. I am almost there. Lend me your wills. Be easy. The god is with us. He will return us to light." Then he pushed a loose stone with his hands and felt it give way and his hand was in the passageway and he began calling to the men outside and they came and moved the stones and took the boys out one by one, being very careful with Meion as he had scraped the skin from the side of his leg.

They carried him to his mother's house and laid him at her feet, sorry for the poor boy, but pleased to deliver justice to Eutorian's old mistress, who had spent her share of the profits. She took him to her room and laid him out on her bed. She was still allowed her house, although Eutorian had taken his favors elsewhere.

"So this is what we have come to," she said, looking down at the injured boy. "Well, we are not finished yet. This family is not finished, no matter who rules the Acropolis."

As soon as Meion's leg healed Niddebaknidde came to take him to Leucippius. Niddebaknidde was an Ethiopian, named for the first word of Greek he had spoken. When he was first brought to civilization he



had seen a bronze Hermes in an entryway and prostrated himself before it, asking his captors, "What is it? What is it?"

"Nikaticius," they had told him, meaning the name of the sculptor. "Niddebaknidde," the enchanted man had said, over and over, thinking it meant God. He was a strong man, fearless and tireless, and Elen and Leucippius used him as a courier between the mines and the camp.

Now he stood in Elen's doorway waiting to take her son to the mountains.

"You must go too," Meion said, turning to his mother. "You said we would go together."

"That is not possible now. I have work to finish here."

"I won't leave without you. I won't leave you here."

"You will do as I say. There are plans you can not know of until you are safe. Now, go with Niddebak. He can't wait all night while you cry like a woman."

He looked down at his mother's face, which was like stone. "Go," she said. "Now, you take me with you when you leave." She relented then and allowed him to put his face against her face, folding him for a moment into her arms. She looked very beautiful, standing in the torchlight, wearing an embroidered gown from Lydia. She had just come from making the arrangements that would be his safekeeping across the mountains. It had cost her many pieces of expensive jewelry.

"You go to the mountains," she said. "You will breathe light there. You will make me proud."

"Who will watch out for you when I am gone?"

"I watch over myself," she said. "I am Alkmeionadae. Nothing touches me ever again. With you here they could blackmail me. You must go now. Meion!" He had come back over to her and taken her face in his hands.



"I won't go. I won't leave you."

"Then you doom us both. Eutorian threatens anything, even to make you castrati. Now go. The mountains hold your destiny. We are not slaves, even though we are fallen on bad times."

He took his pack then and followed Niddebak through the corridors.

# Chapter XI

As long as he lived Meion would remember the climb from Chaeronea to the high camp. It was summer and the meadows were blooming with wildflowers as big as his hand, yellow and white and red, and the sky was blue and he was free, walking along beside Niddebak, the air as soft as a song, the sun pouring down on the bleached stones of the mountains.

Niddebak sang as he walked, whistling little tunes under his breath. He would hear a bird in a tree, or the wind in the leaves, then whistle back whatever it was he had heard. The trip took five days. The last night they slept in a meadow, rolled up in their cloaks, the donkeys grazing nearby, the call of katydids and frogs the only thing to interrupt the silence. It was cool in the night and Meion dreamed of the cave-in, the darkness and the smell of limestone and power rising in him like a dream. He woke thinking of Pelly and Methos and Eleckamenes, who counted themselves lucky any day the overseers didn't break their fingers or let them go hungry. I will return for them, he thought. I will bring them here. They can come here too.

He slept again. This time the dream was darker and the stone did not move and no light came. He woke sobbing. Niddebak got up from where he was sleeping and came and sat beside him, stroking him like a mother. "We leave much sadness behind on the plains," he said. "Here it is better. You will be with Leucippius and with Penelaiaa. No one is ever sad with Penelaiaa. Too much work to do."

"What of you?" Meion said. "Will you stay here? Will you stay with me?"

"I come and go," Niddebak said. "I am allowed to move."



So he had been taken to Leucippius, with a bag of silver tetradrachms and a letter from his mother:

> *Greetings, here is my son. He is sixteen years old and of a questioning and arrogant nature. I trust you will find work for him in your vineyards.*
>
> *Things are well here. Much silver moves to Athens. So we do our part as you do yours. Loyal citizens sleep best. Haven't you found it so?*
>
> *I thank you for this service you do me and look for a way to repay your kindness. Meanwhile, honor the gods and know that your cousin Elen holds you in her heart and in her prayers.*

Leucippius looked up from the letter into the face of the boy before him. "Did she tell you what we do here?" he said.

"No, only that I was to trust you as you were of my blood." Meion looked around him. He was in a tent made of animal skins, in a camp high in the mountains overlooking a lake. The last day's journey had been through country so wild it would have seemed impenetrable if Niddebak had not been there to show him the way. They had walked into the camp past groups of men and women wearing the rough clothes of mountain people and gone straight to the tent of Leucippius, who had not gotten up to greet them. "We are an army," he said. "Although our real work is only to stay alive and wait. We dream of rebellion, of freeing the slaves in the mines. How does that seem to you, young kinsman? Could you lend your heart to that?"

"With all my breath," he said. "With my life."

"Good," Leucippius said. "Come nearer. Let me feel those strong arms. You must forgive me that I do not rise. I am not able to use my legs. A gift from our enemies when I was among them. Well, I shall have my revenge."



"How will it be done?" Meion said. "How will we free them?"

"We have friends in Athens. In high places. And in Corinth and Cyllene. But our real allies are the Spartans, who do not even know we exist. They are itching to take Attica. When they do there will be no law. Then we will take our ragtag band and go down to Laurium and Kos and bring back any that care to come. It is drawing near. Only a few more years and we will see our plans made manifest." He looked off into the sky outside the tent, lost in some dream that Meion could not follow. "Well, have Niddebak take you to Penelaiaa. She is the real chieftain of this place. She will be in charge of your training and see you have work to do."

He might as well rip out his heart and throw it at her feet right now and get it over with, Leucippius thought, as Meion bowed and left the tent with Nidde. She will have that one on her conscience before it's over. He sighed and looked down at his hands on his useless legs.

It was true he could still come in to her. They had not done that to him as well. And it was true she loved him. Every day she proved her love. Still, in dreams he stood up beside her and took her into his arms as a whole man might and only in those dreams was he happy. When she lay across his body in the complicated ritual they had devised for making love it was only her inventiveness and tenderness that made it possible.

She was a beautiful woman and Leucippius burned with jealousy when any new man came into her presence. Now, seeing Meion being led off to meet her he looked down at his hands asking them to take this burden of jealousy off his chest.



"Who is Penelaiaa?" Meion was saying. He was walking with Niddebak across the compound to her quarters. "She is the chieftain? They have a woman for a chieftain?"

"You wait," Nidde said. "You will see." Then she was there, coming out the door to meet them, a tall woman with a soft face. She looked more like a mother than a warrior. "You are a kinsman of Leucippius. Good, we need strong men here. Has it been a long journey? Walking with Niddebak is not easy. He is like a mountain goat. Well, come inside and tell me what you like to do. There is much work to be done. A man who could make weapons would be welcome. Have you ever worked with wood?"

"I can make bows for you," he said. "And javelins. I can throw the javelin. I will do whatever will be of the most use to you. Whatever you need I will do." He lowered his eyes. She reached out and drew him in. "Come inside," she said. "Let us tell our stories."

# Chapter XII

When Auria woke the next morning Meion was sitting beside her holding the baby. "Give her to me," Auria said. "Let me take her."

"She's eaten all the bread and half the honey. She seems better. The cough is better."

"Give her to me. I want to hold her. Kleis, look here, Auria is here. Auria is all right now. Did you miss me? You did not even miss me, did you? You like him as much as me. Meion. Say Meion." She looked up at him. "She did not even know that I was gone. Well, I thank you for caring for her. I will find a way to pay you back for your kindness."

"It's warmer today," he said, getting up. "The sun will shine. When your foot is better I wish to take you to Penelaiaa, to a place of greater safety. You should not be here all alone like this."

"And where is that, this place of safety? Where are you from?"

"High in the mountains. A two days' journey from here. A band of herdsmen live together. Leucippius is our leader. And Penelaiaa is there. You may have heard of her." He paused, then went on. "We are runaway slaves. Like yourself, I think."

"I was never a slave," she said. "Although there is a man who thinks he owns me. I was apprentice to a healer. I can write. I can do numbers."

"Have it your way. I did not mean to offend you. Now, let me see your foot. Does it feel better today?" He moved the covers from her leg and unwrapped her foot. As soon as his hand touched her skin, as soon as his fingers moved against her ankle, he began to desire her again and he kept his face turned from hers. "It will heal," he said. "There is nothing broken." He busied himself wrapping the bindings back around the ankle. "Do you know where you are?" he added. "I tried to tell you yesterday but you were too worried to listen. You are in Clarius's sanctuary. This is where the great statesman and warrior, Clarius, lived when he first came to the mountains. I have looked for this place before but never found it. It is all just as Penelaiaa described it to me."



"I know his name," Auria said. "There's a pottery, in the mountain, and his name is written there. Who is he, this Clarius? And how do you know of him?"

"He is our leader, even Penelaiaa listens to him, even Leucippius. He is in hiding, in the city. But soon he will come back here to the mountains. I saw him once, and talked with him, when I was a boy. He is a strange man, with much kindness. I remember he pulled me into his arms as if he were my mother and asked me about the stars and if I ever thought how lucky we were they never fell on us but moved in their own spaces and were constant. It was the first time anyone had talked to me like that. He filled me with ideas."

"We would be dead if I had not found this place," Auria said. "I ran away with no plans. I only wanted to save her. They had put her out to die. I was following a dry creek bed, the four of us, Phoebe and Metis and Kleis and I. I was looking for water. Then I came to the ledge. Then I was here. It has been, oh, many months ago. We have been here alone a long time. . . ." She shivered and curled down into the bed of covers. "I am so tired. I can't understand this tiredness. I don't know what's wrong with me. I am never tired. I am never sick or tired. I should get up. I should help you." She sat up and tried to stand, then gave up and lay back down. "Oh, curses on this cursed dungheap of an ankle. Oh, curse the godless, soulless, nonexistent gods that did this to me."

He reached down and took the baby from her. He had never heard a girl or woman curse as much as Auria did. Even the roughest women at the camp were not that profane. He moved the cover back over her legs. "It will heal soon. It does no good to curse it. Will you go with me then, to Penelaiaa, when you can? There are women there and children. We have herds. There will be milk."



"Then I will go," Auria said. "As soon as I can walk. I don't know why I am so tired. Oh, curse every cruel, unknown, cursed, ox-dung god to the rivers of hell. Can you take care of her? Can you see to her? And Phoebe must have hay. See that she has hay. . . ." But Auria was falling back to sleep even as she gave him orders. Meion stood above her, holding the baby, wondering at everything, the strange tenderness he felt for everything in the room, the snow falling outside the window, the baby touching his face with her hand, and desire, which was upon him like a dream, as Penelaiaa had told him it would be.

He took Kleis over near the fire and played with her, teaching her games with her hands he had played with his mother when he was a child.

By the time Auria could walk, the weather had improved. On the first nice day she took Meion to see the pottery. Standing at the entrance of the workroom she felt a shiver, remembering how lonely and alone she had been the day she found it. She hung her head and was quiet at the thought, as if loneliness was a shame that must be hidden.

Meion was tracing the letters on the wall. HERE I STUDY THOSE

THINGS THAT ARE MADE OF CLAY AND HARDENED BY FIRE. CLARIUS. "Clarius is a strange man," Meion said. "No one is like him. Perhaps you will meet him someday at the camp. You can tell him of taking shelter here."

"I have been happy here. I am a philosopher and prefer to be alone. Still, I want to go with you. For the milk for Kleis." She moved into a shaft of light coming from the ceiling. "I'm cold in here," she added.



"Wear my cloak," he said, and took it from his shoulders and put it over her, leaving his hands on her arms for a moment. He sighed, then looked down, thinking how strange she was, how hard it was to know what would please her.

"I have a lot of work left to do," she went on. "I have to finish writing down some things. Here, I will show them to you. I have been writing poems in the style of Esappho. I have written five of them." She walked over to the table and lay the tablets out upon it in a row.

Meion looked at the tablets. He picked one up and looked at it, then put it down and picked up another one. "I know nothing of such things," he said finally. "I am a warrior."

"I can tell you what they say."

"If you like. Here, tell me this one." He handed her the one about winter and she read it to him. He looked away. "Oh, well," she said. "It's just something I do to keep busy." She took the tablets and stacked them up in a pile. Later, during the next few days while they waited for her foot to heal she would find him sitting on a bench with the axones, studying them, turning them around and around in his hand. "I could teach you," she said finally. "It isn't hard to read and write. It just takes practice. It's no shame if no one has shown you how to do something."

"I wish nothing to do with writing," he said, getting up. "My mother could write. I could have learned if I wanted to. I only look at these because Clarius made them. Writing is not something I care to know about. It is how the rich keep their riches. They make up laws and write them down and tell us they are gods' words. They take clay or stone or the bark of a tree and write down laws and say gods sent them.

But just because they make marks on clay or stone doesn't mean they may command me. They are still just pieces of wood or clay or stone."

"There are other things written down. It is not only laws."

"It is all a way to make men believe what you say."

"Yes. That is true. I'm sorry I showed the tablets to you. It's nothing to read and write. It's of no importance. I don't want those old tablets anyway. I'm going to leave them here."

"We should leave in the morning," he said. "My people will be worrying about me. Can you leave by then?"

"As soon as the sun rises. I will pack us food. Forget the tablets. You are right. They are of no value." She was feeling sorry for him now and decided to be kind.

In the morning they began their journey. Metis bounded ahead of them but Phoebe had to be coaxed and led. The camp they were making for was a three days' journey to the north and west, deeper and higher into the mountains. Meion led them across meadows and up and around a series of passes and catwalks. Every few miles Auria would make him stop and explain to her the way they had come. Philokrates had been very particular about directions. He had taught Auria to look far off into the distance when she traveled with him and leave landmarks and take bearings.

"Why must you know all this?" Meion said finally.

"I want to know my way back in case I don't like it there."

"You will like Penelaiaa. She is a lady of great kindness and wisdom."

"They might not like me. I might not be welcome."

"Men and women with skills are always welcome with us. We are building a city of our own. The land is not much good for growing food but it is beautiful. Well, you will see."



They camped the first night beside a lake. Meion built a fire and they sat beside it and ate the food they had brought with them, bread and nuts and fruits, the last of Meion's honey. "I desire to lie with you," he said finally. "It is not something I can keep from saying."

"I do not wish to speak of that. It is not something I wish to hear."

"I thought you were so enamored of men speaking truth. This is the truth that is between us now."

"It was done to me once, what you wish. It was very unpleasant. I do not wish to do it anymore."

"You will never lie with a man?"

"I do not know. Perhaps I will, some day. A long time from now. When I am older."

"You are as old now as many wives."

"I do not wish to talk of this." She got up and moved away from him. The sun had left the earth. It was almost dark. The world was very quiet. "However, I will think of it. If you do not speak of it again I will think of it." He was beside her then. The world around them was very still in the last of the day. He touched her arm and she allowed him to leave his hand there for a long time. Perhaps Philokrates was wrong, she was thinking. Perhaps there *are* gods who come and visit us. Perhaps a god is upon me now making me feel these strange things.

• • •

On the second day the trails became harder and they wasted several hours finding a place to ford a river. By night they were not as far as Meion had hoped they would be. "Tomorrow will be better," he said. "We will take our time and not be hard on ourselves. The goat's hooves are cut. We must be careful with her."



"I will breed her when we get to your flocks and pastures. Then she will give milk again. Her milk makes the best cheese in the world. Philokrates was always very careful with her. He fed her the sweetest grasses and kept her as clean as his own beard. I have been careless with her. If he saw her now he would be displeased."

"You would breed your nanny but not yourself."

"It is different with animals. They do not die giving birth." She looked up at him. There was no way to stop talking of it. It was all either of them was thinking of. Phoebe was playing with Metis. Kleis was asleep.

"If you do not use what nature gave you it will shrivel up and die. There is no evil in men and women loving each other." He moved nearer to her. "You could lie with me one time. You could do this once with me. There are many women at the camp who would share my bed. But you are the first one I have desired." She looked at him again. He looked so terrible and pitiful. There had been girls in the kitchen who talked of it as though it were the best thing anyone could do. "When it is dark I will attempt to do this thing," she said at last. "One time I will do it with you. When the stars come out and when Kleis sleeps for the night. But do not talk of it anymore. Do not speak of it until it happens."

Then they did not look at each other and busied themselves setting up a camp and building a fire. Kleis was fussy and had to be walked for an hour before she would sleep. It was black night when she finally settled down. A moonless night. Meion sat by the fire with his hands on his knees and Auria spread their cloaks on a bed of rushes and walked on them until they became smooth. Then she called him to her. "Now," she said. "Show me what is so different from what I suffered at Polymion's hands. Show me what men and women do that has such power over them they blame it on a god."



"I do not know any more than you do."

"Then we will do what we can," she answered. "I was apprentice to a great healer. There is no form of knowledge that is foreign to me."

"How did it seem to you?" he said. It was many hours later. They had been wrapped in each other's arms asleep. It had seemed like wrestling to Auria, like a new world of strange sensations and pleasures only dimly guessed at and much sweating and pulling and pushing and wrestling.

"It was not so bad. Some of it felt good, like things I have felt in my sleep. I would do it again, I believe." She sat up, moved away from him, thought of animals she had seen mating, wondered if she looked like a dog or sheep or goat. She imagined Aphrodite, the statue Philokrates had drawn for her. Perhaps she looked like that and not like a sheep.

"We should move closer to the fire," Meion said. "There are panthers out here and leopards. What were you thinking of? I think you are thinking bad thoughts of me."

"I was thinking of what Philokrates told me of men and women of long ago. They roved in bands driving flocks before them and had no homes or settlements. We are like that now. You and I and Kleis. And still we seem safe enough." She put her face down into his chest and wound her arms around him. She thought of the loneliness of the winter before he came. Only animals live alone, she thought. Only panthers and the wild cats go off and have no other people to talk with them and help them in the world. She sighed. It all seemed very complicated and now she was afraid that he would leave. It had not been good for him, she decided. This mating. He would leave her there and find a woman who was good at such things.

"We must move closer to the fire," he repeated. "Get up and let me move the blankets." She did as she was told and they moved their pallet back to the fire. Kleis was asleep with Metis curled around her. Auria covered her with a robe and made a bed for herself and Meion. I am changed now, she told herself. Now all things are changed.

So Auria and Meion slept beneath the stars. Kleis was beside them wrapped in Philokrates' old cape. Phoebe was curled up with her legs beneath her stomach, half-sleeping, smelling an old smell of leopard on the stones, for leopards still roamed the land of Hellas and preyed on lambs and goats and had even been known to take a child. Metis slept fitfully also, raising his big head every now and then to sniff the air.

They were camped in an old shepherd's campsite, with a limestone bluff to their back and stones arranged in a circle for a hearth. The stars moved in their courses. A fire burned inside the circle of stones and they slept. Below them the life of Hellas went on.

The beautiful land of Hellas, a land of islands and bays, mountains and valleys. Many different peoples had settled there over hundreds of years, arriving in ships or walking or on the backs of horses or oxen or mules, the wildest sort of people, seafarers and wanderers, exiles and runaways. They had created a land of walled cities and fortresses, separated from each other by mountains. There were few roads from one settlement to the next and the ones there were were dangerous. Robbers were everywhere who would kill a man for his sandals.

The largest cities had been created by a few powerful old families. Meion's mother's family, the Alkmeionadae, were one of these. They had made their fortune in Athens and in Delphi, where they built the temples and gave the Pythia her power.



The greatest statesman of the Alkmeionadae family was Pericles, the present ruler of Athens, but he could do nothing for his cousins outside the city as he was busy fighting a war with the Spartans, a cruel and conservative people who enslaved their own kinsmen and sent their sons into the army at an early age. They were so conservative and cautious that it took a great deal of provocation to make them march out to war. Still, the Athenians had goaded and frightened them into it, and on this night, while Auria and Meion lay in each other's arms, the Spartans were camped outside of Athens and the Athenians were crowded together behind their walls.

In the camp where Meion and Auria were headed, Meion's cousin, Leucippius, was drinking wine and worrying about the safety of his little band. Athens was under siege and its citizens dying of plague. The demagogue Cleon, who hated the Alkmeionadae, was on the verge of seizing power from Pericles. If that happened he would surely send a force to rout out Leucippius and his men. Worst of all, Leucippius had made a treaty with a barbarian named Braseus and now Braseus and some of his men had moved into Leucippius's camp. They were little better than outlaws and followed no laws. Leucippius sighed. He was reading a letter from Elen Alkmeionadae, Meion's mother. It was in answer to one he had written before Meion went away.



*To Leucippius Alkmeionadae, most beloved friend and kinsman. Greetings and salutations from Elen Alkmeionadae, on Delos, at the feast of Apollo the Healer.*

*Dearest friend, your letters concerning Meion have reached me at last. So good to know that he is in your bosom and that you love him. Remind him to read if you can. How can a son of my womb be so untouched by books? Perhaps he has seen too much of the real world. When I think of the months he was in the mines, day after day. Why did it take me so long to gather the courage to send him to you? Such questions plague me. Still, he achieved two ends. His own freedom there with you and my untiring hatred of Eutorian. My beauty is fading now and my mind is not as keen as once it was but my hatred grows and festers. It will not be long now and I will end this. Only the house must fall with the master. Nothing short of the entire disruption of the mines will satisfy me now. Mark me, cousin, we will have our revenge for everything.*

*Do not let Meion know my mind is filled with such dark thoughts. Give him the letter enclosed with this one and say I am happy and will join you when I can. It is the very heart of night as I seal this and send it to you, with my love.*

*Elen*

*Never underestimate the danger we are in at this time. Make plans to move the camp at word from me. They think you hate Athens for hating them that use her like a whore. And yet, who has loved her better and longed to cleanse and heal her? Keep my child safe for me. I am ill at ease, sweet cousin, I am impatient and at sea.*

Leucippius called a boy from inside the house and sent him to fetch Braseus.

The boy returned with the man. Leucippius poured wine from a stone jar and offered it to his guest.



"I am worrying over Meion," he began. "He has been gone too long."

"He went searching for bear. He'll be back."

"I'm responsible to his mother for him. Why didn't you go along since you know so much about this bear hunt?"

"He was scouting along the way and I had other plans. Is this why you have called me at this hour of the night? To worry over young Meion?"

"No, I want to talk to you about raiding down into the farmlands. You have to keep your men in check, Braseus. We can't be a hideout for outlaws."

"What are we, then?" It was not insolence. He was really curious about what Leucippius saw himself as doing.

"I do not know, young friend. When I came here it was to hide my shame over losing the use of my legs. I went away to die. Then Penelaiaa followed me and others and I decided to live to serve them. I would take us back to Athens but there is no Athens now. Only a battlefield and sickbed. So, we must begin again up here. Keep the flame of civilization alight. Keep the law."

"Whose law?"

"The law Athena decrees, the daughter of Zeus in her wisdom."

"There are other gods, other laws."

"I have decided that you will study with me. We will study the laws of Zeus's daughter and we will talk of what the courts are and how they serve man and make a better city."

"So the weak can overpower the strong."



"No. So that men know right from wrong and treat each other justly."

"And what is just?"

"Before anger clouds the mind men decide what the outcome will be of arguments and then abide by that when the time comes. It is a great and noble thing, the law. Yet sometimes it errs, as all things human do."

"I will come and read these laws with you then. But it will not stop my men from gaining what they need on the highways. What are we to do who have no land to till?"

"What is the man to do whose horse you steal?"

"Walk home glad he was not killed. Praising the mercy of Braseus."

"Come tomorrow in the early hours. Sit with me awhile then. Do this for me. In the service of harmony."

"I will come. If that is what you wish." The younger man held out his cup and Leucippius filled it and they talked of other things.

In the morning Auria was curled up against Meion's shoulder. She shook him awake to talk about what they had done. "That was very good to do," she said. "It is worth all the talk it makes. Do you think that I was good at it? Did it please you also?"

"Oh, yes," he said. "You are as good at it as I can imagine any woman being, or a goddess even."

"I would like to do it some more with you," she said. "Later we will try it again. But there are clouds gathering in the sky. We must hurry if we are to reach shelter before it rains." She touched his shoulders, where the hollows were. She fitted the ball of her hand into the hollow of his shoulder and thought of the strangeness of another human being, how she might never understand a single thing, much less be wise.

"We can do it later," he said. "We will do it whenever you wish. As much as you wish." Kleis cried out and Auria disentangled her legs from his and got up to tend to the baby. She was glad of an interruption in so much strangeness.



Past noon they came around a cliff and down into one of the pastures that fed the flocks of the camp. A shepherd was warming his hands beside a fire. He called out to them and Meion returned his greeting.

They crossed the pasture and started up the path to the camp. It was beautiful along the path, which wound between boulders and pine trees and led to a flat outthrust of land which looked down upon a clear blue mountain lake.

"Is it much further?" Auria asked.

"A little more," he answered, and even as he spoke the trees opened up onto a clearing the size of a small town. Spread out before them was a village of huts and tents. Fires were burning. Children were playing around a wooden horse painted blue and yellow. Men were working on the foundation of a building, moving stones and mixing mortar.

So Auria arrived at the camp, knowing nothing of the events that would change her life, knowing only that she was going to a place where Kleis would be safe, where there would be food and milk, following this beautiful young man the earth had sent to her. Trust the forces of the earth, Philokrates had taught her. *Theoi,* the forces men call gods. They work for good for those who trust them. Do not set them against each other. Neither let them push you about like waves on the sea. Walk among the men and women of the earth and wish them well and heal them as I will teach you to and you will be safe. He would take her into



his arms when he told her such things and her soft young arms would wind around his old grizzled neck, his old strong shoulders and his wonderful hands would hold her to him. She walked into the camp thinking of him now. He is in Kleis, she told herself. And perhaps in Meion also, now that I am a woman and have done this thing a woman does and mixed my history with this creature who does not even know how to read and can make me feel inferior and like a slave if he stops looking at me for a moment.

They continued up the path. Through the breaks in the trees were fabulous vistas, mountain after mountain spreading back into the sky.

"Once I went to Cirrha," she said. "This is like going to Cirrha. Everything is new."

A tall woman came running out of a house at the end of the clearing. Her hair was braided and coiled around her head. She wore a long wool garment of a style Auria had never seen and she ran across the clearing and took Meion into her arms. Then she turned to Auria, who was standing to one side with the animals beside her, holding the baby in her arms.

"This is why I was delayed," Meion said to the woman. "Her name is Auria. She was alone in Clarius's sanctuary with this child. I have brought her to stay with me. She is under my protection."

"You have brought us a child," Penelaiaa said. "Always a good gift. But aren't you young to have a child this size? Is she your own?"

"As much as my eyes. But not of my own body. I took her from a dying mother. I ran away from the place where I was raised. It was not a good place. There was no one left alive there who cared for me."

"The child is very beautiful," Penelaiaa said. "With golden curls. Let me hold her for you." She held out her arms to Kleis and the little girl went to her eagerly.



"She is dusty from the trip," Auria said. "She will soil your garments."

"I do not mind. I wish to hold her." Kleis reached up a hand and touched Penelaiaa's hair. The older woman laughed and curled the baby closer into her arms. "Come along then," she said. "We will go to Leucippius. Meion, you had us all scared to death. We thought the wolves had you days ago." Then Penelaiaa took Auria by the arm and the three of them moved like a phalanx through the smiles and inquiring faces of the people of the camp.

They were moving towards a dwelling at the far end of the clearing. A man was seated on the porch in a leather chair. He held out his arms and Meion embraced him. Auria felt strange suddenly, watching Meion embrace this man. It must be true, as he had told her, that he was a kinsman of Pericles, the man who ruled all of Attica.

"What is happening in the city?" Meion asked. "Has news come while I was gone?"

"Athens is in turmoil. Plataea is under siege. But the news has been that you were lost. We couldn't imagine where you'd been." Leucippius smiled at Auria as he spoke. He was a beautiful man, with wide shoulders and strong brown arms. He had high cheekbones, like Meion's, and a large head covered with gray hair. He was very powerful and graceful. It seemed impossible to believe that he could not stand up if he chose. He held out his hand and she went to him. This is what it means to be a leader, she was thinking. We all draw near him. She was too young to know her own wonder, too young to know that Leucippius saw the same thing in her face that she read in his. She lowered her eyes and stepped back towards Penelaiaa. For a moment no one spoke. Dreams moved between them. Understandings, compromises, agreements.



"She was in Clarius's old shelter," Meion said. "She found her way there with this child. She was raised in a villa. She brings us many skills."

"In Clarius's sanctuary?" Leucippius asked. "However did you stumble upon that hidden place? Clarius is our ally. Well, you will meet him sooner or later. The gods are busy."

"I followed the sound of water. For my goat. May I tether her somewhere near? I do not turn her out to pasture." Auria paused. "I like to keep her near me." She stepped back, embarrassed to be known as a girl who must keep a goat by her side. And what did they see, these two Athenian aristocrats, as they gazed upon Auria? A girl with a riot of black curls around her head. A beautiful face with high cheekbones and a brooding look around the mouth that made her seem older than she was. Clear blue eyes that burned into any that returned her stare. She was dressed in a tunic of homespun white cloth, scrubbed so many times that it was brilliantly white, and a long cloak of brown cloth made of beautiful old wool, with a deep hem sewn around. On her arm was a bracelet woven of vines. Around her waist a girdle of leather and a sheath holding a finely made Persian knife. She wore leather boots laced up the sides and a string of leather around her brow. Long fine legs and hands which were composed and still at her sides. A girl who would be noticed and stared at anywhere. Leucippius and Penelaiaa looked at one another and agreed it was safe to love the girl. Safe, Leucippius's eyes said. Reasonably safe, Penelaiaa's answered.



"Of course. There are plenty of places to keep your goat. Let Meion show you." Leucippius held out his hand and she took it and held it. A shaft of sunlight was pouring down upon the porch where they stood. The light pressed upon them. The strange understanding moved among the four of them again. They withstood it for a moment, then laughed to shake it off.

"We will keep the child," Penelaiaa said. She reached for Kleis, and the child went to her again and wrapped her arms and legs around the older woman and laid her head against her chest.

"Where is Braseus?" Meion asked. "Is he around the camp?"

"If he isn't off hunting," Penelaiaa answered. "He took a stag last week and had a great feast for everyone. He was so pleased with his success he is probably out hunting for another."

"Do not underestimate Braseus," Leucippius said. "Or make fun of a man's pride."

"You are the one who underestimates Braseus," Penelaiaa began. "Never mind. It is of no importance now. Go and find him, Meion. Say you heard he made a great sacrifice of a heroic stag with many antlers. I am going to take this child inside and bathe her face and hands."

Then Meion and Auria took their leave and found a spot to tether Phoebe and started down the path to the lake. As soon as they were out of the sight of people they began to desire each other again and stopped beneath a tree and leaned against it talking in low voices, as though love were a terrible secret that must be hidden from the world, as though they were the first man and woman in the world to find this secret.



"Did they think well of me?" Auria asked. "They seemed so grand."

"You would have known if they had not. It is good you brought Kleis here. Penelaiaa had a child that died. There has never been another. A girlchild. Afterwards, she walked all the way down the mountain carrying it in her arms. She was wearing a long white himation and the child was laid out across her arms and she did not look at anyone. She walked all the way to the river without speaking. I had not been here long when it happened. She made us dig a grave as the Egyptians and Persians do, a square grave. We lined it with stones and then with flowers and we laid the child down in the ground in a hole filled with blossoms from the lemon trees and then we covered her back up and laid flat stones on the earth and built a cairn to mark the place. It was the worst day I have ever suffered in my life. It is good you have brought Kleis here. She will bring solace to Penelaiaa."

"How did the child die?"

"Of a fever carried by mosquitos. More than one died, but she was the youngest. There were not many children with us then. There are more now."

"Why have so many come here?"

"To live a free life. There are too many outlaws in these hills for men to live alone. And Athens is too crowded and men spend their lives there fighting among themselves. Our family has been banished twice on false charges of impiety. Leucippius will never return. He says the will of a democracy is too fickle. That a man must become as dumb as an ox to lead oxen." Meion paused, then went on. "Still, one must lead or be led. For now, we are only trying to live our lives as best we can. Later, there is always the chance that we will return to power. Then I will go to Athens and see about the life of politics. I might be good at making speeches. Who knows what the fates have in store for us? I would never have expected to find you when I thought I was stalking a bear." He pulled her close to him. They were on a pine-covered path leading down to the lake. Willows grew along the lake's edge; their strange configurations were leafless now, mirrored in the water. Behind the lake a grove of cypresses rose like spears against the cloudless sky. Auria moved close to him, feeling a chill, like a premonition, as if she knew that one day the two of them would fight for their lives not ten feet from where they were standing now. She pushed the vision from her mind and buried her head in Meion's chest.



"Come along," he said. "I want you to meet my friends and see the exercise field we have made." She shook off the chill and took his hand and they continued down the path that skirted the lake. At a cleared place on the far side three men were throwing spears into a target. "There is Braseus," Meion said. "With two of his guard. He's a barbarian, a wild hill man, but important to us. I am fond of him for all his wild ways. Oh, he's seen us now." The tallest of the three men threw his spear down on the ground, pulled off his outer garment and dove into the lake, swimming towards them across the water. Meion laughed and threw off his own cloak and swam out to meet him. They met where the sandy bottom allowed them to stand and began to wrestle, laughing and straining against each other's bodies. Auria stepped back. She couldn't tell if they were serious or in play. The others came and stood along the bank cheering them on. Several times both men sank below the surface of the freezing water, then came back up, choking and gasping but still holding on. Finally, they collapsed onto the shore, still in each other's arms. They stood up and walked towards her. "So this is where he has been," Braseus said, standing before her with water dripping from his body. "Where did you come from, little darkhaired mistress?"

"I am Auria," she said.

"Come and eat with us later," Meion said. "We will tell you the story. I never saw the track of a single bear in those parts but she says there was one in that area. She thought it was a pig."

"I've been away also," Braseus answered. "To the high plateau. I shall take my men and go and spend the summer up there. There are too many here now. Will you go with us?"

"And leave Leucippius here alone?"

"I'll make an outpost. He knows. I have spoken to him of it."

"Who would you take with you?" Meion was shivering, rubbing himself with his cloak as he spoke. There was an edge to his voice that Auria had never heard. Everything was strange to her here. This camp was unlike anything she had ever known. The villa had been a little country farm where they only heard rumors of the world. Now, in this camp, so far away from the settled part of Attica, there seemed to be great things going on. Things of importance that she could not understand.

"I will take whoever wishes to go. It's beautiful up there, very near the gods. There are herds of wild blue sheep. A man could live without working if he could hunt."

"We will talk of it later. Come and eat with us when the sun leaves the earth. We'll be in Darian's old dwelling. Penelaiaa said it was unoccupied. You will find us there." Meion crossed his fist on his forehead in a gesture of fellowship. Braseus did the same and they took their leave of each other.

"Are you a warrior?" Auria asked Meion later. "Is this a warrior's life?" 

"Yes, I suppose you could call me a warrior. Since I must live."

"There is no war up here."

"There is always war. A man takes territory and defends it. A family must have land and others wish to take it from them. Unless you wish to be a Phoenician and trade for a living. Take Braseus. He is seething because none of this belongs to him, although some of the same blood runs in his veins that runs in mine and in Leucippius's. He admires Leucippius above all men and also seethes with jealousy of him. He would gladly be a cripple to have Leucippius's woman and his reputation. Since he cannot, and since Leucippius will not give him a share of the pasture land, he will leave and go up to the plateau above us and start his own camp. Then our forces will be split and if either of us is attacked we will be shorthanded. I will try to make him stay, but it will do no good unless Leucippius changes his ways."

"I do not understand these things. Why can't men and women live in peace and not give in to jealousy and fight over who is in command? Why must a man throw himself into freezing water to prove his worth?"

"You ask a million questions."

"It is how I am. Philokrates said questions are answers we did not know we sought."

"Come and let me hold you for a while. We are safe tonight. When

Braseus comes later you can tell him why men should not fight. Perhaps he will listen to you." He was laughing at her but she did not care and she went to him and undid his chlamys and then her own and lay down with him and forgot for a while the strangeness of men and the things they believe and die for.



Braseus arrived late. Auria set out a supper of bread and cheese and wine, a bowl of black beans and a bowl of nuts in honey, and they ate and drank and told their stories.

"It was a quiet life," Auria said. She had been talking about the trading post. "We heard of war and battles but I had never seen soldiers or men who fought."

"I would live at peace if I could come upon a woman like you in a valley filled with snow." Braseus laughed. "As it is I must content myself with hunting and the campgirls who have become my sisters from so much intimacy. My tent is filled with them. I don't know one from the other unless I'm drunk. Yes, it would be a good life to live on the coast and have a villa and be a tradesman and buy and sell. Perhaps I will try it one day." He filled his mouth with honeyed nuts and washed them down with wine. He was wary of this creature Meion had delivered to the camp but he couldn't help liking her—the way she swung the baby girl from her hip as she walked around filling the cups, the seriousness of her speech, as if she were a girl who had lived always among very old people and had never been a child or run through the woods on summer nights chasing and being caught. She drank little wine and although she laughed at his jokes she was strange. He shuddered, thinking what a task it would be to mount and subdue her.

"Meion says it will be bad if you leave the camp," she said. "He said it will make everyone unsafe. Is he right in this?" She waited for his answer. He looked at Meion before he spoke.

"I would come to your aid if you needed me. Meanwhile, yes, I am leaving, and soon. Leucippius has forbidden us to take anything from travelers as far away as the second turning of the river. How can my men live this way? They will all desert me."



"Promise to stay until spring," Meion said. "It is madness to go off before the winter storms are finished. Wait until the rivers are full and if you must leave then I will understand."

"I will try." Braseus cut into a cheese and Auria filled his cup again. They began to discuss the wall they were building along the exposed sides of the lake and after a while Auria took Kleis and walked out into the cold night air and left the men to talk. It was very beautiful up so high. Even in the cold the night was fragrant with pine. Artemis seemed near in these woods and Auria closed her eyes and imagined the virgin goddess brooding over the forest. "If you are there, keep us safe," Auria said. "Stay near Kleis and do not be angry if I blaspheme you in the daylight hours. We are what we are. We are only men and women. Not gods or heroes, although some of these up here seem to think they are." She laughed at her joke and cuddling the baby close she walked around the circumference of the camp before she returned to the hearth where Meion and Braseus were drinking wine and talking about battles and weapons and hunts.

So Auria's life in the camp began. The dwelling they had been given was in a grove overlooking the lake. Auria set to work to make it habitable and Meion moved his things from the men's quarters and piled them in a corner. The next morning he announced that he was going bear hunting with Braseus. "He has seen the tracks of a great brown bear that has been around here for some years. No one has seen its track in a long time. We thought it must be dead. Braseus is very excited. Perhaps this will keep him from thinking of leaving. We will stalk it with dogs. Could I take Metis and give him a run? Would he follow me?"



"Why did you move into this dwelling if you are going to leave as soon as you arrive?" She sat up and began to dress. "You did not tell me you would leave as soon as you brought me here."

He said nothing, so she went on. "Why should you stalk a bear? What good is a bear to a man?"

"I told Braseus I would go. He is waiting for me." Meion was tying on his leggings, choosing arrows for a quiver.

"Then go. I would not keep you. I have never kept anyone from their desires." She stood up and adjusted her chlamys and reached for her cloak. She looked down at her hands, waiting. Meion picked up his bow and walked out the door without another word, going off in the direction of the lake as if she weren't even there. It did not occur to him that she was really angry because he was going hunting. Why would anyone keep another person from going hunting?

In three days he returned and begged her forgiveness for going.

"There is nothing to forgive. If you wish to spend your time fighting and hunting it is nothing to me." She was mending a gown for Kleis with a needle Penelaiaa had given her. She bent over the gown as though it were the most important thing in the world. She pulled the thread through and bit it with her teeth.

“I had to go with Braseus. I am the mortar between Braseus and Leucippius.”

“The women talk of him leaving. They said there will not be enough to guard the wall when it is finished. Why does he wish to go? The land is not as good for lambs and it is even colder.”

“He wishes to raid down into the villages and Leucippius won’t allow it. Braseus is a hill man. They are not accustomed to law, and resent it.” 

“Then you must let him go. With him here there will be strife and trouble.”

“We will be too few if he takes his men. Anyone could attack us.” Meion bowed his head. He was tired. It was true he had stayed at the hunt to keep Braseus’s good will. It had been a long trek and hard sleeping on the ground and now Auria was confusing his mind.

“Who would come to bother us here?” she went on. “What do we have that is of such value?”

“Leucippius has enemies in Athens. As long as Pericles is general we are safe from attack but he is old now and when he is gone they will come for us when they have time.”

“Who would come?”

“A man named Cleon. A commoner raised to think he is as good as any man. A rabble-rouser. He hates the Alkmeionadae but Leucippius first of all. It was Cleon’s men who set upon Leucippius and destroyed his legs.”

“Why hasn’t Leucippius had revenge?”

“There was none to revenge him. Cleon has a guard of thirty with him always. Do not speak of it more tonight, Auria. It is great sadness to me that I can not revenge Leucippius. I would go there in a moment if he would allow it. If I were not needed here." He looked so tired that Auria was ashamed of her questions and went to him and touched his arm.

"You must eat now. Then rest."

"Where is Kleis? I brought rabbit skins to make her a warm shirt. Is she sleeping?" He sank down on the bed and Auria removed his sandals and set about finding food for him to eat.



"She is staying with Penelaiaa tonight. I think she would live there if I would let her. Penelaiaa gives her honey cakes all the time. Tell me of the bear. Is it like that little dwarfed furry creature I told you of? The furry pig?" She laughed, thinking of Braseus and Meion and the others in pursuit of such game. "Is that what you come home half-frozen from hunting?" She put food on the table and moved a bench near to it.

"It is a large creature and very dangerous. It kills horses and sheep with a slap of its paw. In the winter it sleeps in a lair and you can surprise it if you are careful and take the cubs. The coat makes a wonderful rug and you can fashion hats of the skin. Auria, will you lie with me?"

"And when it is over you will go off hunting the next day?" She put down the bread she was holding and allowed him to take her into his arms.

"I will stay by the hearth and haul water for you like a slave. I will be your slave."

"I do not want a slave," she said. "I do not know anymore what I want. You have brought me here and confused me with your hands and mouth and arms. Now I am like a kitchen slave and without knowledge of myself or anything." She began to cry, strange confused tears coming from nowhere. They were the first tears she had cried in a long time. She did not know what to think of these salty confusing terrible tears.

"I won't go off again. I promise you."

"It isn't that. It is nothing at all. Except that he is gone who taught me everything. All things he taught me. There is no one to talk to now. No one in the world will ever talk to me that way again."



"I will try," Meion offered. "I will do what I can for you."

The next day the weather warmed considerably. It was a beautiful bright winter day that lightened the spirits of everyone. Auria and Meion went down to the exercise field in the afternoon. The sky was bright. The rocks thrust up from the field like red flowers. The spears of the cypresses crowded the sky. "Why do you say there are no gods?" Meion began. "How could anyone look at the skies and believe there are no gods?"

"If gods ruled our lives we could see them. If they are in the clouds they could come down and speak to us. The gods in temples are only stone dolls. The Asclepiads laugh at men who believe in gods."

"What of clouds in the skies, the beautiful patterns? How do you account for them?"

"They are water in different forms. Like spray on waves or your breath on cold days. Like snow, which melts into water. Clouds are only water, no matter how beautiful they may seem to our eyes. Don't get mad, Meion. I can't help it if I was raised by a philosopher. He told me what the truth of life is."

"You mustn't let the others hear you talk like that. I heard someone the other day saying you cursed like a witch."

"Then I will go back to Clarius's hut if these ignorant women do not like the way I speak. I talk as I choose. I am a Hellene and free."

"Come and join us, Meion," Braseus called from the field where the men were practicing with bows. "Let's have a contest. You've rested long enough. Come on. Let's see if this woman has unmanned you."



Meion held his hands over his head in the sign for victory. Braseus ran towards him and the two of them began to wrestle, rolling around the ground as they had done in the water. Auria walked back up the hill alone.

When she was almost to the top she turned and looked back down. They were still wrestling, laughing and rolling around the ground. They stopped finally and picked up javelins from a pile on the ground and began to throw them at the targets. Braseus picked up a javelin and hurled it down the course and into the side of a target. Meion placed one beside it. They threw again. This time Braseus was closer to the center. Meion took his time, then threw the shaft down the field and dead center into a target. "Best of ten," Braseus said. "You can take that one for a beginning." Meion nodded his head and began to choose among the spears lying around the ground. The other men had moved back. Auria watched until the second throw began. Then she turned and walked back up the hill. Soon I will be great with a child, she was thinking. I will sit with the women and nurse children all day long and he will be throwing spears into targets. This will be my destiny. And what of this Braseus? He is not even civilized. He cares for nothing but fighting, spears and swords and falling all over the ground on top of Meion. What am I doing in this place with these violent people? Penelaiaa takes Kleis off and cares for her but I do not think Penelaiaa cares for me. She gives me strange looks when Leucippius holds out his hand to me. And she is not easy to talk to, grand and imperious. Once I thought a man or woman lived only to question things and listen, to sit beside ones they loved and share morning bread and evening bread. Once I came down a long dark road on a wagon and he was waiting at the end for me and now he is gone and there is no one but me who knows the clouds are made of water.



Auria went back to her dwelling and began to straighten all the things inside. She took a broom of willow whips and swept the ground outside the door and then went to Penelaiaa's dwelling and found Kleis playing with spools from the loom. "Why are you sad?" Penelaiaa said. "On such a nice day."

"They are fighting beside the lake. There is no enemy here and yet they practice every time the sun comes out. I am not used to living with warriors. Where I lived we grew food and raised sheep and ships put in and caravans came and traded goods."

"If we are attacked you will be glad Meion has a good eye and hand."

"Will we be attacked?"

"I pray not, but it might happen."

"Then we should go further up. We should not stay here if we are in danger."

"We could not move forever." Penelaiaa stood beside a chest. She seemed very tall and distant. Auria picked up Kleis and held her.

"I am sorry. I am unhappy because Meion said the women of the camp were whispering about me."

"They whisper about anything. One thing is the same as another to them. If something seems wonderful to them they must try to make it less so. Otherwise they would be too ugly in comparison. Take it as a compliment that they talk of you."

"Too much has happened. I thank you for letting her stay here so long. I forget to thank you for all your kindnesses."

"We will be better friends," Penelaiaa said. "We will talk more on these matters."



~

That night an altercation broke out in the men's quarters. Braseus and his guard were quarreling over dice with two older men and a man was killed. It was an accident, but it brought things to a head.

"They must be cleansed," Leucippius said. He had set up his chair in the middle of his main room. The chair was covered with skins and a red robe was across his knees. He looked like an old king of a mountain fortress. Braseus stood before him, his feet spread wide, his hand resting on his sword, his head back and to the side. Meion was outside the door, on the porch. Half of Braseus's guard was in the yard, waiting. Others of the camp had come to stand on the porch. They were quiet, listening. Penelaiaa left the room where the men were talking and walked out onto the porch to stand by Meion. She was wearing a long tunic of homespun white cloth. Her hair was braided and tied around her head. She had put on her court bracelets from long ago. Meion pulled her to his side.

"They must be cleansed and pay a blood price," Leucippius was speaking in a loud voice. "We are not barbarians. We can not let murder go uncleansed."

"It was no murder," Braseus answered. "Letis became angry over dice and pulled out a knife. It was a fight, not a murder."

"Still, it must be cleansed. They can go together to Delphi, all three of the men who touched him, or down to Olympia. Yes, Olympia would be better, then no one could say we used influence to have them pardoned."

"They are not guilty of murder, Leucippius. This is nonsense. I need them here."

"Letis has relatives in the camp. It will end in more murders and bad blood. Bring the men to me." 

"They do not answer to you. They answer to me." Braseus shifted his weight from one hip to the other. Through the open door the men and women on the porch could see the way Leucippius hardened. As they watched he took his sword from beside his chair and laid it across his knees. Nothing was said for a moment, then Braseus spoke again. "I will take my men and animals and go tomorrow to the high pastures above the waterfall. I won't submit to your authority, Leucippius. Your ways are not our ways. My grandmother was the Pythia at Delphi. My blood is as rich as yours."

Leucippius sighed and looked down at his hands. A shaft of light fell across the floor between them, splitting the room in two. They took it for a sign.

"Then go your way. Clarius will be here soon to aid me. I have no need of barbarians for friends. If the murder is not cleansed we all will suffer. You also, Braseus. You were in the room and did not stay his hand."

"I do not submit to laws that come from city gods. Dionysius knows these hills and the Apollo of the Parnassus needs no temples. Nor priests to interpret our ways." It was a long speech for Braseus. He raised his voice as he said it, so the men outside could hear him. "I will make my own camp and rule it the way mountain men have always ruled. The strongest man wins and the others do as he wishes. So men continue to be strong and do not submit to priests and pederasts." Braseus took his sword hand and raised it to his brow in salute and turned and left the room. As he walked out onto the porch he stopped and spoke to Meion. "Will you go with us? Will you be my hearth-brother and share my fate, or stay with this cripple?"



"I can not leave here, Braseus. But let me walk with you a moment and persuade you not to give up old friends." Braseus turned his attention to Penelaiaa. "Will you go with me, Madam? Will you share a man's tent for a change?"

"I live with a man whose dungbucket you should worship," she answered and turned and went into the house.

"Walk with me to collect my things," Braseus said to Meion. "I will leave before the sun does."

"Let the light of another day shine on your decision," Meion pleaded. "Wait a day." But nothing would change Braseus's mind. He packed his belongings and called his followers around him and by dusk they were gathering to leave. He took thirty men and struck off the back way, a wooded path that led up and around the mountain and across a wooden bridge over a waterfall. It was a three hours' hike or an hour's ride. The men with horses led the way. The women and children came next and a guard of ten to bring up the rear. The rest of the camp stood around in silence and watched the preparations. Leucippius was still sitting in the middle of his room. He had hardly moved from the spot all day. Penelaiaa had walked down the stretch of meadowland to the grave of Ai. Auria followed her. Penelaiaa looked up and saw the girl's short brown tunic coming across the meadow, the dog, Metis, by her side and the child, Kleis, in her arms. She looked away and turned back to her work, pulling weeds that were growing in the stones of the cairn. She did not look up until Auria was almost to her side.

"Will I intrude on your sorrow?" Auria asked. "Shall I turn back?"

"No, we will go down to the river and let Kleis wade in the smooth rocks. It does no good to tend the dead. What does Ai know of white vine and yellow spider climbing over her piece of earth? She is far from here now. Chasing butterflies in other meadows." Penelaiaa raised her face. "It was kind of you to come. So, what have they done up there? Has Braseus left yet?"



"They were gathering. Could Leucippius stop him?"

"He would not to save us all. I am the cause of this. So the fates catch us in their nets. I was kind to Braseus when he first joined us and he mistook it for something more." She paused and took Kleis from Auria's arms. Auria was quiet, not knowing what to say to this woman whom she was only beginning to understand. Penelaiaa seemed so wise in many ways, with such knowledge of the world, and in other ways, so clouded and mistaken. I must be quiet, Auria told herself now. I must learn to listen if I am to live with all these people and their ways.

Penelaiaa continued, "So he makes this gesture to show me he is a greater man than Leucippius and for a return I will be left with no way to secure the ones I love. I love the men and women of this place, Auria. One by one they chose to come and cast their lot with us. Well, I will charm Clarius into returning." She brightened up at the thought. "And we are not without strength. There are still two hundred men and boys. And the wall grows. Here, this is the way to the river." They moved down a rocky path to a beach of stones and held Kleis by the hands while she stuck her feet into the freezing water, screaming with delight each time. "We have today and its glories, do we not?" Penelaiaa said. "Let us go back now and be an example to the rest."

Auria waded out to her knees in the freezing water and looked around her at the beauty of the world. A garnet tree laden with nuts hung out over the bank and she made a note to herself to pick them when they dried completely. The dried nuts made a poison so deadly that a drop of it on an arrow would kill a man in an hour. So I am a warrior now, she thought. And take joy in knowing I could kill. Like a barbarian who does not even sacrifice when he kills his cattle. Like Braseus himself. I am glad he is gone. We will be stronger for it.



"What are you thinking?" Penelaiaa asked. Auria was standing very still in the freezing water.

"Nothing that needs speaking," the girl replied, and waded out and tied back on her sandals.

"She is the strangest young woman I have ever known," Penelaiaa told Leucippius later. "In Athens she could have been the high priestess in any temple. Who was this man who raised her, this Philokrates? Did you know of him?"

"The Asclepiads are strange men. They reach into the heart of life with their arts. You are beginning to trust her then, are you not?"

"To love her, I think. She has been delivered to us by Athena. How many lambs did Braseus take from the flock?"

"Do not speak of it. Let it go."

~

Auria was seated with Meion beside the hearth. Kleis was asleep beside them in a basket of rushes. Meion had his head in Auria's lap, his foot crossed upon his knee. As he moved his leg the shadows of their bodies played against the wall. Metis was near them, curled into a fat red ball. Phoebe was against the wall, eating an apple.

"Does it matter so much that they are gone?" Auria stroked Meion's forehead, smoothing away the lines if he wrinkled his brow.

"He is the best archer in the camp and his men are the strongest. Besides, he was my sworn brother-in-arms. We have hunted elk and boar and deer. He is a man you want beside you in a battle."



"What will he do up there?"

"Gather around him all the outlaws he can find and build an outpost. It is Penelaiaa who is the real cause of this. But not of her doing."

"He has plenty of women."

"Many women are not Penelaiaa." He reached for her then and they got up and moved to their bed and lay down upon it and began the thing that seemed to Auria like a long road winding between silver olives.

"Where do we travel?" he asked her, when she told him that. "To what destination?"

"To the bay of Itea, to run out onto a pier and take a ship for Sicili where men live in trees and children are born in pairs."

# Chapter XIII

1. The freewoman, Penelaiaa Metella, in the high camp near Cithaeron, to Clarius Arasistratus, in Athens:

*Braseus is gone with thirty men. Also, he has taken the best arms. We will buy more. A Sumerian trader out of Cirrha will supply us soon. You must come to us. There is no way Leucippius can lead us from a chair. This is a promise you made to me and I will keep you to it. You are more important here than there.*

*Meion went off hunting. He returned after three weeks with a girl he found in your old sanctuary. She is a strange girl and educated. She read things you left in your workshop and says she is your disciple. Her name is Auria. She has a child with her, a funny little thing with blond curls, like Ai. I keep her by me often. She is learning to speak and mimics everything, even the dogs and the birds in the trees.*

*Meion is in love. How tall he seems and more serious than ever. The girl returns his love but they argue incessantly. It is all a nice diversion. What else? The shoemaker, Aeneas, asks to be remembered to you. He sends word he will make new boots for you when you come. Answer as quickly as you can. Hurry to us. If Braseus becomes strong enough he might attack us himself. You must talk with him. P.*

II. Clarius Arasistratus, from his villa in Athens, to Penelaiaa Metella, by way of Corinth:

*As soon as the weather permits I will be on my way. Things are harried in the city. There is much hoarding and petty theft. Unsolved murders of two citizens. A suicide at least once a week, or a poisoning. Rumors of plague in Lemnos. The Spartans could walk in tomorrow.*



*We must remember what our ends are. We could hold the mountain passes forever with a thousand men. We will talk of this when we meet. Braseus must join us then so we can make peace with him and not work at cross-purposes. Send word to him that we will meet together in the spring.*

*I am intrigued by news of my disciple and look forward to hearing about my gardens. Until we embrace. C.*

III. Penelaiaa, in the mountains, to Clarius, in Athens:

*I am turned into a grandmother and can not keep my hands off the child the girl brought to me. Kleis, they call her.*

*When will you come to us? Destiny weighs upon my heart. I have written Braseus telling him to meet with us in the spring. There must be alternate plans for the women and children. There are thirty-eight children in this camp alone. What provisions can we make for them? Answer by Eurobeaus, who comes this way in March. Or come with him. P.*

IV. Clarius Arasistratus, on the island of Exaria, to Penelaiaa:

*I will be delayed in coming to you. There is a chance of making an alliance with our kinsman, Philomenes, who is here with fifty followers, all strong men. Half the island is under their power. Philomenes says we must stay in our strongholds, build stockades, fortify the passes. Plague rages in Athens now and the Spartans are in Laurium.*

*How is my little disciple? I wonder what she found of mine to read. It seems so long ago that I was there. I can't remember what I was thinking then.*



v. Penelaiaa to Clarius:

*Such a spring. I have never seen a lovelier one. The light of morning is like wine. It is dawn as I write. Cocks crow, a dove calls in a meadow, all around me the camp is waking. Fires will be lit, food cooking, a new day.*

*The child Kleis is asleep in my bed. Often she stays with me now. Meion and the girl Auria sit in my rooms talking of everything beneath the sun, arguing like children, showing off their knowledge. Meion is the practical one, always returning to what he knows and can defend. She follows her mind wherever it goes. I listen to them and remember how we talked, all of us, a strange mixture of knowledge and ignorance, young and unfinished. As we all are until we become old and unfinished.*

*I await the solace of your company. P.*

vi. Clarius Arasistratus, in Athens, to Penelaiaa, daughter of Phidias, wife to Leucippius Peisistratus:

*Madness everywhere. Pericles announced he will divide his lands among the citizens if the king of Sparta spares them on his way to the Thrisian plain. You know they were friends when they were young and fought together at Thermopylae. It is not the war that is destroying Athens but this sickness. Thucydides contracted it on Andros years ago and is able to walk among the sick. He comes back to us with tales of horror. I am staying in the villa, being a coward where disease is concerned and unashamed of it. Kos, the physician, says it is caused by overcrowding. He has seen disease spread among the crews on boats in this manner. Pericles is to blame for this for calling the citizens into the city. What worked once and saved us from the Persians destroys us now. HAVE YOU HEARD FROM ELEN? C.*



VII. Penelaiaa to Clarius:

*Last night I lay out all night upon the stones beside that little spring to Hera, halfway up the eastern side of the mountain. Do you remember it? A little bower. I wished to watch the stars as I used to when I was a girl. We would dress in new robes and lie out all night dreaming of our weddings. Last night I saw again how small we are compared to the gods, who hide their nature from us. Leucippius's arm is weakening. He tries to hide it from me and drinks more wine and is haughty to everyone and talks like a general instead of a leader of men. Still, the sweet-smelling nightflowers were all around and consoled me with their fragrance. Send hope by eagles or deliver it yourself with your beardless boy's shaven chin. How I miss you. P. No, we have not heard from her.*

VIII. Clarius to Penelaiaa:

*I will come when it is possible. There is still much to do here. I envy you the mountains this time of year. When I was there the meadows would turn blue with cornflowers overnight while I slept. On clouded days the white weed would lie upon the grass like dew or a web spun to catch the sunlight. I was clear then about all things, and knew how a man should live. Still, it was my destiny to go back into the world and live among my fellow man. Confusion grows among us. I do not believe our fathers suffered this disease of the mind. They were not ashamed to be strong or send colonies out to carry their offspring into the unknown days ahead. If I go back to worshipping gods I will choose Athena, the one whose eyes are not clouded by desire. Love from your old graying Clarius.*



IX. Penelaiaa to Clarius:

*It is all as Leucippius predicted. When men go into the city they lose sight of both the practical and the divine. Leucippius says even the poorest men will now begin to worship money, as it is all they see that is powerful. Rich men putting on plays or contests or sharing out burned meat at sacrifices. Some of the mountain men up here still eat meat hot and raw the moment it is killed. They say if a man eats another life he must do it while it still lives and not fool himself about what he is doing. In the city such reality disappears. Honor is left by the wayside and pride becomes the tyrant. I hear there is much theft in Athens now and that even garments are stolen. Is this true? Penelaiaa*

X. Clarius to Penelaiaa:

*I have visited Megales. We could go there if we needed to leave Attica. Our cousins there are in a strong position.*

*Pericles is a fool to serve the mad children of Athens. They blame him for everything that happens and scream out insults and demands at the assemblies. They are angry about your father's great buildings and say Athens looks like a vain woman wearing too many jewels. Pericles said he would pay for the buildings himself in that case and dedicate them to himself. At which they screamed out that he could spend all he liked, even the treasury of the Delian League.*

*Elen has written me. She is enraged at Pericles because he won't grant her a divorce from Eutorian. But what is he to do? Without silver there would be no ships built and Athens would be lost. Eutorian is still very powerful. Even with the Spartans knocking at his gates and the workers and slaves hating him. He has treated the slaves very badly. Everyone in Athens speaks of it but no one goes to stop it. Athens will suffer because of its slaves, as Leucippius knows well enough. I long to talk to both of you.*

*I must tell you of my trip to Kos, where I met a young man named Hippocrates, who is of the cult of Asclepius and is performing many strange cures and talking in a wonderfully clear manner about the arts of healing. Tell my young disciple that I will tell her all about the latest developments in medicine when I come. He is writing a book of aphorisms which he allowed me to see. We had several pleasant evenings together with wine and bread while he showed me his work. I was taken all over the hospice where the sick come to be put on strict diets and given large doses of* water. *Here are some of the writings of this Hippocrates, that he allowed me to copy. "Life is short and art long, opportunity fleeting, experiment dangerous, judgment difficult."* Writing *of* epi*lepsy: "It is not any more sacred than any other disease, but has a natural cause, and its supposed divine origin is due to man's inexperience.* Every disease has its own nature and arises from external causes."

*This Hippocrates is a great admirer of Pythagoras and wished to talk of him without end. He was brought as a child into the presence of*

*Empedocles and learned from him the notions of harmony of elements. I liked the young man enormously and wish to see more of him.*

XI. Penelaiaa to Clarius:



*How are you traveling in such times? Be careful, dear friend, and if you must risk your life in travel come in this direction. You can meet your disciple, Auria, and watch the love affair. There should be a marriage of these two.*

*My father has relented of his rage at me and sent a shipment of oil and wine and a pair of mules that were used to build the Parthenon. They are called Ke and Katake and are a beautiful strong pair. A mule is a strange creature. Trust a Persian to invent a creature that is barren. The Persians are the great castrators of history, are they not? Well, we are fortunate to be born Hellenes and Athenians and I never forget that, no matter that the rabble are ruling Athens now. It will rain later in the day and clear my head of these resentments.*

*Kleis of the golden curls lays her hand on my arm and I am as sentimental as any grandmother. She grows every day and pronounces words correctly now. She was calling me Pepeepeee. Now says Penelayee. I will have this wedding now that I have conceived of it. P.*

Penelaiaa sealed the letter and looked up from the table, thinking of how far away she was from the world she was raised to inhabit. Who would have thought I would consort with slaves, she thought. Or live in a dwelling with a porch made of hides. She got up and went out into the clearing and walked around the camp speaking to the men and women she found there and then walked down to the pass to find the runner from Clarius who had been waiting two days for her reply.

. . .

Auria and Meion were fishing far out on the back side of the lake in a boat made of reeds and planks, casting nets for the small fish that ate the lilies. "I did not know about lakes until I came here," Auria was saying. "Although I had seen pictures of them on maps. It would be easy enough to make one by damming up a river. I have heard there are small animals that do such things."



"Do you never stop thinking of such things? I have never known a man or girl who had such a need to change one thing into another."

"Why do you say cruel things to me when I have ideas growing in my mind? I wish you would go hunting again if all you wish is to make me think I am wrong to open my mouth and speak."

"I did not say you were wrong in anything." He stood up and shook the boat from side to side with his feet, making water spill over the sides.

"Don't do that, Meion. You will make it sink." She pulled in the net and settled down onto the floor of the boat. "You must not swing it from side to side."

"Will you say I am a gentle dog that does whatever its mistress says and never complains?" He swayed once more, from one side to the other, and water poured in over the side. Auria began to bail it with a stone bowl.

"Stop, for the sake of Poseidon and all the water nymphs, please stop." He sat down and helped her bail but it was too late. The boat was sinking. He paddled as hard as he could and made it almost to the bank before the whole thing was submerged in the water. Auria waded ashore and sat down on the bank while he saved the sodden boat. Across the way the bluff on which the camp sat was glittering in the sun, the tall cypresses leading to the water were brilliant green and the leafless willows threw their shadows on the grass. He climbed up onto the shore and lay down beside her. "I was not alive upon the earth until you appeared to me," he said. "I can not remember a time when you were not here."



"And also with me," she answered. "Swear by Apollo that you will not die in battle or leave me ever."

# Chapter XIV

"We shall have a wedding feast," Penelaiaa said. Leucippius was not listening to her. He was bent over papers on a desk he held on his lap. "They must marry," she repeated. "He is Elen's son. We will uphold our honor even though we eat stew made of squirrel and rabbit and make galleries of animal skins. I will arrange a ceremony."

"Perhaps you should ask them if they wish to marry. They fight all the time. Perhaps it will not be wise."

"All young people fight when they fall in love. It should have been done weeks ago when they came here."

"Then ask them. It will be a good excuse for a gathering. It will cheer the camp up."

"Don't laugh at me, Leucippius."

"I'm not laughing. I'm quite serious. Who shall we say she is? A physician's daughter from Thisbe? A girl he found in a cave?"

"We will have a wedding at the new moon. There is little enough happiness in the world. I am elated that the girl is here, and the small one too. They give me great joy. If I only see them cross the compound in the morning on their way to the lake it charms me like music or a flock of birds going across the skies." She turned and faced him, very tall and proud, her head to one side as it had been the first time he laid eyes on her.

"Come here to me," he said. "Close the curtains and sit by me. A runner came today from Piraeus. Pericles is ill. It is rumored he has caught plague. Cleon is gathering his forces. If he takes power he will come for us, you know that, don't you?"

"Yes." She was very still. Her hand was on the flap of cloth that was the door. She slid her hand down the length of it, closing out the light. "All the more reason for a wedding feast."



"You could go to Megales. The Pythagorean circle there would welcome you."

"And leave the rest?"

"I would not go, but there is no reason for you to stay. You could have another life, with a normal man. You are still young. There could be another child."

"There is one here already. Meion has brought her to me. And twenty more besides and more coming now that Athens is at war." She had not left the door and still held the curtain.

"Then you may help me to my bed if you are so intent on being godlike. And wish to serve mankind instead of selfish ends." He folded the maps and papers and stored them in the desk and put it on the floor. "You are very beautiful today, Penelaiaa. Have I told you that?"

"I know," she said. "I have felt all day that I was beautiful." She tied the curtains together with a string and walked over to where he was and gave him her shoulder while he moved himself from the chair to the bed. "It is the young lovers," he said. "They have the whole camp in heat."

Later Leucippius brought it up again. "There is a small island about ten sea miles from Lesbos, in the direction of Adrean. It has not been inhabited for many years. There are stone huts there that could be converted into dwellings. There are lemon trees and a grove where you could grow vines and vegetables. Anticulous would protect you from Lesbos. No one would bother you there. I have long had it in mind that you could go there if it became dangerous here."

"How large is this island?"

"About seven miles on the longest side. It is rocky and without trees but habitable. I was there on a sea voyage as a boy. You could go there with the children. Auria and the children and other women. I could send a few men with you."



"How would we get there?"

"We would have to send money to procure a boat from a port somewhere on the western side of Attica. Shall I see about it?"

"It would not hurt to have a boat paid for and waiting. Is there enough money?"

"I will use what we do not have to spend on wheat."

"Then do it. Not for me but for the children. Surely you don't really think they would try to invade us here. The passes are impossible to take."

"The lands below the lake are easy. If they didn't mind traveling seven days they could come that way. I have known Cleon to go to more trouble than that to kill his enemies. Especially if he is frightened."

"Sleep now. Do not think of it anymore. We will suffer what must be suffered, but not before it happens."

"Plans must be made, Penelaiaa. Then I will sleep."

"Think of the wedding feast. Think of me standing beside them holding the wedding torch."

"Oh, so this is the part you have assigned yourself in this marriage drama."

"Yes. I will hold the mother's torch. Someone must do it." She turned her back to him then, imagining it. It seemed as real as anything else in the world at that moment.

# Chapter XV

"Penelaiaa says we must marry." Meion sat on the edge of the wooden bed holding Auria's ankles in his hands. The bones of her ankles fit into his hands like the handle of a sword. He turned his eyes from hers. She was a strange girl for all her talk of truth. Also, she was the most impious person Meion had ever talked to in his life, more than his mother even. Now Penelaiaa said he must share a long procession and take marriage vows with her. He looked down at her small beautifully shaped legs and said it again. "Penelaiaa and Leucippius say that we should have a wedding feast."

"Do you wish it?" Now it was Auria's turn to be thoughtful. Meion was the grandnephew of Pericles, a descendant, through his mother, of Xanthippius and Megales. Who was he to ally himself by law with a Thracian captive? She moved her legs from his hands and got out of the bed. She pulled a woolen chlamys over her head and tied it around her waist with a belt. "I will tell you who I am," she began, turning to face him. "Here is what I know. This was told to me by Philokrates, who never lied to any man. I am the daughter of a chieftain's son, a swift runner, a brave man. Our city was besieged and captured and the men put to death and the women and children enslaved. My mother died and my grandmother came with me on the journey to Hellas and lived until a day before our caravan arrived at Meldrus's door. I was alone and orphaned from the time the sun rose on that day until after dark of the next. That night I was delivered to my teacher and friend, Philokrates, who cared for me from that day until his own death." She squared her shoulders and went on.



"Here is what I remember of those dark times. Much running and stones falling from roofs and hands pulling me along in the dark and my grandmother singing to me in a dark room. Then many days on donkeys and carts and walking along paths that led beside the sea and one night I could not wake her and wept and beat on her chest and face but she wouldn't wake and speak to me." She paused and looked at him again. "I have never spoken of this. I have never spoken of it even to Philokrates for I feared it would make him sad. Never have I shared this sadness with anyone. This old woman who was my grandmother was beautiful and small, with hair as white as bleached stones and breasts as soft as the air above the most beautiful meadow in the world. So I remember her, and she would put pieces of food into my mouth and pull me into her body in the night. So I was bred well also and much loved.

"When she would not wake, another woman sat me on the cart beside her and there I rode all day and sometimes walked. There are kind people everywhere. I have remembered that woman and wondered where she is and if I will pass her somewhere in my life and not know who she is or that she comforted a strange child on a sad day.

"This is what I know and remember of myself before I came to the villa where I was cared for by Philokrates. Also, I recall a man who held me in a chair and that must have been my father. I recall my mother only as a pair of hands that dressed me and a voice that called some sort of warnings. I have thought of these things many hours while I was alone at Clarius's sanctuary. When the mind is alone it must draw upon all it knows to stay well. As I nursed Kleis I would remember things from when I was small and wonder if the way I held her was the way my mother held me. Such little things I know."

"I do not need to know any more about you than what I see and what we know together of each other."

"You would always think yourself above me. No, you must hear my lineage as I remember it. I am almost through. There is not much more. So then I was given to the wisest man in all the land around Cirrha and the Gulf of Corinth, who had been in the inner circle at Epidaurus and left in anger and went off to pursue his studies in his own way. He was a free man and taught me all he knew of everything. No woman you could marry has ever had a better education or been loved by more worthy people. Also, I was treated as a whore and a slave by a man named Polymion and someday if I live I will cut his eyes and hands from his body and destroy him utterly. Aside from that I have no debts in the world." She was still then and stood with her hands at her sides waiting for him to speak.



"Will you marry me then? Shall I tell Penelaiaa we will do this thing?"

"Who will hold my wedding torch?"

"She will."

"What shall I bring you for a dowry?"

"You could bring Metis, and Phoebe." He walked over to where she was and took her into his arms and began to pull her towards the bed. "You could bring your terrible mouth and your soft skin and your legs and the place between them that talks to me when I sleep and when I wake. You could bring your hands and feet and ankles."

"Then I will do it," she answered. "And we will see what happens."

So the wedding feast was planned for the next new moon. Penelaiaa found a bolt of pale yellow cloth for a wedding gown for Auria, and began to embroider a belt for it. The shoemaker made them new sandals and a plot of land was set aside for the house they would build to replace the tent they had been using for a home. It was the first wedding feast in a year and everyone was very excited about it and argued a great deal about whether the procession should be from the camp to the lake or from the lake back to the camp. In the end it was decided that the procession would begin in a meadow where the flocks grazed in winter and follow a path down to a summer pasture, then around to the back of the camp where the wall was being built beside the lake.

"An ox must be sacrificed and a wheaten cake broken and ten witnesses must stand in a circle while you make your vows. So it was when I was married and so it shall be for you." Penelaiaa pulled the yellow cloth across Auria's shoulder and held it while Auria adjusted the folds. "Yes, like that. That will do."

"There is a law that says a man may not marry a slave."

"I thought you said you were never a slave."

"I say a man who fears nothing can not be a slave. In that sense I am not a slave. But I belonged to Meldrus. There is no reason for us to have this wedding. I am not sure we should do this thing." She let the cloth drop and faced Penelaiaa. "Why do you wish us to do this thing?"

"Because this polis, this little city or camp, is a creation of our minds. Here all men are equal. Auria, listen to me. This is how we Hellenes lived for many years before we were crowded into cities and began to have empires and enslave one another and bring men and women on boats from other places to move the stones for temples. I can remember a simpler time in my own life. The servants on my father's land were equal citizens in the life we led. We did not have some who could marry and some who were treated as cattle. I wish you to have this marriage as a lesson to the camp that we are more than a band of exiles."

"I am not sure I wish to bear children. It is hard enough to care for Kleis all the time. If I become large with child how will I fight if we have to fight?"



"How have you kept from having a child so far?"

"I put sponges into my body and I pray to Athena although I do not believe that gods intervene in our lives. Still, when we love each other I always pray to her to leave me as I am."

"You believe a marriage ceremony will change that?"

"It might. I have thought of it." Auria walked over to the other side of the room and pulled Kleis away from a trunk of robes she was rummaging in. "I feel strange about all this. We have been happy as we are. There is no need of this wedding." She looked at Penelaiaa, who was sitting down now, looking suddenly old and tired. "I am sorry," Auria continued. "I do not mean to refuse your gift. You have planned this because you love us. I will take this wedding feast and marriage that you offer me and say no more about it." She carried the child over to Penelaiaa and put her into her arms. Kleis reached up and began to play with the older woman's hair.

"We are here as on the wings of a great falcon being carried to a destination we can not know," Penelaiaa began. "All my life I have tried to create goodness in the world and to love beauty wherever I find it. My father believes a man must raise monuments to beauty but I have been content to worship it in its human forms. I found and loved it first in Leucippius. No accident or loss of limb will ever change for me what I saw in him when he was young. He would climb aboard a chariot and ride it like a god. But none of that. What he is now is not less than what he was. Meion possesses this power also. But you yourself have it as greatly as I have ever seen it in a man or woman. You have brought great pleasure to my life at a time when the world around me seems a place of madness and uncertainty. I wish to have this wedding for my own pleasure and to capture one day from the dark encroachment of what may come." She set Kleis down on the floor and took Auria into her arms and held her there. Kleis grabbed them around the ankles and stuck her head in between their legs, and the camp wag, a harness maker named Dian, passed by the open gallery and witnessed the scene and spread the news all over the camp that the women were already beginning to weep with joy that one more of their number had captured a good man in her net.



So an ox was brought up from the pasture and prepared for the sacrifice and wheaten cakes were baked in long pans and women gathered flowers for garlands and the days until the new moon slipped away.

While they waited for the wedding Meion traveled up to the high pasture to see Braseus. They talked and drank and threw dice and Braseus promised to come to the wedding feast. "Our families have been through much history together," Meion said as he was leaving. "Let our grandchildren know the friendship our grandfathers had."

"This girl has made you into a farmer, with a farmer's mind. See, you are hurrying back to her now."

"I do not see you sleeping in an empty tent."

"How is Penelaiaa? Is she well?" Braseus held the rein of Meion's horse. Meion took it from him without answering. "Be careful of the bridge over the waterfall," Braseus continued. "Lead the horse across."

"I will see you at the new moon."

"With an empty stomach to receive a feast." The men laughed and held each other's arms, then Meion mounted the little mare and rode out of the camp. All around were the men Braseus had taken with him, idle and unkempt, drunken and half asleep before their tents, gone back to living like outlaws in a month's time.

# Chapter XVI

On the day of the wedding Auria was awakened before dawn by the women of the camp. They dressed her in the new himation and the embroidered belt was tied around her waist and her new sandals put on her feet and a wreath of small white flowers tied around her hair. When Auria was dressed, the procession of men, with Meion among them, arrived at the door and a man named Eudoxe asked Auria to come out and greet her husband. She walked out to him and held out her hands and he took them, and then, with Meion and Auria leading the way, and the children running ahead and singing and throwing flowers, the procession wound its way down the path between the pine trees and on down to the pasture and back around to the terraced vineyards and the olive trees and the lake. Auria walked along holding Meion's hand and watching everything that happened as if she were not the center of it, but its historian. This is how it has always been with me, she decided. I come to my own wedding and think of everything except the truth, which is that I am walking along on my wedding march, holding the hand of my husband, and will become a wife before the day is over. I never meant to marry or be a wife to anyone. I was to be a healer and a philosopher and find the numbers that would express the truth of all things. She held on tighter to Meion's hand and he turned his face and looked at her and she saw that he was as much a stranger to this wedding march as she was herself. "We are in a wedding feast," she whispered. "I am going to be your wife."

"I know," he answered and smiled his first real smile of the day. They were quiet then and went back into the strangeness. By the time the procession arrived at the lake everyone was sweating and the flowers had wilted in Auria's hair.



They arranged themselves in a circle and Penelaiaa raised the marriage torch and they said their vows and the wine was brought out in thin black cups that had been especially made for the wedding. Leucippius's chair had been brought down and he was sitting in the center of a table made of boards. Braseus was beside him with three of his lieutenants. When the ceremony was over Meion and Auria went over to receive Leucippius's blessing. A man named Zenthius, who was Braseus's advisor, was speaking. "It is the fashion now for men of wealth to hide their power," he was saying. "The assembly demands displays, sacrifices, contests and dramas, all sorts of excesses, and so men of honor are taking their fortunes and withdrawing to their estates, the ones who are fortunate enough not to live in the path of the Spartans."

"But surely they are not holding contests with plague everywhere. I heard there was barely room to pitch a tent or make a cookfire, and that Piraeus was as bad as Athens. We have different informants, Zenthius, that much is clear. Who are your heralds?"

"Dependable men. If you need to know anything about Athens, just ask me. I'll find it for you." Zenthius raised his cup and drank off his wine. He wasn't letting these citified exiles get ahead of him.

"Have you heard from Anakratus?" Leucippius asked. He was going along with the pretense that Zenthius had a perfect spy system in the city. "Or his brother, Zennoble?"

"No, but I am sure they have left Athens. One of my informants said Pericles stopped a plan to send carts of dead people to the Spartans to spread disease among them. The people were angry with him for not allowing them to do it." Leucippius drank his wine also and a boy came and filled the cups. Zenthius went on. "I'll say one thing for your noble kinsman, he holds his own against all comers. He's a tough old bird to be his age."

"I wish I was there to help him," Leucippius said. "I often wish things had gone differently in my life. Hand me that winecup, Zenthius. Enough of politics for now. We will toast to love and marriage." Zenthius handed the cup to Leucippius, who held it aloft to make a toast. The gathering quieted and he began a speech about the heroic lineage of the groom and the heroic story of Auria's escape with Kleis. Halfway through the story, with all eyes upon him, his hand began to tremble, his arm failed, and although he raised his left hand to support the right it was too late and the cup fell, spilling wine everywhere. Meion rushed around the table to help and with two others carried him up the hill to his dwelling. The people of the camp were quiet, talking among themselves, then the musicians gathered and began to play and the pourers filled the cups and the wedding dances began. But the wedding was ruined now and after dancing two dances with a group of men and women Auria excused herself and went off to find Meion. She found him standing outside of Leucippius's dwelling. "His arm has failed," Meion said. "Perhaps it will have to be removed. There is no one to take his place, Auria. I am not old enough to lead them. Only Leucippius can hold this ragged band together and Clarius is far away. The worst thing of all is that Braseus was here. Has he left? Yes, I think he has left."

"Then I will heal him," Auria said. "Take me there."

She went into the room and stood halfway between the door and bed. She looked at all of them, talking to Leucippius and to one another and shaking their heads. Then she asked them all to leave. When they were gone she had Penelaiaa tie the door curtains and light all the lamps and sent a girl to heat water in a cauldron. Then she removed all of Leucippius's clothes and laid him out on the bed. "You must tell me where the feeling is," she said. "My fingers will go in deeper and deeper and as soon as you feel pain you must tell me. I do not want you to be brave, Leucippius. I am looking for the places where the nerves still live. Here, sit up, I will draw it for you. This is how the muscles join together." She took a stick and drew on the dirt floor a design of the muscles of the arm and back. "All creatures share this design," she said. "Man and beasts. Philokrates showed it to me many times. How many times I was made to draw this. All is controlled in the head and brain. The messages come down from the head, like seagulls flying down from a precipice or doves from a roof. They arrive by secret rivers in the arms and legs and make them work like pulleys. If one goes out there are others that can take its place while it heals. Sometimes at Epidaurus they would study cripples or dogs that had lost a leg in fights and see how the body would compensate and bring itself back into harmony. That is what we must do with you. We must bring back order and harmony into your body. Turn over and let me see these legs that you have lost the use of. There, like that." She turned him over onto his back, marveling at the beauty of what was left of his body, at the width of the chest and arms. His ribcage was as wide as her own shoulders. The muscles along the waist and hips were still large, strong and well defined. "We will make these hips do some work," she said. "We will begin now." She asked for oil and Penelaiaa brought it to her and she oiled her hands and began to work her fingers down into the muscles, moving her hands into the hollow places of his body, listening, feeling, pushing blood into the muscles, waiting for the body to tell her what she must know. She had stood beside Philokrates a thousand times while he massaged the men and women of the villa, and he had taken her small hands and shown her what she was looking for, how the nerves could be found inside the intersections of the muscles.



She was so intent on what she was doing that for a long time she didn't notice Penelaiaa standing across the room, jealous at the sight of another woman with her hands on Leucippius. Finally, she looked up and saw the older woman's face and she lowered her eyes and went deep into herself and thought for a moment before she spoke. Learn stillness, he had told her. You must learn silence also.

"I have done all I can do today," she said finally. "You must care for him now." She stood up and went to Meion. "I would like to dance now," she said. "I would like to join my wedding feast." He took her hand and led her down the hill and they joined in the circle of the dance, which continued until long after the sun had left the earth and the great constellations of the night had come to rule the sky.

Then, every day for many weeks, Auria worked on the muscles of Leucippius's hips and legs, pushing and rubbing and probing, until finally she thought she had found the source of the trouble and she began to work very deeply into the muscles that seemed affected. "Talk to me," she told him. "I do not need a hero. I need information from inside this skin that is stretched over your amazing frame."

“In another world you might have been my woman,” he said. He was breathing very hard from the pain she was causing him. “Has that occurred to you?”

“Not in a world where Penelaiaa lives. Since I value my life.” She moved around to the other side. Leucippius was stretched out face down on the bed. She began to work his legs. “Tell me when you feel this in your waist, in the muscles that go from the back up along the waist. Tell me about one leg and then the other and when you can move the arm. When you can feel the muscle move in your leg, move your arm. First one, then the other. Yes, like that.” 

“Truth will not harm us.”

“Truth comes in many guises. Try to move only the bad arm now. Really try, Leucippius. Concentrate. Breathe into the muscles. Oh, yes, that's it. That's very, very good. Do it again. Yes, just so. Athena and Zeus, gods and shadows. You are moving it. Once more, oh, that's the way. Penelaiaa, come here. He's using it. He moved it all the way to his shoulder. Oh, now it begins to work.” Auria began to rub the muscles below the ones he had moved. “Rest now. We will work more later.” Leucippius raised his hand again, lifting it from the floor beside the bed to his shoulder.

Then Auria was more determined than ever to cure him and devised exercises with leaded weights so he could work the arm when he was alone and made a tea of bryony and mint for him to drink and put him on a strict diet and forbade him wine. “Penelaiaa does not like it that I touch Leucippius,” she said to Meion. “Should I give up curing him? Should I speak of it to her?”

“You could teach the skill to her.”

“Perhaps I can. Yes, I will try.”

• • •

When his arm became stronger, Leucippius asked to go down to the lake to oversee the construction of the walls. The camp was accessible only from the south, where a series of terraces led down to the lake. The lake itself formed a barrier for part of the exposed area but on either side was a stretch of land that had to be fortified. On one side the open land ended in a bog and a forest. On the other it ended in a rock bluff. On the side that met the bluff the work was almost completed, a double wall with two wooden towers. It had been possible on that side for the builders to drop stones down from the bluff, breaking them into usable sizes in the fall. The other side was more difficult. The stones had to be moved further, across softer ground. They were being moved on dollies pulled by mules.



Meion had been overseeing the work while Leucippius was bedridden, bringing reports on how high the walls had grown and how the building of the towers progressed.

"I will turn this camp into an impenetrable fortress," Leucippius was saying. Men were loading his chair onto poles so it could be carried down the hill. "A citadel, an acropolis. I will build a row of towers behind the walls, a boardwalk will join them and from that we could rain down boiling water and stones upon any that come that way. Yes, a second row of wooden towers will be next."

He pulled himself into his chair and six men picked up the poles and carried him down the hill and set him down beside the carpenters who were fitting the joints for the towers. Auria rigged up a tripod so that he could exercise his arm with the weights while he watched the construction. The men were very interested in the design of the pulley, and Auria's reputation increased among them. She set up the pulley and showed them how it worked. Then she left her patient and went to find Kleis. Halfway up the path she turned and looked back down on the construction site. Men were taking measurements with a rope. Other men were using surveying rods along the marshy edge. A wagon load of foundation stones was making its slow way up the hill from a quarry below. Hodcarriers and masons and bricklayers, carpenters and woodcutters were all working away, in good spirits now that Leucippius was returned to them. Meion was working on the second wall. With two other men he was struggling to move a rock into place, sweating and shoving, bruising his back and arms and hands. Men are very strange creatures, Auria was thinking. She was remembering him above her in the night and how, afterwards, he would lie on his back and seem to think of the whole world, as though no man could ever rest or be satisfied in any way. Every man I have known is stranger than the next, she decided. Even Philokrates and even Leucippius, who rose up from his sickbed to tell me he would have been the man for me in another time. Yes, they are unlike us. More courteous and more civilized, when they wish to be, than any woman, and the next moment tearing their shoulders to prepare for war. They love war, every one of them. They are useful when war is coming and can work together without argument. Sometimes I believe they want an army to come up the meadows and lay siege to our camp. Auria shook her head and went off to find Penelaiaa and tell her what she had been thinking.

"It is what men do," Penelaiaa agreed. "If they can not find an enemy they will invent one. Now Braseus and Leucippius are at odds but if we had been attacked last year they would have gone out together like brothers to fight and die. Elen Alkmeionadae understands this. She loves power and battles and likes to be in the midst of politics. You will meet her one day and talk to her of these things."

"Will she like me? Will she care that he married a Thracian?"

"She will love you as we all do. For your beauty and courage and happy face. You have helped Leucippius. I will not forget that." Auria



bowed her head. "Will he recover?" Penelaiaa went on. "Will he be strong again?"

"I do not know. I was thinking of how you look at me when I am touching him. I am sorry, Penelaiaa, if I offend you. But we are women. We can speak of love and jealousy and not be at war. I have worried about you while I nursed Leucippius. I wish you to speak your mind on this."

"You are a strange wise girl. Were you ever a child, Auria? Did you play as children do?"

"I do not think so. It was play to me to talk with an old man and examine everything. I am sorry I am not gay."

"As to Leucippius, I burn with jealousy when you touch him, yes, that is true. If you are old beyond your years, I am a child forever about this hero I have for a husband. It has been a terrible long sadness to love him, torn in two like a tree struck by lightning and still as strong and wildhearted as a great stag in the forest. I am tired of it, Auria. It has worn upon me like water in a cave. He is tired now, too. It is almost over, all that we have lived for. If Clarius would come that would be a blessing. But he stays away. Perhaps he thinks this camp is nothing but a hideout and a refuge. Perhaps he doesn't want to come and tell us that."

"Will Elen come one day? Meion's mother?"

"I pray so. I do not understand a woman like that. She says she lives for Meion and to return the family to our lands so that he may inherit it. But she seldom sends messages to him and never comes this way. The strangest thing of all is that Clarius loves her. The gentlest man I have ever known loves the coldest woman. We are strange creatures when we love, are we not?"

"We are always strange. Life is a mystery man can not solve." Auria put her hands together into a pyramid and held the pyramid up to her forehead. She was laughing now. "This is what Little Aeo used to do when Philokrates would say things like that. It was Aeo's way of saying we were talking like Egyptians."

# Chapter XVII

Niddebak arrived in the middle of the night. At dawn Meion found him outside the tent. "The Peloponnesians have taken your mother," he said. "Eutorian is dead and all the guards. The mines are torn apart. Many have fled. I don't know where she is."

"Was she hurt?"

"She was talking to them in their language and was unharmed. Perhaps they will use her as a spy or an interpreter. I don't know where they have gone. I was hurt in the fighting and could not follow." He held out an arm, which was festering from a wound. Auria sat down beside him and inspected it. Nidde allowed her to minister to him, sinking down on his knees and holding out his arm at shoulder length.

"We will find her," Meion said. "If it is not too late. If they haven't taken ship."

"Many people are sick and dying in the towns. It is not a good time to go down there."

"You don't need to go back. I can go alone."

"If you go, I will go with you. As soon as I sleep."

"I'll have to tell Leucippius. It's a bad time for me to leave here." He clasped his hands before him. "Still, she is my mother and I must look for her." Auria stood in the doorway, holding a basin of water for Nidde's wound. "I'll go too," she said. "I can speak their language. Not much, but I can understand it."

"No. You are needed here to care for Leucippius." Auria knelt beside Nidde and began to bathe the arm. "You don't have to leave," she said. "Your mother would not wish you to be in danger."

"Only honor matters to my mother. It is all she knows."

"I also know honor," Auria said. "But I also know slavery and I know death." No one answered. She went on bathing the wound. "Never mind. It is for you to decide. I know nothing, not even who I am." She bent over the arm. "I will make a salve for this. I must go pick comfrey by the lake." She stood up to leave. "Let it dry until I return."



"She knows the healing arts of Epidaurus," Meion said. "She can read and write."

"You are his woman?" Nidde asked. "You are his wife?"

"I don't know." Auria said. "I don't know what I am." Meion reached for her and pulled her to his side. "She is my life," he said. "She is the tree of which I am a branch."

"Athena's goat," Auria began, then stopped herself from cursing in front of his friend. "Go on, see Leucippius and tell him you are leaving." She pulled away, but kept her fingers on his arm. "If you allow yourself to be harmed in any way do not return to me. I will not live with a cripple as Penelaiaa does. Come back dead or alive but in one piece." She pulled away then, and went from the tent and down to the water's edge to look for rue and comfrey.

"That one is much like your mother," Nidde said, when she was gone.

"Yes," Meion said. "Do you think she is unfair to me, Nidde?"

"They are unfair," Nidde said, looking down and shaking his head. "It is the price we pay for lying with them."

• • •

Auria was not alone in her disapproval. Penelaiaa showed up next, just as they were leaving. "This is unwise," she said. "You will not find her. Clarius is coming. Stay until he arrives."

"If she is taken on a ship I'll never see her again. I have to go."

"She knows what she is doing, Meion. She had time to get away. She has a plan or she wouldn't be with them. Perhaps she is making overtures for us. She would not want you wandering around looking for her now."

"Then why hasn't she sent word?"

"Perhaps there was no way."

"I am going, Penelaiaa. I must search for her."

"Wait two days. Wait until the morning of the second day from now."

"I will wait till then. Then I must leave." Auria stood aside and said nothing. Later she walked back down to the lake carrying Kleis in her arms, thinking how full of storms the world continued to be. "I will teach you to swim in this water," she said to the child. "Inside the body of your mother you were in an ocean of water. When you were born the ocean poured out upon the floor and so you know already how to swim in water." She waded out, holding the child, and began to float the little girl around, holding onto her arms. Nidde came down the path and squatted on his haunches watching her.

"I saw you in a dream many years ago," he began. "Many seasons and much time ago I dreamed of you and Meion sitting grayhaired before a fire and I was there also and you gave me bread. In this dream the time that is before us is given to the day we are walking in. Because of this dream he will not die although he should go down to the ports to find the Lady Elen Alkmeionadae. I come to tell you this to ease your heart." Auria waded closer in to shore, holding Kleis around the middle. The child paddled in the still clear water of the lake. Auria was quiet, looking at Nidde's face, the strange nose and sharp high bones of the cheeks, the wide thick lips, skin as black as a starless night. There was no dishonesty anywhere, in his face or the lines of his arms and legs. He was seated all the way down on his haunches, completely comfortable, folded up like a crane. A long silence went on between them while Nidde remembered his dream and Auria studied his face.



"There were painted chests along a wall with letters on them like the words of writing on parchment. The walls were very pretty, like the color of flowers. Perhaps it was a dream of another world but I think that it was here."

"Thank you for coming to tell me of this dream," Auria said. "Now if he leaves, I will console myself with your pictures. What did the writing look like? Can you see it in your mind?" She had waded up on shore, dragging the wet child. "Could you show it to me?" Nidde took a stick and drew some letters in the clay beside his feet. They were very good reproductions of Greek letters, theta and epsilon and omega.

"It is part of a name," Auria said, getting very excited. "Lockers with names on them. But I do not know whose name it is."

"It is a very good dream," Nidde said. "Very clear dream of time we are walking to in this time." Kleis took the stick from his hand and began to draw her own things in the clay. Round circles, tight little happy circles. She looked up after each circle, and Nidde and Auria exclaimed at the beauty of the circles and she drew on.

That night a runner arrived with messages from Elen, two letters on long rolls of expensive parchment, written in fine black ink. One of the letters was for Meion. The other was for Leucippius.

From the Lady Elen Alkmeionadae, to Phidius Megales Alkmeionadae, Meion:

*My son, have no fears for me. I am in good hands. This Brasidas knows more than all the generals of Athens put together and knows also my worth to him. I have given up all allegiance to Athens. The Spartans will return our lands to us and do for us all those things our kinsman, Pericles, would not do. I am Alkmeionadae first and Athenian only by lines drawn on a map. There is no Athens now anyway, only a rabble waiting to befoul the temples our fathers raised.*



*Stay by Leucippius and do not travel. The roads are like battlefields now with all the highwaymen and robbers turned loose to do as they choose.*

*Do not reply to this letter. I hold you near. My thoughts are all of you.*

From the Lady Elen Alkmeionadae to Leucippius, kinsman, commander:

*I have given up all allegiance to Athens. Brasidas will return our lands to us when this war is over. Another year and the Peloponnesians will control all of Hellas. Athens is dying of plague. The mob will have its way with what is left. Do not grieve for what was beautiful and is no more. All things change and pass away into the new. As the sea eats the coast, time takes our lives. May the gods preserve you until we embrace.*

*Elen*

*No one must send word to me. Do not chance a messenger. Brasidas is watchful and his men are absolutely loyal. I do not wish him to know where my allegiances are. Tell Clarius not to search for me. He is such a fool about practical matters. I fear him more than I do Cleon. Do not tell him where I am until he has left the city.*

"I will search for her anyway," Meion said. "Or at least I will travel to Sounion and see what news there is." He was talking to Leucippius. Penelaiaa and Auria were listening. Nidde stood in the door leaning on his spear. Kleis was playing with a wooden doll Nidde had carved for her that morning, a doll with arms that moved like limbs set into a tree. It was a trick Nidde had learned from a Cretan prisoner at Laurium, to hollow out the trunk and insert the arms on wooden pins. Kleis was fascinated by Nidde, and had been standing by his pillow when he woke that morning.



"Go if you must," Leucippius said. "But take Nidde and return to us quickly. What route will you take?"

"Along the coast and down into the Peloponnese, then to Sounion. We must know what is happening, Leucippius. If the Peloponnesians are overrunning Attica we must know of it and make alliances as my mother says."

"I would never work against Athens." Penelaiaa went to stand by Leucippius's chair. "I could not side with Spartans against the city of the goddess."

"We will not work against Athens or betray her," Leucippius added. "Still, it is human to save ourselves and these we have with us. No man would judge us disloyal for that. Perhaps we will save Athens by some act."

"I think my mother has written these letters knowing they would be read," Meion said. "It would be like her. Else, why would she address me by such a long name? I have never had such a letter from her before. I think the letters are a ruse."

"It would be like her." Leucippius took Penelaiaa's hand and pressed it against his cheek. "Let the young men go and find out what they can for us. Fix food for them to carry and bid them godspeed. The city of law will not fall to childbeating Spartans or perish because of disease."



"I wish I could believe it." Penelaiaa turned to the young men and offered to prepare food for their journey but they refused her offer.

"The earth feeds me when I travel," Nidde said. "I do not insult her by carrying dead meat about me like a Persian. I can smell it on a man a mile away."

"Go catch the horses you need." Leucippius smiled. "Before the women change their minds and make you stay."

Then Auria was with Penelaiaa and Kleis, on the path above the camp, watching as Meion and Nidde rode away.

"They have gone," Penelaiaa said, taking up Kleis, who was crying for Nidde to return. "So what will you do with this day, Auria? While your husband goes off with his Ethiopian?"

"I will practice throwing javelins," she answered. "I will teach Kleis to swim. Nothing will harm them. Nidde had a dream of our old age and he has told it to me. So they will escape their dangers."

"Nidde has strange powers. I have often thought I would like to travel to Ethiopia and see where the dark people live. My father has gone there. To search for wood for his statues."

"Why was he angry with you?"

"For leaving the city. He loved Leucippius and was glad of the marriage but they quarreled later. It was my father's surgeons who kept him from dying. Sometimes I think it was wrong of us to force this life upon him. Still, he has achieved much in his way, has he not?"

"I never think of him as a cripple."

"You have made him less of one." Penelaiaa stepped back, holding Kleis, stroking the child's hair. "I have wronged you in my mind, Auria. I have forgotten to thank you for your kindness."



"I thank you for letting me come here. I was alone in the world and you have made me part of this."

"If Athens were alive again and like it was when I was young, oh, I could take you there and we could walk its streets and sit beneath its lovely trees and shop in the stalls."

"I never have been to Athens, or to any city."

"Perhaps we will go one day. When the time of war and plague is over and the land is returned to health. We will take horses and ride down into the city and you shall see the temples my father built and be an honored guest among my family."

"I will wait for that." Auria smiled and pressed her hands together at her waist. "I will talk with the philosophers and poets and go to see the plays of Aeschylus and Euripides and wail at the tragedies as Philokrates told me of them. He knew these plays and would recite them to me. And from the poet, Homer. The great lays and tales of ships and battles."

Meion and Nidde went first to Delphi to consult the Pythia. Delphi and its prophecies were an invention of the Alkmeionadae. The first Pythia had been a mistress of Megales. In the years since then Delphi had become so rich and added so much to its treasuries that the townspeople and the priests and finally the Pythia herself had come to believe the prophecies, to believe that Apollo himself reached down from heaven and gave a common village woman the power to foretell the future.

"You will step on the soil of many free countries," so the priest interpreted her answers to Meion's questions. "Do not fear a stranger bearing gifts. Learn stillness and to save your speed till you have need of it."



"You will be the right arm of a king," she told Nidde. "Your name shall be sung on the earth."

"What did she mean about the king?" Nidde asked. They were leaving Delphi the next morning, leading the horses down a steep road to the sea. "In my country are many kings, but not here. Does this mean I shall return to my country?"

"She is only a woman of the village. Her prophecies are a pretty sad lot nowadays. Still, it is not wise to pass so close to Delphi without paying Apollo his due."

"We heard nothing of your mother."

"I heard that Brasidas was near Corinth in the past week. She is with them."

"If we find the Lady Elen will we rescue her?"

"No. We might cause them to harm her if we tried to take her from them by force." He laughed and looked at his friend. "She is a strange mother, is she not, that causes me to think it is the Spartan general who is in danger?"

"She fears nothing. I have seen this before protect a man from anything." Nidde paused, then went on. "So why are we seeking her?"

"To know what we should do with the ones in the camp. Leucippius wishes to send the women and children on a ship to Andros, where we have friends. If the news is bad in Piraeus I will go back and tell him and we will send them away."

"We should all go to this island," Nidde said. "Why stay and fight for a mountain fortress with the women and children gone?" Meion did not answer him and they rode in peace for a while. Nidde was thinking of how the men of his tribe fought against the neighboring tribes in the spring, for the sport of it and to take hostages and slaves and come home smeared with blood. In my heart I am an old man now, Nidde decided. I have lost my taste for battle and would be content to sit among the women and watch them weave and cook and talk to the children. Next I will lose my speed and then my eyes will dim. He counted on his fingers, trying to remember how many winters he had lived on the earth, but he had lost track many years ago.



The next few weeks were lonely for Auria. She tried to keep busy. She walked in the woods gathering plants, she built a fishtrap for the stream. She set up a loom and tried weaving, but the conversation of the women bored her and the threads kept getting tangled and her mind wandered. She was spending a great deal of time listening to Penelaiaa talk about the life she had left behind in Athens. Auria never tired of asking questions and listening to the answers.

"How did you come to know Leucippius?" she would say. "Tell me from the very beginning. How did he come to be your husband?"

"We followed a man named Dondoneian, who was a disciple of Pythagoras. Clarius lived near us. He and his sisters were very wild and entertained all sorts of ideas and people. They were wealthy and his father was so decadent he was the talk of the countryside. None of us ever went to Athens back then. People came out from Athens to visit the country and would stay for weeks or months. Clarius and his sisters were allowed to do whatever they wished. When my father was away my brother and I would go over there. We wanted to purify the city of superstition. Mystic cults that promised extra lives were already beginning to steal men's minds from sanity. Well, we were quite young, not much older than you are now, and it was a fortunate time, good crops and good weather. There was more of everything than we could use. It was a time for ideas to be born." Penelaiaa got up and went to stand in the doorway. "Finally, we went off to live as a brotherhood. Leucippius had just won a famous chariot race when he came to join us there. It was very gay, the life we were living. We drank wine all the time, even in the mornings, and talked of ideas that would change the world. Then my father accepted Leucippius's proposals to me and there was a great wedding feast and we freed twenty slaves to bring luck to our union. Then the bad times began. Shortly after the wedding feast Clarius was sent to Laurium and then went to live in the hut you found. Then Leucippius was set upon and injured and our brotherhood was broken apart. Still, the ideas we believed in were good ones. Better than the ones we believe in now, with Elen allying herself with Spartans and Alcibiades making God knows what trades and treasons. I lived in an age where honor was the chief desire of men and I have lived to see the end of that."

"Tell me more of the order. Of this Pythagoras that you honored. Philokrates spoke of him too."

"He founded a colony on Crotona, much like the one we later founded in his honor. He wished to see if man could live in harmony, as in music, or the order of numbers. We are at the dawn of man's life on earth, Auria. It will take a hundred generations to finish what we started. You do not finish ideas in a lifetime. All you can do is keep them alive for those who come after you." Penelaiaa picked up a basket and began winding a spool of thread.

"No one is happy, are they, Penelaiaa? We search everywhere for happiness but we never find it."



"Surely you have known someone who was happy."

"Philokrates. But all he ever talked of was ideas, or maps. He liked maps a lot." Auria paused. "And Kefallinia. She was too busy baking bread to be unhappy. Yes, she was happier than Philokrates even."

In the morning Penelaiaa called Auria to her. "I have been thinking of our conversation yesterday and I have decided to give you work to do. I wish you to start a lyceum for the children, to teach them to read. There's an extra tent we could set up in the grove. If it's too small we will enlarge it. Well then, will you do it?"

"A lyceum? And I would be the teacher?"

"Yes. You would be in charge. No one would interfere with you. Well, it's settled then? You will do it? I'll send word that the children are to come to you tomorrow."

"I'll have to go to the lake and bathe," Auria said. "I'll have to repair my sandals. I must cut my hair. And wash this filthy chiton. I am to be the teacher? Kleis, did you hear that? We are going to have a lyceum and I'm going to be the teacher." She lifted the child up and swung her around and around in the air.

In the morning Auria began. She gathered sixteen children of different ages into the tent. There were fifteen more outside listening but too afraid to go in.

"We will begin by reading," she said importantly. "First I will read to you. Then I will show you some of the letters we use to make words. The letters make the words. The words make the stories." She paused and looked around. Sixteen spellbound faces were turned her way. She took a breath and went on.

"Myths make men believe in gods," she said. "But all they are is words made out of the letters I will show you. Men believe in gods because they hear myths and think they are true. But there are no gods. If there were gods they would have done a better job. They would have made us perfect and happy and at peace. They would have made us unselfish and fixed it so we would not have to die." She paused again. "So, if gods are only words made out of letters, then man must be his own god, must rule himself. A wise man taught me this when I was smaller than most of you. Well, I say good for us that we must rule ourselves. We will think of better things than a bunch of crazy jealous undependable gods can think of." She was rambling now. She looked around. Several children had hidden their faces in their arms. Others were looking around at the patches in the tent. One was picking his nose.

"All right," Auria said in a louder voice. "Now I will read you one of the myths that men teach their children to make them obedient and afraid."

A hand was raised in the back of the room. "Why do they tell these myths if there aren't any gods?" he said. "Who makes them up? Why would they tell lies to their children?"

"Because they don't understand what makes them think," Auria said. "They hear voices in their heads made of memory and think gods are talking to them. Or they have dreams and think they are true. While all the time it is only the workings of the mind that are fooling them. Surprise a rabbit on the forest floor. His ears stand up. He listens. Sounds are all around him. Suppose he imagined those sounds were orders from a god. It is the same with men. They hear the wind blowing off the sea, which is the same as the steam rising from a kettle, only infinitely larger. But men see only the wind and say a god is blowing his breath in a cave. You see, there are warmer parts of the earth. I know a man from there. His name is Nidde and his skin is black and thick to ward off sun. Anyway, the wind starts in those hot places and blows here."



"I thought we were going to learn to write," a girl said. "I thought this was a writing school."

"Some people think goats are gods," a boy piped up. "My momma said she knows a town that won't sacrifice a goat except one day a year. . . ."

"I had a goat that talked to me," another said. "It was always talking to me. Whenever there wasn't anybody around."

"Lie," the first boy said. "You never had a goat that talked. You're always going around telling about that goat. Everybody knows you're lying. . . ."

"They do not," the enraged young herdsman said, leaping to his feet, grabbing the other boy by the hair. "I did have a goat that talked to me. You ask my sister. She heard it too. . . ."

"Stop it," Auria yelled. "Sit back down before I take a spear to you, Ion, you let go of him right now. Now every one of you sit down before I send you home. Sit down and be quiet and don't say another word. Do you hear me? DO YOU HEAR ME? Now we are going to settle down and be students. First we are going to make some tablets to do our writing on. I have wet clay and wooden sticks to form boxes and we will each make a tablet and then find an oak and pick new branches for styluses. Then we will begin to learn the letters. We will save this talk of gods for later."

"I could show you how to talk to goats," the young herdsman said. "You come with me some afternoon and I'll show you what they say."



"Maybe they should exercise first," she said later to Penelaiaa. They were sitting beside Leucippius. Kleis was playing nearby with Metis.

"Run them up and down the mountain half a dozen times," Leucippius said. "Then sit them down to learn."

"Don't laugh at her, Leucippius," Penelaiaa said. "Ignorance is dangerous. The more educated young people we have around us the safer we will be. Have you stopped believing in knowledge now? Has the mountain air made you a barbarian?"

"It has made me a realist. Besides, now Auria has made me into a physician and I dream at night of the mighty muscles in my waist which will move the muscles in my arm and then all will be well. In my sleep I talk to the parts of my body like a child. It is a fitting end to an athlete, no doubt." Penelaiaa was frowning at him as she always did if there was the slightest trace of self-pity in anything he said. He watched her face, amused to know he could play her like a harp when he wished. Life has its consolations, he reminded himself. "Go on with your plans," he said out loud to Auria. "Make them exercise. Then teach them a small lesson, then exercise them some more. If they don't learn the lessons at least their waist muscles will speak a stronger language to the muscles of their arms."

“I have to go now and find the others,” Auria said. “I will return this evening and see how you are coming along.”

When she was gone Leucippius spoke again. “Why teach children to read and write? Build them a temple. That’s something they can understand. Tell them the world is full of mystery and terror and in the end we die. Tell them to eat and drink and be prepared to suffer.”



Penelaiaa turned to him. “Don’t talk this way. Don’t say such things to Auria. She is enthusiastic about her new work. I do not want you putting darkness into her heart.”

“We were all fools together,” he went on. “Drunken fools who believed we were better than other people.” She was moving away. He had gone too far. “Come back. I don’t mean that, we were heroes and great philosophers and seekers after truth. Our ideas will live for all time and be a light to men.” He held out his hands and pulled her toward him.

“I don’t know what you’re thinking,” she said. “Your mind is a stranger to me.”

“Good. Then you can never leave me because you will never be finished trying to sound me out.”

# Chapter XVIII

The second day of Auria's teaching went better. The young herdsman brought a goat to illustrate his point and one of the girls brought a carved wooden image of a goddess and a small boy brought his sister, a girl Auria's age. Her name was Leiakes and she was tall and broad-shouldered with a wide smile. Whatever Auria said, she nodded her head in agreement, looking right at her the whole time.

Auria did not know how to teach people to read. She was making it up as she went along, trying to remember how Philokrates had taught her. She remembered going with him to the potter's shed to get clay and making the first tablet on which she wrote the first word, and so she began with that. Later, he had taught her the letters, one by one, then taught her some words, then shown her how the words were made of the letters. It had all seemed a game, so she made it into one now.

By week's end Leiakes was her assistant, learning things as fast as Auria could teach them and helping with the younger children. Auria even had an attack of jealousy one morning at the speed with which Leiakes memorized the words. All morning she had to say a poem Philokrates had taught her against jealousy:

Let me welcome beauty wherever it grows
And not poison my heart with barbs of envy.

Some of the children who had stayed outside came into the tent now and the grown people of the camp began stopping by when their chores permitted. It was all very gay and lightened the spirits of everyone. Even Leucippius got over his spell of cynicism and agreed to come and lecture the class on geography.

In the midst of this intellectual outbreak a group of refugees arrived at the pass. Auria went down with Penelaiaa to question them. They walked down the path and turned a corner and the refugees were there, about twenty altogether, standing in a group. Auria saw the tall head of Kefallinia and beside her, Little Aeo, with a red cloth tied around his hair and a pack on his back. She waved her hands in the air and called out to them, and as soon as Penelaiaa had questioned their leader and satisfied herself that they carried no sickness, Auria ran to them and threw herself in Kefallinia's arms. The wonderful soft places on the bottoms of her arms wrapped around Auria as they had done when she was small. "Oh, good fortune," Auria kept saying. "Oh, this is too much good fortune. How are you here? How are you here?"



"They are all dead," Little Aeo said. "The Spartans took the others and we met these ones by the river and they brought us here. I have dreamed of you and wondered where you were. Meldrus said you were dead but none of us believed it. No one who knew you believed you would die."

"Who is dead?" Auria asked. "And by what manner?"

"Meldrus and the children are dead, thrown off the rocks, and all the metics. Our Lady Eleuria died soon after you ran away so she was not there to witness it, may the gods have pity on her. And the kitchen help and the shepherds all carried off for slaves on the Spartan galleys. They came by sea on their way to Thrace. They took everything, all the supplies, and laid waste the fields. They threw the dead in the wells, some of them that tried to defend the harbor, not of our household. There is only Kefallinia and me." Little Aeo paused. Auria let go of the woman and hugged his small body to her own. He only came up to her shoulders now.



"All gone?" she said to Kefallinia. "All of them, the Thracian brothers with their tattoos?"

"They were glad to go," Kefallinia said. "They were among the ones that went out to meet the soldiers. I'll warrant they aren't so happy now, rowing galleys all day. They believed they were sailing home. Well, perhaps they will find a way to escape once they are there."

"All gone," Auria said, hugging Little Aeo to her, talking to Kefallinia over his head. "Our villa with its painted walls. Our water, which was the sweetest water in the world, everyone said so. I have dreamed of that water, with its golden color like Kleis's hair. Oh, Keffee, listen, you do not know. I have a child with me, Eleuria's child, that was put out the day I ran away, the day Philokrates died. His spirit inhabits her. Anyway, she is here. I took her."

"I wondered about that!" Kefallinia said. "It was something I imagined happening. I told Krakes so one evening, but he said it was not likely."

"Then the story is true," Penelaiaa said. "Forgive me, Auria, for I doubted it."

"Oh, it is true," Kefallinia said. "There was an infant born that day and exposed. The mother was so drunk I don't think she knew what happened. The child is here? She is the last of her people then, poor little thing, that were a powerful family in the country and had much land. No one is left anywhere now. Well, the world will start up again."

"Come with me," Auria said. "And I will show her to you." Then she led Kefallinia and Little Aeo to her tent where Kleis lay sleeping beneath Philokrates' cloak. And Kefallinia and Little Aeo marveled at this living child after so much death and looked on Auria with different eyes for having done such a thing.



"You will stay here with me," Auria said. "Put your pack down, Aeo. We will have a celebration." Then Auria went out and killed two rabbits and Little Aeo found roots of tamarind, and Kefallinia cooked a stew so delicious it seemed to Auria it was the first real food she had tasted in years. She mopped the last of it out of her bowl with a piece of panbread. Then she moved over to Kefallinia and snuggled down into her breasts, which were as soft as her arms. Little Aeo was teaching Kleis tricks with his tongue, rolling his lips up against his nose until he looked like an Ethiopian. "You have become a woman," Kefallinia said to Auria. "I had no idea you would grow so tall. You were such a tiny thing."

"I am four ducats," Auria said. "I am a warrior now, Keffee. I can make bows and throw a spear eight times the length of my body. I will be ready if we must fight."

"There is no one to fight," Little Aeo put in. "The Spartans have laid waste the farms and gone home. They burned the stables and tore branches off the olive trees and dug up the vines. Why anyone would do such hard work just to leave I do not know."

"You saw them! With your own eyes!"

"Yes. They wear tunics with no trim and march in lines like bees. There was a boy with us in the woods named Ionius who could mimic them talking. Oh, it was very funny. I heard they haven't a single poet in all their cities. Anyway, they have gone home now for fear of the plague."

"The villa is burned?"

"Only the stables. But no one is there. It is deserted."

"We could go and claim it in Kleis's name. Leucippius told me about inheritance of land. It becomes yours if it is written down. We could claim it for Kleis if her family is dead."



"How would you prove who she is?"

"I would tell them," Auria said. "I would say so." She moved closer. Keffee was wearing a cotton gown that had been brought to the villa when Auria was a child. Auria rubbed a piece of it between her fingers. "I have a husband, Keffee. There was a wedding feast and a long procession and many strange things happened on that day and at the end of it Kleis slept with us in our wedding bed. Oh, I love him very much. He is beautiful and strong and he is gone off now but you will meet him when he returns. If he is not killed. Everything he does is dangerous. He has no sense of caring for himself. And what would become of me if an animal killed him, or a man?"

"Love is very sad," Little Aeo said, getting up and going to sit by her. "There is always much suffering for it."

Kefallinia spoke of it to Penelaiaa later. "Is he kind to her? Is he a good young man? She is very dear to me. I have loved her since the night she was brought to us out of Thrace and given to the old man. That next morning he brought her to me to be fitted out with proper clothes. A white wool chiton and leather boots made of the finest leather and a little cloak. I took her by the hand to meet the other children and told them her name."

"He is the best of our young men. I am glad you have come to live among us, Kefallinia. It is good for Auria to have old friends. The world is in disarray. We must live the best lives we can in the face of that. Auria says you make bread that breaks men's hearts. If I arrange flour and ovens, will you make it for us? We have wheat Kraseus brought us. Only if you like, of course. We force no one to do work here they did as slaves."



"I would be glad of it. Little Aeo will help me. He will show you what we need." Kefallinia slapped her hands against her sides at the thought of it. "Yes," she repeated. "Tomorrow we will make an oven and begin."

News of Kefallinia's prowess with bread spread through the camp. By noon the next day a crowd had gathered to help with the building of the ovens. Every woman could make bread. But the great bakers, the ones whose bread left a memory in the mind as well as the stomach, were as rare as genius always is. When news that Kefallinia, of the villa of Meldrus Helonai, was in the camp and about to build ovens, people dropped what they were doing and came running to help. Then, when it was discovered that not only was she the legendary Kefallinia, but also a friend of the strange wild girl, Auria, who was teaching everyone to read and write, the camp got very excited and there were rumors that they were about to begin a great high civilization, with arts and literature.

It was not going to be done that quickly. Kefallinia scrutinized all the grinding stones and pronounced them old-fashioned and called masons and showed them what she wanted made—round wheels of stone that moved by a wooden handle with a slot above to drop the grain onto the grinding floor and a lattice of mats to sift and collect it. The masons set to work on the grinding mill and the rest helped build the ovens, three of them side by side above a furnace of sun-dried brick. There was a long argument about what to use to caulk the ovens. A man from Maroussi said he knew a formula that would last a hundred years. He shouted the others down and was allowed to add powdered marble to the usual mixture of sand and lime. When the oven was finished, the furnace was filled with olive wood and set to burning. While it heated, Kefallinia mixed ground wheat with wild onions, tamarind and olive oil, then added curdled goat's milk and began to stir. The loaves went in. The smell rose to the heavens. People gathered around. They brought wine and grapes and cheese. The first loaves came from the oven. The feast began. Musicians pulled out their pipes and lyres. Auria danced with Little Aeo, then with Kefallinia, then with Kleis. Penelaiaa walked out into the cleared space in the center of the dancers and danced a wild maenads' dance she remembered from her youth, leaping and striking poses in the air. More loaves went in, more bread came out. The moon rose above the mountains and the people of the camp danced until it set.

So the days went by while Auria waited for Meion. In the mornings she taught school and in the afternoons she wrote on her tablets or hung around the kitchen helping Little Aeo or playing with Kleis, who had become very jealous of her attention and demanded more of her time than she wished to give. "Aurrriaaa," Kleis would say. "Hold me, hold me, hold me." And Auria would stop her work, whatever it was, and allow the little girl to drag her around by the hand. She was a talkative child and chattered nonstop whenever she was awake. "To think I was the one who taught you to talk," Auria said. "To think I have unleashed this tongue upon the world."

"Don't say dat," Kleis said. "I don't like dat."

"Well, pardon me, your most divine goddess," Auria would answer. "Forgive me for laughing at the little queen of earth and heaven." Some of the tablets Auria made were about Kleis. She would draw an outline of the child's hand, then draw in the veins and joints of the fingers and the whorls of the fingerprints.



"In the hand is the source of mystery," she wrote beside the drawing. "It seems the hand can remember without the spirit to guide it. It is alive all by itself and has a memory of its own, or else, how could we do things without thinking of them first? In the night Kleis reaches for my hair. When she finds it she is content. Her hand *knows* my hair from my gown. I must write down each thing of this sort that I notice as she grows up. By the time she is grown I will know the history of how we develop from babies to finished people. There is a plan inside of us that shows how we are to grow. Is it in the hand? Yes, I think it must be in the hand."

She bent over the parchment, using very small letters, writing as carefully as possible, for parchment was dear and she only used it for important things, such as things she called *concepts,* a word Philokrates had acquired from a friend in Athens he corresponded with. "We must record these concepts as we imagine them," he had told Auria. "They must be stored on parchment or on clay and put where rain can not get to them. We must record them and we must teach them so they will be stored in the minds of men. Also, knowledge of plants and insights into the workings of the mind. If we could find the seat of memory. Oh, I have spent much time on that. Well, there must be much wasted time. Then, when thousands of generations of men have come and gone and left their teachings it can all be put together and we will have the answers we are seeking. If we last so long. If the skies send rain and the sun shines down upon us and the seas do not rise up and cover the land. If all goes well and man lives a thousand generations we will know the answers to all things."

"Would you like to be alive in that fortunate time?" she had asked. They had been in the courtyard, the sun beating down on their heads. A gourd of water was in his hands. Her hand was on his leg. The muscle moved beneath her hand when he spoke and she thought she must record that when she had time or at least always remember it and so she had.

"I would like to be alive in all times and see men through all their adventures," he said. "But I am content to live now. This is as good a time as any. There has been food on the table all my life and I have not had to work too hard. Here," he added, handing her the gourd. "Drink this. I have a theory that our blood is water that swims in us like a river and we must always be adding water to its store."

She thought of that morning now and was filled with questions for which there were no answers. Up, up, spirit, she said to herself. Slave to every emotion that comes like a wind from nowhere. Slave to sadness and memory. She got up and went off to the lake and took off her clothes and swam alone in the cold water, thinking of the rivers of blood coursing around her body. Perhaps this blood carries memory, she thought. Yes, the ocean itself might be a pool of memory and the blood might be an ocean of memory inside us telling each part what to do. Oh, if only he were here so I could tell him this concept I have found.

. . .

The next day Auria changed the program of her school. As soon as they arrived she arranged her pupils in lines and marched them down to the lake's edge and back three times before she began their lessons. She had decided during the night that if the blood was the source of memory she must be sure to keep her pupils' blood moving swiftly so they would learn better.



After an hour of study she lined them up again, and again they marched back and forth to the lake's edge. "Is this all we're going to do?" the young herdsman asked. "Couldn't we race or throw javelins? That would make our blood busy."

"Each morning we will think of new things to do," Auria said. "We will march up and down and also practice each thing we can think of to make us strong. What can you think of that we can do?"

"Throwing rocks into the lake," a girl called out.

"Footraces," called another.

"Javelins," a group of boys started yelling. "Javelins, javelins, javelins."

"Rocks in the water for today," Auria said. "But not just any old way. Choose teams of five and pick a leader. Then figure out a target. Throw a branch in the water. Then each person gets ten rocks to try to hit it and you must keep score."

So the lyceum turned into a gymnasium and the pupils spent at least half the day by the lake or running up and down the hill to and from the lake. The sight of the small brown chitons running up and down the hill amused Leucippius to such an extent that he made a promise to himself to stop his pessimism and resentment. "The greatest wisdom is the least resentment," he wrote on a piece of parchment that he gave to Penelaiaa for a gift. “Forgive me,” he said when he handed it to her. “I have been acting like a small boy. It does no good to curse life. I did not have to continue to live after they broke my legs. I could have killed myself or allowed myself to die. I thought then that I lived to have revenge but now I think I wanted to live long enough to watch Auria

herding those little demons up and down that bank six times a day. What does she think she is up to?”

“She is creating order from chaos. She told me so the other day.”

“Here they come again,” Leucippius said. “Here comes the goddess of order with her little band.” Auria was marching beside the double line, calling out the alphabet as they marched. “Alpha, beta, sigma, iota, let’s hear it for epsilon. Epsilon, epsilon, epsilon.” She had plaited a wildflower into her hair and it fell across her cheek as she marched the children down to the water. “Cosmos, logos, biblian, ge, gamma, dendra, anthropos, arche, logos, theon.”

# Chapter XIX

In the midst of all this a diversion occurred. One morning there appeared at the school two small boys, about five or six years old and as alike as two peas in a pod. They had bright hair and, although they were dressed in rags and in need of a bath, they were so beautiful no one could stop looking at them. The other children crowded around them and around the girl who had brought them there, a tall scraggly girl who said she had found them on the road and brought them along with her.

"I think they are from one of the villages near Pyrrha," she said to Auria. "I heard the Spartans burned it on their way to Mytilene."

"Where are you from?" Auria asked. The boys looked at each other for a moment, then the one with the freckle above his nose spoke.

"We are from our home."

"And where is that?"

"Where the river comes down into the town and goes beside the houses. Where the birds sit on the roofs to bring us luck. We would like to go back there."

"Where is your mother?"

"She is taken somewhere. We would like to go there now."

"You stay with the other children, Leiakes," Auria said. "I'll take care of them. You can leave them with me," she said to the girl. "I will keep them. There is plenty to eat in my tent."

"Thank you," the girl said. "I have two of my own and my husband told me I had to find a home for them."

"It's all right," Auria said. "I have a little girl who needs playmates." Then Auria took the little boys by the hand and they went to the tent, where Keffee was sitting in the sun watching Kleis. "Look what I have,"



Auria said. "Kleis, here are brothers for you. Find them food, Keffee. Kleis and I will take them to the lake for a swim. Have you been in water?" she asked. "Did you bathe in this magic river that flows through your town?"

"Oh, yes," the quiet one said. "Oh, yes, many times. We caught fish and we can swim. Our father has a boat."

"Well, eat something and then we will show you our lake. Kleis, look here. Here are Philippus and Theodorus, who have come to be your brothers."

"We would like to go home now," Theodorus said. "We would like to go to our mother."

"We will have to wait on that," Auria said. "Until I can find the way. Meanwhile, let's be happy while we can." Then she took the day off from school and cut their hair and sewed up their garments and played with them and in the evening she pushed the rugs together and took the covers off the bed she slept in with Kleis and arranged it so the four of them could sleep together on the floor. Kleis was so excited she could not calm down and kept going from one to the other, touching their hair, which was a shining reddish-gold color, even more beautiful now that it was clean.

To quiet them down Auria began to tell the history of her life, a story Kleis had been hearing all her days. Her favorite part was when she was born into Auria's hands, but it was taking a long time to get to that part because Auria was weaving into her own life the story of a magical birth of twins in a town beside a magical river.

"Tell bout dat Meion," Kleis said. "Tell bout dat honey tree. Tell about dat."

"So there was this tree on the path," Auria began, feeling Philippus turn and begin to settle down. "And there was a creature in it the size of a child and covered with fur, and like a dog because it could run on four feet, and like a squirrel because it jumped out from a tree and it had honey all over its nose and paws and bees were swarming and it was going buzzzzzzzzz, and the breeze was blowing and we were afraid of nothing because we are Hellenes and have no enemies we can not conquer and have nothing to fear because we are stronger than anything in nature and stronger than anything in the world and know everything we need to know and recognize all the plants and catch all the fish and fell trees and build our houses against storms. . . ." The children were sleeping now. Auria covered them and sat in the dark looking at the small humps of their bodies, thinking of herself when she was small. Then she thought of Meion and the way his arms had held her the last time she saw him and she got up and found the small polished mirror Kefallinia had stolen from the villa and went outside into the moonlight and tried to see herself in it but all she saw was a shadow. I may have grown old, she thought. And he will no longer desire me. Tomorrow I must wash all my robes and my hair and put fresh pine branches everywhere. When he comes I will show him these children and the school and tell him everything that has happened. If he comes. If he returns.

So thinking she went back into the tent and snuggled up beside the little row of waifs.

. . .

In Athens, led by a pair of servants carrying torches, Clarius proceeded to the pier and boarded a ship bound for Cirrha, a port below Delphi on the Gulf of Corinth. As he stepped on the gangplank he turned and saluted the city that had nurtured him all the days of his life as if he knew he would never set eyes on it again.

# Chapter XX

The city of Athens had a small port near to its marketplace, but its trading vessels and the large triremes of its navy were six miles away at the port of Piraeus. The famous long walls joined Athens to its port.

Meion and Nidde were walking down the main street of Piraeus, a dusty cartroad that ran along beside the wharves and piers. They were dressed in white chitons and carrying small packs. They had left their horses and gear with a peasant on the outskirts of town, an old man who had served Meion's father in five campaigns and retired to raise olives on land the Alkmeionadae had given him. He had recognized Meion before the boy even told him who he was and took them in and arranged to keep their horses while they wandered around the port seeking information.

Piraeus was so crowded with refugees that at first no one paid any attention to them. The plague that had killed so many had abated. The dead had been burned and the half-dead carted off to die further down beside the sea.

The streets were clear of sickness this morning as Meion and Nidde walked along the cartroad listening to the sailors talk and trying to pick up what information they could. There were so many rumors and so much wild talk that it was hard to separate the truth from the stories. Every sailor they spoke to seemed to have just come from an engagement with the Spartans and come away with a victory or a defeat that turned at the last moment into victory.

"Off the coast of Messenia there were five vessels with two hundred hoplites armed with steel-tipped arrows," a man was telling them now. They were stopped beside a large cargo boat that had just come up the coast from the smaller port in Athens.



"How goes it in Athens?" Meion called to a young sailor who was tying the boat to its moorings. "Are things well in the capital of the world?"

"If a world with no head is well," the sailor answered. He tied down the line he was holding, then stood on the gunwales, balancing like an acrobat. His face was familiar to Meion, but grown older, and Meion could not place him for a moment. "Pericles is ill," the sailor added. "They say he is dying but no word comes from the palace. So we deliver olive oil as if the world could live without politicians, and so it may." The captain of the cargo boat appeared and came to stand beside the young sailor.

"What are you telling our young friend?" the captain asked.

"That Pericles is ill. It is not a secret, is it?" Meion's face registered his dismay. He turned and took Nidde's arm and held it. As he did so, the captain raised his hand.

The boat was a supply ship for the Athenian navy. There were soldiers aboard to guard the olive oil. The captain motioned to four of them standing by the unloaded crates, and the four men surrounded Meion and Nidde.

"I am a citizen," Meion said. "You have no right to set these men on me. The black man is my slave. Let us be." The soldier who had been telling them about Messenia stepped out of the way. The guard forced

Meion aboard the boat. Two more soldiers dragged Nidde behind him. The young sailor who had been speaking to them caught Meion's eye and shook his head up and down, as if in assent. It is Methos, Meion told himself, who was second behind me in the cave when the avalanche almost ended all our days. Little Methos, grown as tall as myself. How did he find his way to this ship? They must be in real trouble in Athens now if they are using slaves from the mines to man the navy vessels.



The captain met them in the small makeshift cabin. He was a sturdy grayhaired man, recently come up through the ranks to be given command of a cargo boat. In times of peace he could never have expected such a post and he was nervous about his command, eager to prove his worth to the generals who had hired him. The general he was accountable to was Hyperbolus, after Cleon the chief enemy of the Alkmeionadae in the senate.

"Who are you, wandering around in a time of war? Don't you know the Spartans are on the plain? And if you are a citizen, why are you doing nothing to defend your country?" The captain reached out his hand and felt the muscles of Meion's arms. Meion pushed his hand away.

"I am on my way to join Clarius Arasistratus in Athens. You may have heard of him, that was a senator once and still has power in the city. I came this way to survey the death. I have been in Parnassus, with my servant, scouting for the senate. What is your name, captain? And what is the name of this vessel?" He turned his back to the captain and took back his spear from the man who had taken it from him. "Also, hand my pack here and the things of my servant. You were doing your duty, doubtless, and so we will say no more about the insult."

“I will send a guard with you to Athens then.” The captain had decided to be cautious. “The mistake I made could be repeated since you are not what you appear. I will have my soldiers accompany you to Athens.”



“As you like,” Meion said. “We have horses outside the city. We will ride there. Do you have horseguards aboard?” The captain was uncertain now, afraid of making a really serious mistake. If they had horses, perhaps Meion was a gentleman; certainly he spoke and held himself like one. On the other hand, if he was allowing spies through or missing the chance to take two strong men for slaves that would also be a mistake.

“That’s a likely lad there,” Meion added. “With the silver-white hair. Give us that one for an escort and I’ll forget your insolence. Yes, he’s light enough. He can ride behind my servant on one horse. I’ll take that one for the insult and if the sun continues to shine perhaps my uncle Clarius will not take your ship and command also when he hears of this.” The captain was wavering but he would not be fooled.

“I’ll send a guard with you to your uncle Clarius then. We can’t take chances in these troubled times.” Meion looked at Nidde and the guards moved in closer all around them.

“As you wish,” Meion said. “Tell them to follow us then to where our horses are stabled.”

# Chapter XXI

In the camp Penelaiaa had been writing letters to Clarius. They were slow to arrive and the news they brought was old by the time it got there.

Penelaiaa, daughter of Phidias, to Clarius Arasistratus:

*It is dawn. Today the gray-eyed goddess rules. Harmony prevails. What would I do without the girl, Auria? She is teaching the children to read. Half in jest I proposed a lyceum to keep her busy while she waits for Meion. Now, out of my whimsy she has created a real school. Even the grown people go there when they have time.*

*She says the earth is round, or, more likely, shaped like a funnel. I tend to think of it as a great loaf, out of the oven but still smoking and settling down. There were tremors in the hills last week, one in the morning and one in the afternoon. I went with Father once to Olympia after a tremor destroyed his workshop there. Of course the superstitious think the gods became angry, but Father, for all his lip service to Zeus, told me it was only the earth settling down into its final form.*

*Now I see I have used up almost the whole parchment without telling you that we have a bakery. Three ovens instead of one, very Egyptian. And this lyceum. The walls are coming along slowly. The men work on them without complaint but without great interest either. Would Cleon really send an army here if he came to power? I stood on the precipice above the shrine to Athena, you know the one, and looked down upon the plain and for the first time I could imagine an army coming that way. The fates hold out happiness, then snatch it away. Please come to us. We need you here.*



Clarius Arasistratus, bound for Cirrha, aboard the trireme Hellene, to Penelaiaa, daughter of Phidias, greetings and love:

*Pericles has come down with the plague. May the gods preserve us now. Last night we were tossed by storms and had to put into port at Balis to make repairs. I will send this ahead by a transport boat carrying wheat. Pray the letter or I will arrive shortly.*

*I had thought we would have Pericles another year. As you are aware, it is widely known in Athens that the Alkmeionadae control the Pythia. Cleon has begun making speeches about blasphemy and telling the people not to believe the prophecies. He has not gone as far as implicating Pericles, but has slandered Alcibiades so badly that only Alcibiades' friendship with Socrates, who is a good influence on him no matter what you think, has kept Alcibiades from killing Cleon on the street.*

*The Alkmeionadae create trouble for ourselves with our hot tempers. It is only the loyalty of such as you that has kept us in power this many years. Alcibiades lays himself open to criticism. He is so careless of the company he keeps that he has even been accused of spying for the Spartans. We must all flee Athens soon.*

*Do not let Meion come this way. Elen is with Brasidas. And yes, in answer to your more pressing question. Cleon or Hyperbolus either one would send an army to kill Leucippius if they could spare one. In his absence his shadow grows in their minds.*

*Are the meadows blooming? Is the air thick with the smell of thyme and daphne and pine? Will I eat this remarkable bread soon and have the solace of your company?*

*Your servant,*
*Clarius*

*The ship that will carry this waits to sail.*



The letter arrived one day at noon. The next day Clarius was there, wearing a grey cloak fastened at the shoulder with a pin, his hair white along the sides of his face. He walked out into the clearing and stood very still. Auria was surrounded by students. She had been showing them a word on a tablet. As soon as he walked out from the cover of the trees she knew who it must be and handed the tablet to a child and walked over to where he was standing and spoke to him.

"You are Clarius. I am Auria, that took shelter in your sanctuary and drank from your spring. Whatever you need while you are here I will do for you."

He took her hands and held them. "Penelaiaa has written me about you. We will have much to say to each other." He smiled, still holding her hands. Auria had never seen such kind eyes, not since Philokrates' own. She wanted to pull her hands away but could not. She straightened her shoulders. "I live in a dwelling by the lyceum," she said at last. "You may come and visit me there whenever you have time." Then people were coming from all directions to talk to him and they swept him away in the direction of Leucippius's house. As he moved away he turned and called out something about his gardens but she could not hear what he said.

Then she was very excited and went back to her students and taught them so furiously all afternoon that several of them considered not coming back to school at all.

~



Penelaiaa was cutting up onions and arguing with Leucippius. "But why?" she was saying. "Why let Braseus use our paths for his bearers if he has no loyalty to us? That back pass could be used to attack from the woods. The more bearers who travel that way the more passable it becomes and the more available to an enemy."

"All we made are promises not to interfere. If he wishes to turn his camp into a den of thieves there is nothing we can do about it. We are in no position to interfere with the way he runs his little horde."

"Well, we must meet with him then. I won't live without some order." She turned and saw the crowd bringing Clarius. "Oh, gods," she said. "Clarius comes. Leucippius, he has come to join us." Clarius entered the room and embraced her, then dropped on his knees by Leucippius.

They talked excitedly for awhile, then Penelaiaa sent the others away and the three old friends sat in a circle.

"Here we are," Leucippius said. "Still alive by some miracle and we have this camp and an outpost on an island and confederates here and there. Speak, Clarius, sum it up for me, if Penelaiaa will relent and allow me another cup of wine. The little physician has forbade me all pleasures now that she has taken me in hand. Come along, Penelaiaa, one more cup won't kill me tonight." She filled the cups and Clarius began to speak.

"Cleon and Hyperbolus fight among themselves but Cleon has the upper hand. The moment Pericles dies anarchy will reign. What the plague left undone the Spartans will finish off. The Spartans and Corinthians are building a navy now and plan to challenge Athens on the seas. Then the barbarians will come down from Sicili and stable goats in the temples. I would have died for Athens when Athens was something a man could understand. Well, there is no use to mourn for what can't be saved. We must plan the future of this handful we have led to these mountains."



"I am doing all that can be done," Leucippius said. "We are making a fortress and we will wait and see what comes of it. Well, the donkeys you came on will come in handy, and the corn. How long do you think Pericles will live?"

"He has plague. Word is all over the city that he is ill."

"Leucippius thinks some of us should go to Megales," Penelaiaa said. "He has ordered a boat to take us there. It is waiting on the river Iolus. Hallicus went there with the coins and says it is seaworthy. Meion is searching for Elen, as you know if you got my letter."

"Where did he go?"

"To ask for information at the ports."

"He will not find her. She is with Brasidas."

"He knows that. Nidde came. And is with him now. Tell me of Brasidas. Is he an ephor?"

"More than that. He was the first Spartan general in the war to be accorded a victory celebration. He is very powerful in their military. Also a drunkard, if rumor serves. The Spartans don't like drunks or anyone who pleases their senses. Still, he's a law unto himself among them now. And fascinated by all things Athenian. He traveled with his father when he was young and visited Athens when his father was ambassador there, after Marathon. I suppose she has taken him for a lover." Leucippius looked at Penelaiaa but they said nothing.

"Have you seen Auria?" Penelaiaa asked. "I don't know why she hasn't come here to speak to you. She stays here half the time."



"I met her as I was coming into the camp. What beautiful eyes she has."

"She's done wonders for my old beat-up body," Leucippius said. "She is teaching me how the rivers of blood travel around my body and is so convincing I find myself believing anything she says."

"How Meion must love her," Clarius said. "Well, I suppose he is not afraid of strong women. He may be the only boy in Hellas prepared to match those eyes."

"They fight," Penelaiaa said. "It is not an easy madness."

Across the camp Auria was imagining what was going on in Penelaiaa's house. At any other time she would have felt welcome to go and sit there, but tonight she was waiting to be summoned. No summons came. At dusk it began to rain and Kefallinia moved the cooking pots to the entrance of the house and cooked dinner. Auria kept getting up and staring out the entrance at the rain. Kleis pulled at her chiton, wanting attention, but she pushed the child away. Even the twins could not get her attention.

"Leave her alone," Kefallinia said. "Can't you see she's infatuated?"

"I am not," Auria said. "I wish to talk with a literate man. Is that asking so much in a life that is short and plagued with torment?" She turned her back to them. Kefallinia raised her eyebrows and wrinkled her nose and Little Aeo and Kleis went into gales of laughter. Auria walked out of the tent into the rain and across the clearing and sat in the deserted school, picking up the children's tablets and putting them back down.

It was too maddening. The person who could answer all her questions was a hundred yards away. *He was here this very minute and she could not go and talk to him.* It was too much to bear. She sat on a stone bench for a long time in complete dejection, then sloshed back across the clearing in the rain and went to bed.



A hundred yards away Clarius was writing by the light of an oil lamp.

From Clarius Arasistratus to Cincinnus Eudoxus, on Mount Pelos:

*Greetings. I am at the camp of our leader, Leucippius, who is in good health and good spirits and wishes to meet soon with all the commanders of the camps to clasp the hands of all who share our freedom and our brotherhood. Come lend your wisdom to our own, so that we can plan for the winter ahead. Have you heard news of the lady, Elen Alkmeionadae, or her son, Meion? If any there have come lately from the cities, please question them and if there is word send a runner.*

To the Commander Braseus, from Clarius Gaius Arasistratus:

*Greetings. Good luck in your adventures. You will be glad to hear that Leucippius is well and ready to lead us as soon as we agree on what is to be done. He has made a remarkable recovery from the ills of last winter. We must meet soon. When can you come here?*

*Have you had word of Elen Alkmeionadae? Or her son, Meion? If anyone knows their whereabouts please send word.*

To Melistius Sipyon, on the Island of Andros, from Clarius Arasistratus:

*Melly, has the woman I told you of shown up there, or her son? I must have word of them. Please send out scouts. Would you also send to Sparta if you have spies there. I am indebted to you already to such an extent only five ships bearing silk and corn could repay your kindness. My prayers for your well-being.*

He put the papers aside and walked out into the clearing. It had been raining but he had hardly noticed it. Now the sky was clearing, the moon beginning to move out from behind the clouds. He stood in the grove of trees near Auria's lyceum thinking of Elen and the months he had lived with her while Eutorian was in Thrace. Elen was greatly in fear of Eutorian at the time, as he had taken Meion away with him as a hostage. Still she had managed to come to Clarius at night, and during those months, he had known the only real ecstasy of his life. Then Eutorian had returned and it was over, as swiftly as it had begun.

"What do you want?" he had said to her. "Tell me what you want to go with me and I will give it to you."

"It is not within your power to give."

"I can keep you safe and your child too. If I ask Pericles for this he will grant it."

"No, Eutorian would seek us out and have us killed. Besides, it is not only the child. A hundred men would die because of me and their children would be yoked or starved. He would punish me by killing my friends. He has told me this."

"There must be a way."

"There is no way."

"I could leave Athens. Nothing holds me there."

"Meion is waiting for me, Clarius. I must go see to him now. He is acting strangely since they returned. That dog, that filthy dog. I will eat his heart before my life is done."

"Then you stay to have revenge? Is that it?"

"No, please, Clarius. No more. Don't spoil what we had." He had left her then and gone to live in the mountains. He had not seen her since that time. Now he stood in the grove of trees beside the lyceum thinking of her. He thought that he had lived a thousand years and must live a thousand more. A thousand thousand nights to miss her and wonder where she was.



"Someday we will sit before a fire and tell our stories," she had said. "Someday it will happen." She had promised him that, but he was tired of believing it now and went back into his tent and slept a cold and dreamless sleep.

# Chapter XXII

It was late the next afternoon before Clarius found time to talk with Auria. She was sweeping up the floor of the school when he appeared and asked if she would go for a walk with him. She put the broom aside and pushed her hair back out of her eyes. "I will have to see the baby first," she said. "Let me see how she is."

"Penelaiaa told me you had a child with you."

"She was born in the villa where I lived . . . she was born into my hands."

"Whose child was she?"

"A woman named Eleuria. Her father was a lute player, a minstrel who stayed there for awhile. They are all dead now."

"Eleuria, that was married to the trader, Meldrus, that lived on the road to Delphi?"

"Yes, the very one. How did you know?"

"She was my kinsman. A cousin of my mother. You have done my family a good turn." They had arrived at Auria's tent, which had grown now to twice its size. There was a cleared place along the side where Kefallinia did the cooking. The twins were off playing with a pigeon Auria had captured for them. Little Aeo was nursing Kleis, who was wearing a shift that was smudged with dirt. She laughed at the sight of Auria and threw herself at her legs. Clarius reached for her. "May I touch her?"

“Of course. She likes everyone. Go on, pick her up. She won’t care.” Clarius lifted the little dust-covered blonde thing into his arms. She was fat and strong and pulled at his beard. “Oh, little one,” he said. “Oh, little jewel, how have you come out of all this madness? What a fat little thing.”

“She lives on goat milk and bread.”



“Our lives are very strange. To think I should be holding Eleuria’s child. She used to come and stay with us when we were children, in a different world, a different time.” He took the seat Kefallinia offered him, a makeshift chair, and looked around. “What can I do to be of help to you? Is there anything you need?”

“You have already done it,” Auria said. “By leaving us shelter when we needed it. Kleis is mine. No one will take her from me. They are all dead that could have claimed her. They put her out to die. She is mine. I saved her.”

“No one would dispute your claim. Least of all me. I am persona non grata with all of them. But my mother will be glad to know something lives out of that branch of the family. They drank themselves to death, most of them.”

“Well, bring her along with us then, since she is your kinsman.” Auria picked up the child and wiped off her face. “Come along, we’ll take her with us on our walk.” Then, passing the little girl between them, they started down the path to the meadow.

“You must not think I would ever take her from you,” Clarius said. “I didn’t mean to frighten you.”

“It’s all right. No one could take her because I wouldn’t let them. Well, then. Tell me about the strange writing on the axones. I studied it for many hours thinking I could figure out what it said. Does it repeat the Greek words on the other side? I thought it might."

"It is called Sanskrit, a sacred language of the Far East. The letters are very beautiful and have many esoteric meanings. It was created to write down the words of a prophet who is to come among them. They say their words are boxes to catch the spirit of this man when he appears."



"How long did you live in the little valley?"

"For six years. I wish I could go back there now. Tell me of my gardens. What grows in them? Did you plant new things?"

"I know every plant in the world. I can recognize anything a man can use. I found other plants in the meadow and brought them in and made a new bed, nearer the creek, where there is sun all day. I planted wild orchids and Egyptian potatoes. And many herbs and some moss that is good for stomach cramps." She looked at him. He was leaning into the crook of a tree holding the baby. He did not look at all like a commander, or a hero. She had forgotten he was one. She had been talking to him as if he was anyone at all. "I want to talk about the Eastern writing some more," she added. "What is it called?"

"It is most properly called Vedic, although many are beginning to call it Sanskrit now, which means holy writing. It is not standardized like Greek and each monastery writes its own version so it's very confusing. They need a grammarian to set them straight."

"Where are these cities?"

"A year's journey to the south and east, across land so barren you can not imagine men live there, yet they do, and herd animals and plant grain and irrigate fields and talk in many tongues, but in the end all men say the same things. They talk of the events of their lives and beg mercy from the skies and dream of better times. Don't you find it so?"

"I should like to travel to those lands and meet men who talk in different tongues. The man who raised me had been across the seas and seen such things as you have seen."



"There are places in the world that are much older than Hellas, Auria. We are young here still and on our way to destroying all we have achieved." He stood up and began to walk along the path. Auria offered to take Kleis from him but he was happy with her in his arms and kept her there, wearing the child against his shoulder like a poultice, thinking of her mother and what a funny, happy, little thing she had been. He walked along the path thinking of the waste of the world. Auria moved close to him. She could smell the warmth of his body through his robes; how simple he seemed, how simple and how good. She decided to be his disciple and never leave his side.

"Come and see my lyceum," she said, when he left her at her tent.

"I will do it gladly. It will be the bright spot of my visit here. I once spent a long while trying to decide how we should educate the young, but could come up with nothing better than the same old ways. Show them something and watch them do it, then show them again. Is that your method?"

"Oh, I don't know. I don't think I have a method. I just do what Philokrates did for me. Some of them are better at it than others. Some just come to talk . . . I think most of them just come to talk. The part they like is when I read to them."

"The lazy are always with us. There are worse things I suppose."

"Not if they are at your lyceum." She looked up. It was all right to contradict him. She went on. "You can not teach them all. Some of them can not learn. Some of them are curious and some are asleep. But it is an interesting task and I have learned many things from doing it. Come and visit us and see for yourself. Perhaps you can help me."

"I will come gladly to watch whatever you are doing." He took his leave of her then. She watched him walk away and was filled with a  sense of mystery. Men and women walking the earth, so different from other creatures, and yet, of the earth, and subject to its laws. If I eat one plant I become sleepy and if I eat another I am made giddy. How to learn these laws. How to know one truth from another. She looked down at the veins in her arm; they barely were visible at the wrist. Rivers of life. Roots of trees, geometry of leaves. Mystery after mystery after mystery. Apollo, Athena, order, reason, light. I, Auria, of Thisbe and Boetia and Thrace, of the mountains and the skies. She shook her head and went off to drink at the spring.

# Chapter XXIII

In Piraeus the ship's captain had arranged a guard for Meion and Nidde—two mounted soldiers, another soldier walking beside them, and Methos. As soon as they were out of sight of the ship, the mounted soldiers climbed down from their horses and led them. It was very warm, the middle of the day. Most of the citizens had disappeared into their houses or closed up their stalls for the noon meal. The six men in their tattered battalion walked along beside the piers. "How did you come to be here, with that brand on your arm?" Meion asked Methos. Nidde was walking on the outside of the soldiers, pretending to be unable to understand a thing. He had gone into his darkest, hunted nature. The guards thought he was dumb and ignored him. Their orders were to take the two men to Hyperbolus in Athens and if they were what they said the guards were to give Methos to them in apology and return. They walked along in the hot sun glad of an excuse to leave the life of the boat for a few days but irritated at having to march at noon.

"I was conscripted from the mines," Methos replied. "And a good day that was. Since then I have sailed all over the Ionion Sea and up the coast of Messenia. Also, around the whole of the Peloponnese two times and into the Gulf of Corinth. I have seen the world or most of it." He looked straight ahead as he talked. He was sure of Meion's identity now but he did not want to tip off the guards. The sun beat down.

In the woods above Sounion five hundred men had escaped from the mines to live in freedom, Methos was thinking. If he could reach the trees and grab one of the horses he could join them there. Could find his brothers and learn the fate of his sisters. Could wake in the mornings with the sunlight playing down between the leaves of the trees and live as he chose and call no man master. He will help me, Methos decided, watching the back of Meion's head as it moved along in front of him. For now, walk quietly. And wait.

Methos walked along the dusty cartroad behind Meion. The guard leading the horses brought up the rear. "My black man will tend the horses for you if you like," Meion said. "He is good with horses. Will you give the leads to him?"

"Take this one," the first man answered. He was the junior officer, if there was a ranking in the motley troops that had been aboard the cargo boat. "The bit doesn't fit his mouth. And he's skittish from the boat ride. I think he'll bite my hand off if I turn my head."

"No," said the other guard. "We can't have a black slave pulling the horses. Come along, Feriades, don't complain. It's a trip to the city. We can find a wineshop before we return. Tell on with your story, Methos. I had wondered at that brand myself. So you came from the mines."

"We heard the Spartans had taken Laurium," Meion said. "We heard they had loosed the slaves and taken the women and all the silver. Were the reports honest?"

"Pray Zeus they were not," said the captain. "Well, it's a bad time for the land and impiety everywhere. But it makes work for them that like to travel. Hard sailing on that flat-bottomed cargo boat that Balis commands. He'll have a pretty commission if you turn out to be spies."

Meion laughed. "It will not be long to the place where our horses are stabled," he said. "We'll rest there before we continue. I will treat you to a meal and wine for your trust."

"I'm doing as Balis commanded me, nothing more," the leader said. "As for me, I believe any gentleman until he pulls a sword and sometimes afterwards if he's good with it. I do as I'm told so I get my bread but I think as I please."



"Like a true Athenian," Meion said. "Well, I'm glad of the company with all the rabble on the road. Are you sure you wouldn't care to let my man pull that horse for you?"

"I'll pull him myself," the leader answered. He was a stout man, in a dark regulation chiton that was too tight around the shoulders and the waist and he trudged along in his heavy sandals for a few more minutes. There was not a cloud in the sky. It was hotter every minute, not a breeze stirring now that they were no longer beside the sea. They were moving inland on a road between olive groves. After a while the leader motioned to Nidde and handed him the reins of the horse and they proceeded down the road between the ancient olive trees, Meion and the young soldier leading the way, Methos and the captain behind them, Nidde and the other guard last, leading the skittish Thessalian mares. They were small horses out of the shore stock, with sweet faces and dainty white markings on their legs. Nidde moved the cruel bit from the mouth of the one he was leading. "Ke, ke, ke," he whispered to the horse, and when they stopped for water at a stone basin in a stream he slipped the creature a honey cake he had bought that morning at a stall.

# Chapter XXIV

Meion and Nidde led their captors along a dirt road that wound between olive groves into a small valley formed by the mountains. The road was in shade here and they walked in silence until they came to the hut where Meion and Nidde had left the horses in the care of the old man and his wife. The woman came to the door when she saw them. She was very old and as thick as one of the olive trees that she tended. She kept her black eyes fastened on Meion and spoke to him. "Well, master," she said. "You have picked up a party. Shall you buy food for this crowd before you travel further?"

"Why not, mother." Meion motioned the guards to seats beneath four giant olive trees that ringed the yard. "This shade is welcome and your wine and the sacred water of your spring will revive us all. A boat captain has given me a guard to take me into town to my cousin. A curious and unexpected fate." He took off his outer garment and laid it across a wooden bench and propped his sword against it. Nidde did likewise, keeping only his dagger. Then the two captives sat down together upon a second bench, and the men that had been set to guard them did likewise. The old woman went into the house and spoke with her husband and in a while they reappeared with a stone bowl and cups and a dipper and set it down before the men. Nidde took up the dipper and served each one in turn and then the old man went back inside and returned with cheese and grapes and a round loaf of bread.

All this time Meion was questioning his captors and they were telling him stories of the progress of the war.

"So the men of Mytilene have revolted and they will all be put to death as soon as the revolt is put down. Men, women and children this time to teach the other colonies a lesson."

Meion caught Methos's eye and a flicker of recognition passed between them and then was doused. 

"The big news is that Cleon has won a battle and taken prisoner a thousand Spartan hoplites," another soldier was saying. "Their best troops. He has driven them back to Athens to work on the harbor. He'll be a hero to the people for that day's work. Also, it is Cleon who speaks loudest for killing all those Mytilene bastards who revolted against us. Good for him, I say. I'll lend a sword to that slaughter."

"Cleon won a battle?" Meion said. "How long ago?"

"Oh, it couldn't have been forty days. He's only last week gotten them back here. The victory celebration was last week but we were at sea and missed the party."

"What else happened? What other good news have you?"

"The seige of Plataea is ended, in defeat for us, but what good will the victory do the cursed boyfucking Peloponnese? When winter comes they must return to their lands and we will go with our navy and extract a fine revenge. I want to be in that invasion. There'll be spoils for every man to take all that he wants. I'll need a wagon to carry home the women I'll have for a reward."

"And have to feed them when you get them," laughed a third man. "I'll take my reward in golden cups and grain. Maybe a horse or two." He indicated the brindled mare and the dark gelding that stood side by side in a pasture with Meion and Nidde's saddlebags on them. The old man had saddled them and brought them around while the men were eating and drinking.

"I brought the horses," he said now. "In case you will be leaving before the light gets too far away. The sea eats the sun each night and coughs it back up when the gods rise from love." He straightened his shirt and filled the wine glasses. Meion had been generous with the old man the night before, listened to his stories, then paid him half his wages in advance.



"What else has happened?" Meion said now. "What of the naval battles? There was no word where I was. I'm hungry for news."

"I'm an eyewitness to one battle," the oldest man said. "We were six triremes bound for the Peloponnese and we took on a fleet of ten Spartan vessels in the straights where the Ionian rushes like a lover into the Gulf of Corinth. Such a torrent it pours. May I never sail that way again, every moment your life is in danger. A gust of wind coming up at the wrong time and you can join the others who got too far above themselves and thought Poseiden was asleep.

"We circled their boats for many hours, being faster than their heavy old-fashioned crates. Our rowers were crazy for victory, as manly as if they had a stake in the outcome. We barely had to beat them to keep them rowing. We had the Spartans in our hands. Ten boats, carrying troops and horses and weapons. We circled them, pushing them ever nearer the mainland and were within a half mile of the beach planning to gather what was left when it washed ashore." The storyteller filled his cup for the third time, getting carried away. He had told the story a dozen times already to the other soldiers and it grew better with each telling. They were hanging on his every word. It seemed too good to be true, sent to walk a gentleman and his servant to a senator's house, and then the added pleasure of wine and food and a shady resting spot. Maybe even horses to confiscate if all went well. The soldiers leaned toward the wine bowl and partook of it while the storyteller told his story and the old woman replenished the bowl as it emptied.

"As we were circling their boats for the fifth time . . . ," the soldier was saying. "It had been a long day, all morning and all afternoon we moved and pushed them and they sought a way out. It was growing late and we were sure of victory. The men on our boats were beginning to yell insults at the Spartans, laughing at the design of their boats and their audacity in calling themselves sailors, when suddenly, such is the spoil of hubris, a squall came up out of nowhere. In part of an hour it rose up on the horizon, a black cloud that spread out to cover the sky and was upon us like a hawk, sweeping Athenian and Spartan alike onto the sand. The boats had nowhere to go but onto the beach. They were all wrecked but two, one of ours and one of theirs. I was on a boat that crashed into a rock, and had to throw off all my gear and swim for my life."



"What happened then?" Methos asked.

"We climbed ashore and fought on the sand but the heart was gone out of the battle with the ships crashing all around us and the weapons gone." Meion had gone to stand behind the bench where his spear was leaning against his cape. He waited until Nidde was poised over the oldest man with the wine dipper in his hand and then he picked up the spear and drove it into the chest of the leader and took his sword and decapitated another. Nidde had killed his man with his hands, breaking his neck. "Will you run, Methos?" Meion asked. "Or go with us to higher ground. It is I, Meion Alkmeionadae. Did you not know me?"

"I knew you by the black man," Methos said. "Gods go with you and watch you as their own. As for me I will run away somewhere in the forest. There are many there now. Hundreds from Laurium that have escaped." Meion dropped his weapons and went to the younger, smaller boy and embraced him and gave him several gold coins and asked the older couple to outfit him with food before he left. Then he paid the older couple and told them to tell whatever story they wished to tell if soldiers came for the bodies.

"I will dispose of them," Methos said. "They were no friends to me. Also, I will take one of those horses if I may."

"Take them both," Meion said. "If one tires you will have the other." Then Meion took up his sword and spear and with Nidde by his side mounted his own horse and began to ride.

"We must go straight home now," Nidde said. "We must go back and tell them what we know."

"First to Sounion," Meion said. "We are in the hands of the gods. Today has proven that. We will finish what we began before we leave these settlements."

They said goodbye to Methos and mounted the horses and began to ride.

# Chapter XXV

Clarius fell into the habit of coming by the lyceum and watching Auria teach. They had several kinds of writing materials now—tablets made from wax Little Aeo found in the woods, clay tablets for everyday, a scroll of cloth and one of parchment. For ink they used the juice of berries boiled in a copper pot.

The children were learning words now and were beginning to make up their own sentences. Two half-grown boys, carried away by learning, had stripped the bark off half a beech tree and were recording the history of the camp, starting with the numbers of men, women and children, then listing their names and occupations, then a catalog of animals and supplies, horses, donkeys, mules, sheep, pigs, goats, and measures of grain and corn.

The children came to the lyceum after their morning meal and stayed until the sun was high. As the summer wore on it became too hot to study at midday and Auria let them go home earlier and earlier. "I would like to climb the wooded part of the mountain until the path stops," Clarius said to her one day, as the students were leaving. "I've been thinking of it all morning. We could take food and have a picnic in a glade. You make my heart young, Auria. It makes me understand why Socrates risked his life to save Alcibiades at Plataea. It was for love of the ideal of youth, he told me once, not only the beautiful young man he was saving. Do you know these people I am speaking of? Do you know of them?"

"I have heard Leucippius and Penelaiaa speak of them. Alcibiades is Meion's kinsman. And this Socrates is the one they argue about. Penelaiaa likes him but Leucippius says he does not value freedom."



"No one knows what Socrates believes. All he does is ask questions. Then too, he drinks quite heavily and pretends to be a slave to his passions but I do not believe it. He is the most disciplined man I have ever met. He wears the same cloak winter and summer. Anaphon said if a slave was made to live as Socrates does he would run away. He is a mystery but I have never regretted time I spent in his company and always seek him out if he is near. What made me think of him is that he is always saying the young keep him alive. I have seen him down on his haunches talking with children while they played in the dirt, talking baby talk or garbled street language. He can speak in the clearest Ionic or Attic one moment and the next be talking in the most common koine. Here, I will help you with that." Clarius helped her stack the tablets under a cover. Then they went by Kefallinia's bakery and got bread and a wineskin and started up the mountain. Auria was running ahead of him, pulling leaves off plants and smelling their stems, stopping to inspect moss or breaking off pieces of bark and tasting the juice. "I will lose my skill for plants if I don't come to the woods," she said. "It isn't just the names. You have to know which ones are kindred, how they are alike, and how they change with the seasons. It's the smell that tells you things. You see, if you know how things smell and what that means, you can go somewhere you have never been and know what is good to use. Philokrates believed the earth was made of water shaped in different forms with different smells. Well, that's one thing he believed. He did not believe in gods of any kind. Or luck. Or even words themselves. He said words were only tools, like a plow or a chisel or a net."

They arrived at a little knoll and sat down to eat their bread and drink their wine. "What shall we talk of then?" Clarius began. "In Athens, when philosophers go for a walk together, they choose a subject and explore it as they talk."



"Then tell me about politics. I love to hear of politics and the ecclesia and such things. Philokrates told me of them."

"As you know I am a kinsman of Pericles and I thought at one time he would save Athens but in the end all he has done is create a system that will be inherited by men who lack his genius. They are my bitterest enemies."

"Who are they?"

"A man named Cleon, and one called Hyperbolus. Cleon is the worst. A violent man with a violent character. It was Cleon who voted to kill all the citizens of Mytilene when they revolted. He is a drunkard as well and without judgment of any kind. Still, the rabble love him and will raise him to power as soon as Pericles dies."

"Go on."

"Our lives here are being influenced by events that began long ago. Attica can not support a growing population. So we sent out colonies to the islands and the lands of Sicili and the eastern coasts. At first we left the colonies free, as good fathers free their sons. Then we turned into fools and demanded tributes and ransoms. When Pericles dies Athens will be left in the hands of greedy men, sophists and frauds, cursed with a system of laws and courts that will create further injustices and excesses. I heard, as I was leaving Athens, that Cleon had won a great battle and taken many Peloponnesian hoplites as prisoners. So he will be swollen with victory and on to further madness I am sure." Clarius paused. Auria was listening intently, hanging on his every word. He went on. "Perhaps it is not hopeless. Perhaps the citizens will come to their senses and see through these demagogues. Perhaps Cleon will rise



to the occasion of greatness and change his ways. But I doubt it. I do not know what will ever stop ignorance and greed and brutal lust and war. Well, enough of this bad talk. Today is a day of peace. I think I will strip a beech tree like your students and record every day of peace."

"Perhaps Meion will find his mother and bring her here so you can see her."

"Perhaps he will. She promised me that one day we would sit beside a fire and be toothless together." He laughed out loud. "Well, my teeth are beginning to ache in the night so that happy time may be drawing near."

"Philokrates was interested in teeth. He said if he had another life he would spend it finding a way to repair teeth. There was a priest at Epidaurus who was carving teeth of elephants' tusks and putting them in people's mouths but they would not stay. They could not find a mortar that would work. I told him they should build a little bridge, or a catwalk, inside the mouth of very fine metal and suspend the teeth on that. He said it was a good idea and he was going to write it down and send it to someone he knows on Kos. I don't know if he ever did it or not."

"What a good mind you have." Clarius reached over and touched her shoulder. "Well, come along, we must go on if we are going to make the top and get back before dark. It's hotter than Hades, even under these trees. I warrant this has watered down the spirits of the armies of the plains."

A runner arrived that night with bad news. Auria and Clarius and Penelaiaa and Leucippius were on Leucippius's gallery eating their evening meal when the man was brought before them. Pericles was dead, he said, and Cleon and Hyperbolus were ruling as joint generals. Cleon had brought his captured Spartan hoplites to Piraeus and put them to work dredging the harbor and the citizens were celebrating the death of Pericles as if he had been a tyrant and Cleon and Hyperbolus great saviours of the people.



"Now it will begin," Clarius said. "All the worst things I have imagined. Come, let us walk down to the lake and consult the stars. Nothing will come of sleeping with this bad news in our heads."

"I will go with you," Auria said. "Penelaiaa, will you come too?"

"I will stay with Leucippius. In the morning we must work even harder on the fortifications."

Then Auria and Clarius walked down to the lake and sat on the stones by the half-finished wall and other men and women came to join them. The news had spread around the camp, and there was a feeling of uncertainty in the air.

# Chapter XXVI

Meion and Nidde approached Sounion from the north. When he was a child, before Elen lost favor with Eutorian, Meion had been brought to a villa near Sounion each summer. He had been old enough to be allowed to wander and so he knew the region.

"There is a shrine to Artemis along this road," he said. "We used to bathe there on hot days. If I can find that shrine I will know the way from there."

"We must find a house and ask questions. We can't wander on the main roads like this. We must find fresh horses."

"We will find a villa and say we come with warnings that the Spartans are on their way. Look, there's a path. We'll follow that." They turned a corner and followed a path that wound down through an olive grove. The trees were very old. Some had three and four trunks coiled around each other. The ground beneath them was carefully tended and raked. Above, on a rise of land overlooking the sea, was a white house surrounded by pink and red flowering bushes.

A group of young men were beside a grape arbor, leaning on their shovels in a desultory manner. A girl stood near them with a water pitcher balanced on her shoulder. Her hip was stuck out at an angle and her breasts were bared beneath her short robe.

"Hello," Meion called out. "What is your master's name?"

"Olynthia is our mistress," the girl called back. "We lost our master in the war. Who are you, coming to our villa with a black man by your side?"

"We come in peace," Meion said. "But bearing bad messages. It was to Olynthia that we were sent. Could it be the same as your mistress?"

"Who was the wife of Philip of Crete and settled here and built this house and has given both her sons and her husband to die in battle for our country? Is she the one you are seeking? She stays in the garden, looking out at sea and does not care what we do. I would run away but there is nowhere to go."



"Well, you are lazy slaves then," Meion answered. "And not worth the bread your mistress feeds you. Take me to her." The girl shifted the water bottle to her other shoulder and led the way up the path to the house. A woman was sitting on a bench looking out across the ocean. She turned her eyes to them but did not get up. Meion held out his hands. "I bring you messages from the senate in Athens," he said. "They send love to the mother of heroes and the wife of a hero and bid me warn you to take measures to insure your safety and that of anyone dependent upon you. The Spartans will send a fleet this way soon. They have taken Laurium already and will have you in a vise before the leaves fall from the olive trees."

"Who are you?" she said. "And why have you come to this house of mourning to tell me lies? No fleet could put into this port. They would have come years ago if that were possible. Now, what do you want of me that the gods have not already stolen?" She had not moved. Her face was very beautiful, with clear skin and wide gray eyes. "Tell me who you are and I will not harm you. There are twenty men within reach of my voice who could kill you in a minute. Sit down. There, on those benches. Altaii." She raised her voice and a servant appeared, a huge man in a yellow chiton. "Bring wine and cheese for our guests. They have come to warn us of invasion." She turned back to them. "What do you want here?"

"I am seeking my mother," Meion said. "Who was wife to Eutorian, the overseer of the mines at Laurium. She was taken when the Spartans  invaded. I wish to know if any have heard of her. This is my servant, Nidde. If your servants kill me, he will take five of them with him."

"There'll be no killing. No, I have not heard of her. But further down the way the Spartans occupied some villas for a time. They are frightened of the disease in Athens. As I am." She sat up. "Do you come from there?"

"No, we were near Piraeus but we saw the carts and departed." The servant reappeared with cups and a plate with cheese and set it down beside them and they began to eat.

"You may sleep here if you like," the woman said. "From here it is half a day's ride to Laurium. Do you know it there?"

"Yes," Meion answered. "I know it there."

"Well, go inside and Altaii will show you to the bath. You will dine with me later, after you have rested. Will your servant wait on you or will he stay here? He is very interesting to look upon. I have not seen an Ethiopian since I was small. One waited upon my grandmother in her old age. A gentle people, they make good nurses and are not contemptuous of weakness." Nidde moved out and stood before her, as if on display.

"I would be glad if you treated him as you would your own," Meion answered. Nidde bowed, first to the lady and then to Meion. "The sunset will be beautiful this evening," he said. "It will bring many colors to the world."

“I will have Altaii call musicians. We have not had music here in many months and days. When you have rested we will eat and have music. There has been no life in this house for a hundred days. More than a hundred, isn’t it, Altaii?”

“Many more,” the servant answered. He led Meion back to a large chamber with many beautiful hangings on the walls. There were porcelain jars with painted designs. There was a cage of briers holding two small yellow birds. The room was joined by an archway to a pool covered by an awning. A fountain played in a corner. Meion bathed and washed his hair and put on the fresh chiton Altaii left out for him.



Olynthia was waiting in the courtyard when he came out.

“Let us walk down to the ocean and see how this sunset looks on the sea,” she said. When they were away from the house she spoke again. “Tell me what you are really doing here. I am an old woman about to die of grief. I would not harm you or give you away. When you appeared this afternoon, I was wondering whether I would drink lye for my dinner or slip into the bath and cut my wrists. I was trying to decide which would cause the least mess for Altaii to clean up, who has always been a kind servant and has no family of his own. He has grieved for my lost children as much as I.”

“And your husband? Do you also grieve for him?”

“He was killed leading an expedition against Sicili and my sons by his side. Now grief is my husband and my child. But enough of my troubles. You could read them on my face. What are you doing here? Tell me what you need and I will help you.”

“I am searching for my mother, as I told you. Also, I need a safe passage back to the mountains. Fresh horses would be the best thing of all, if you have horses, but I might never be able to return them to you."

"There are horses in the stable. Take your pick if you can ride them. They were broken by my sons. The stable boys ride them now. What does any of it matter? What is your name?"



"Meion Doryphorus, son of the Lady Elen Alkmeionadae. Kinsman of Pericles, descendent of Megales and Alkmeion. It was my family that built Delphi. You may know of us that way."

"We hear that Pericles has died. Has that news found you?"

"No. But we expected it. Then I must hurry more than ever." He turned. They were on a promontory looking out to sea. "Our enemies will be in power now. Great luck has brought me here if you will lend us horses."

"Come then before it's dark and see the stables. Rest tonight, then I'll speed you on your way. You have done me a service by coming to remind me that the world is going on beyond my grief. You may take anything that will be useful."

Musicians came that night, bearing citharas and lyres and an instrument for keeping time, a lambskin stretched over a cylinder of wood, upon which a boy beat with hammers. Wine was passed in cups and the people of the farm danced on the terrace. Nidde danced for them and they applauded and then each of the men came out onto the floor and danced a turn, trying to imitate his steps. There was much stamping and turning and much wine was consumed and it was almost sunrise when the musicians played the last song and fell asleep on their cloaks beside their instruments. Olynthia took Nidde by the arm and led him back to her bedchamber. The sun was high in the sky when they emerged.

In the afternoon horses were saddled for them and saddlebags filled with provisions. Olynthia handed Meion a sack of silver and gold coins. "These will buy you a safe passage," she said. "I will send prayers for your safety."



"Do not leave the world," Meion said. "There is much you can do that is of value. If you die, a cruel master will come here and command these people. Couldn't you stay to prevent that?"

"I will try. Perhaps I will run away and join you in your mountains."

"We would welcome you. Ask where Leucippius and Penelaiaa have their band. Anyone can tell you once you pass the foothills and can see the clouds of the Parnassus. They will tell you where we are, if you say our names."

"I will remember that." She held out her hands and he clasped them and then she went to Nidde and embraced him and the men mounted the horses and began to ride.

"When I first came to the land of Hellas I was surprised to see horses," Nidde said. "It still seems to me an unusual thing that a man climbs upon the back of an animal and rides it. Who do you think was the first man to do this thing?"

"You're worse than Auria with your questions. Just pray to Poseidon, who is their god, that these borrowed horses take us where we're going. This one of mine has not been ridden in a year. Well, how was the night? How did it go with this white-skinned lady of sorrows?" Nidde turned his head from Meion and would not answer. He would never understand the Greeks, who must talk about and question everything they did and ruin all their excitements and their pleasures.

They rode across pastures and fields, taking a path beside a watercourse. By late afternoon they were within a mile of Laurium. Nidde stayed with the horses while Meion worked his way along the ridges overlooking the mines. He returned with bad news.



"The mines work as always. I saw old Dirius, the head of the guard, talking with others. Several hundred slaves were on the western face, most of them children. I suppose the older ones got away. Methos said they were banded together in the forests. If we could find them we could tell them to join us. We could make the camp strong again." He paused, thinking of it. There was no way a man could do all he could imagine. He went on, in a softer voice. "There is no Spartan overthrow of Laurium now. It is the same misery that was here before."

"Shall we seek out the ones who have escaped? We could take them to the hills."

"There is no time. Pericles is dead. Peace must be made with Braseus at all costs now." The sun was going down behind the mountains. They were dismounted, standing on a rise of land where lemon trees crowned the crest of a hill, the land all around them so beautiful it was impossible to imagine that men could fight and die in such a place; there seemed to be plenty of everything for many men. Sky, fields, sunlight, olive groves, vineyards, lemon fields. Yet half a mile away children dug in the earth for metals and slept in cold beds and were hungry. All of this was in Meion's mind and he nuzzled his horse's face and looked up into the beautiful colored clouds and was quiet.

"Let us go," Nidde said. "It is time to leave this sadness and return to our friends."

"Yes, we must go back. I am worried about the others. Last night I dreamed of Auria and the dream was very bad. There was a waterfall high in the rocks and I was holding her by the arms to keep her from being swept away. Below were torrents of water and black stones and I held her by the arms but the water came over us and would sweep us all into the ravine below."



"We will go back then. Do not be sad over a dream."

"I am sad that I ever left to go off on this useless adventure."

"We will ride these horses to the hills," Nidde said. "If I do not fall off of this yellow one we will be home tomorrow."

# PART III

# The Lands Laid Waste

*Pericles was dead. It was the end of an epoch, of the golden age of Hellas.*

*Pericles was dead and Cleon ruled in Athens. Historians of the time described him as a boisterous demagogue, the most violent man in Athens.*

*A second wave of plague had swept through the city. There were bloodbaths everywhere. The vines were broken at the roots, the wells poisoned, the lands laid waste.*

# Chapter XXVII

In a room near the Acropolis, Cleon was arguing with Hyperbolus about the captured Peloponnesian hoplites. "I don't care what the butt-fucking Spartans want. Of course they want their soldiers back. And I want their soldiers to dredge my harbor. I don't want peace with them, Hyperbolus. I want to conquer them once and for all and rid the Delian League of their influence. I captured the hoplites and I will do with them as I please. Now stop talking to me about them before I start crucifying them to shut you up. I captured them. They are mine."

"What would you trade them for? The envoys said to make an offer. Would it harm you to make an offer?"

"The head of Clarius Arasistratus and the head of Leucippius and throw in that traitor, Elen Alkmeionadae, who married my cousin and cuckolded him and has disgraced my family a thousand ways. I heard she was with Brasidas now. Spying for him. If he wants his hoplites back so badly, tell him to go up to the Parnassus and rout out that boil in my neck, that viper's nest of Alkmeionadae, and then deliver my kinsman's wife, Elen, in one piece and not diseased or pregnant, and I will consider his offer." He drank from his wine, getting really angry now. "I want Alcibiades more than all the rest but this crowd will do for now. I can't touch Alcibiades yet. His friends are too powerful. The Alkmeionadae have harmed Athens more than any plague, but I will be their nemesis. See if I'm not."

“Are you serious about this offer?” Hyperbolus got up from his couch and went to stand by the balustrade, keeping his back to Cleon, trying not to show how excited he was. If he could take Cleon’s hoplites away he would have a chance to end Cleon’s sudden absurd power. “May I tell them that is your offer?”



“Yes. Tell them I want all three, Leucippius, Clarius and Elen. Better dead than alive, except for Elen. I would like her alive if possible. That should be easy if she’s really with them, which I do not doubt. It is like something she would do. No loyalty to anything.” Cleon moved across the room to a table where wine and food were waiting. He was in a good mood, full of himself after a night of pleasure. He was beginning to feel like a leader at last. It had taken awhile after Pericles’ death for him to feel really powerful. The harvest of what he had worked for all his life had overwhelmed him. Now he was beginning to enjoy his power. The more he exercised it, the more it grew. Now, with Hyperbolus groveling before him and the Spartans suing for peace and Brasidas embarrassed over the loss of his troops and messengers running in from all over the Aegean bearing greetings and pledges of support, he was full of himself and ready to begin running the Athenian democracy any way he liked. First, he would rid himself of his enemies. The Alkmeionadae in general, and especially Leucippius and his little band of malcontents, had been an irritation to Cleon for years. The chance to get rid of them and his cousin’s disgraceful ex-wife all at once seemed too good to be true.

“It’s late in the year for a military action in the hills,” Hyperbolus said. “Brasidas should be getting back to the Peloponnese for the winter. It’s almost October and the water becomes rough. No one sails after the end of October. Still, I will take the envoys your offer.”

"He isn't planning on going back. He's at Corinth, isn't he? Planning to attack Piraeus, so I heard. Ironic that his own hoplites will be fortifying the pass against his boats. Where are his headquarters? In the bay of Corinth?"

"He's at some little port a few miles away. The fleet is at Corinth, but he has his headquarters in that old villa of Doriakutus. An old fortified house from the olden days, with a little amphitheatre of its own. Perhaps Elen is acting plays for him while he waits to get his soldiers back." Hyperbolus turned to Cleon, smiling his famous charming smile. Cleon picked up a loaf from the table and broke it and handed half to his visitor. "They are doing a new play tonight at the Dionysius. One that is being gotten ready for the festival. Aeschylus wrote it. That old doomsayer. Still, he does the dialogue right. Will you sit with me?"



"Of course. I will meet you there after dinner." Hyperbolus bowed and left the room. A servant, who had been standing quietly by a table all this time, filled Cleon's cup. It was a clear rose-colored wine that had just come from Mykonos. The servant wiped the edge of the cup and handed it to his master. Then he excused himself and left by a side door and went down a set of stone steps and into the kitchen and found a boy and began to tell him a message, teaching it to him very carefully, word by word, then making him repeat it over and over until the message was perfect.

The boy, who was named Cynthias, took off his stained kitchen garment, drank a glass of water, put on a short wool skirt and left the building by a side door. He ran down a cobbled street until he came to a road leading to the country and began to run along it, taking great, loping strides, saying over and over to himself the message until it became a song. In five hours he had covered twenty miles. He passed an orchard of olive trees where boys were beating olives to the ground with rods. He went another mile and found the house he was seeking, a long white stucco house with a pink roof on the crest of a hill. He ran up the path and was greeted at the door by an elderly man and a young woman. They took him inside and called another man from the back. Then two women appeared. They listened and gave him food and drink. A runner named Merculi appeared and Cynthias told him the message and had him repeat it four times. The second runner left the house and disappeared down the path bound for Leucippius's camp.

"Someone must also take a message to the Lady Elen Alkmeionadae who is in Ianthe on the Bay of Itea with the Spartan forces," Cynthias said. "The message must seem to come from Myron, a sculptor of Aegina. It must be an invitation to bring Brasidas to visit him."

"We have no one who can run but Merculi, who just left for Leucippius. Could you go further today?"

"Perhaps, in a few hours. Could I have a cart to carry me part of the way? I could rest and then begin to run when we reach the paths that go along beside the ocean. Could you send me in a cart?"

"I could take him," a girl named Cleo said. "Nikki and I could carry him to the market at Aphaia and he could run from there."

"Done," the older man said and the young women left to borrow a cart from the olive harvesters. In an hour they were on their way. In two more they had come to the town of Aphaia. They left Cynthias on the outskirts of town. He began to lope along a path running along beside the ocean. He went back into his message song. "You must beware. Cleon has offered to trade the captured Peloponnesian hoplites for members of our friendship. Do not trust any but the ones whose names you know. He is asking Brasidas for the heads of Leucippius and Clarius and for you to be turned over alive. May Athena protect you in this time of danger. From Aetiia, son of Petri, friend of the Alkmeionadae." Cynthias was loping along, practicing a second message, a fake message that would gain him entry to the camp. "Myron of Aegina, greatest sculptor of Greece, and his apprentices and family invite the lady Elen Alkmeionadae and her guests to come and visit his studio and kiln in Galatea, in the hills above Itea. Please be so kind as to give the runner food and drink and return him in good health to me."



The second runner, Merculi, was taking the message to Leucippius by a shortcut which wound its way through old pastures that had not been used since the time of the earliest Hellenes. Nothing was left of their settlements now but stone ruins and packs of wild dogs who fought with the mountain goats and preyed on the wild sheep. Merculi knew it was dangerous to go that way but he was a haughty boy who always did as he pleased. He sprinted happily around the old paths thinking of the good time he had had the last time he was sent to the high camp and how beautiful it had been to swim in the clear blue mountain lake and afterwards to lie on the grass and tell stories of messages he had taken and people he had known all over Attica and the Pindos. There was a girl with funny ears who had been kind to him. He turned a corner thinking of something she had told him. Two large black-and-white dogs came out from behind a rock and began to bare their teeth. He had forgotten to carry a stick. He picked up a rock to throw it. As he did, the largest dog pounced and sank his teeth into Merculi's leg. The muscle tore loose from the bone. Merculi found his knife and killed the dog and picked it up and threw it into the face of the second one. Then he dragged himself into a position behind a rock and ripped off his tunic and tied it around his leg. It was almost a day later when a sheperd found him there and carried him back down the mountain to be cared for. He was delirious by that time, and besides, who could he have trusted with the message? Who could have found the way?



Cynthias delivered his message to Elen and quickly left. Now Elen stood on the balcony overlooking the harbor and wondered how much time she had. No one had come to the villa since Cynthias left, by ship or on foot, so the offer had not reached Brasidas. It might be days before a messenger arrived. On the other hand it might be any moment. She went into her bedroom and opened a chest and took out a short brown chlamys a boy would wear and put it on. She pulled on leggings and short brown leather boots and tied her hair back from her face with a colored scarf. She left the room and went to find Brasidas. He was bathing in the atrium. She knelt beside the pool and kissed his shoulder and whispered something in his ear. He laughed and she picked up a gold chain he had thrown down on the floor beside his robe and put it around her own neck. "I am going riding," she said. "Will you join me?" She tapped one of her boots on the stone floor and pulled her shoulders back. "I will ride slowly so as not to have too long a start."

"Who says I will come to look for you?" He slipped down into the water, admiring the tops of her legs. She was a piece. A woman ten years older than he was, and still taking up his whole brain and making him talk like an Athenian fop, even using the foppish Ionic they used to talk about philosophy and art. Well, she was Alkmeionadae. A woman who was good enough for him, for a change.

"You'll come," she answered. "I'm going to take the brindled mare."

"Don't stay after dark. There are wolves in those woods."

"You won't come then?"

"I might. Go on. I'll come or I won't." She turned on her heels, pretending to pout, then looked back over her shoulder, pretending to flirt. Then she was gone.



She went down to the corral and took the mare and led her out to the path. One of the sentries gave her a leg up and she smiled at him. "Don't tell him which way I headed," she said. "It's a race. Say you didn't notice." Then she was gone, making straight for the road that led across the isthmus and along the Gulf of Corinth in the direction of Delphi and on into the mountains. By the time Brasidas had dressed in his riding leggings and embroidered Persian riding shirt and chosen his headband and tied it just so around his head and made his excuses to his lieutenants and caught his stallion and given in to spending the afternoon engaged in one of her silly Athenian games, she was over the isthmus and into Attic territory. She stopped in Thisbe and traded horses and bought food and made for the hills. Clarius will be there by now, she was thinking. The kindest of men, the one who never wished to harm me. The one who loved me.

The woolen chlamys rubbed against her skin, the hair of the horse's neck chapped her face, the fields led upwards in the darkness. A new moon climbed the sky and Elen forgot her danger and amused herself with the thought of Brasidas's rage when he found she was gone.

She made first for Delphi, where she took shelter with the priests of the shrine.

"Will the Spartans come this way?" the priests asked.

“I think they will come to Itea in boats and march this way to the Parnassus. Is the treasury safe?”

“Pericles moved it to Athens long ago. Haven’t you heard?”

“I have been with the Spartans many months. I thought to learn how to save us but it has done no good. This war is insane. No one knows



what’s going on. The college of ephors sends different orders to Brasidas by every courier. Well, I will go to Leucippius if you will lend me fresh horses.”

“We could hide you here. You could stay with the Pythias. There are three of them now. They live quite well. They don’t stay in the huts now but are housed in the temple of Athena.” The priest laughed. He was an old friend of Elen’s. “Nor do they sleep alone.”

“They must be getting younger. Have you changed the age? I thought they had to be old settled women.”

“The town profits from our visitors. We try to give them their money’s worth. I myself have been interpreter for the sacred ravings in the past year. Would you like me to intercede for you?” Elen closed her eyes and smiled and the priest called for wine. “Old friends are best,” he said, pouring the wine. “To Delphi,” she answered and raised her cup. “To prophecy.”

In the morning she stopped at the sanctuary of the Castaglian Spring where the ancient olive trees grow straight out of the mountain. She drank of the water and touched it to her eyes and stood in the stillness of the mountain asking questions of the empty shrine.

Will my son live? she asked. Will my line survive? A long ray of light fell across the spring and touched her garment. Everything was very still. The only sound was the hum of bees in the distance. We do not know what we are doing from one day to the next, Elen decided. So I will go to Meion and see this girl the fates have woven into the fabric of our lives. Then she bowed her head and left the way that she had come.

# Chapter XXVIII

Auria had begun to go to the pass every afternoon and look down on the plains to see if Meion was returning. She did not really expect to see him. Everything she knew made her believe she would never see him again. Her mother had been taken from her and Philokrates had died and so it would be with Meion. She stood on top of the rocks that guarded the entrance to the path. Standing with her feet planted, she gazed out across the mountains. Many thoughts came to her then—the knowledge of longing, how it stays in the heart. She remembered lines from the poets Philokrates had read to her and they had all said the same thing. Man's sadness was real and all the gaiety and joy we create are only our puny weapons in a battle we can never win.

So be it, she decided, standing above the path with her feet on the boulders. If that is how it is, then I will tell no one who does not already know it and I will stay with children who do not know it yet and I will sing all day and make bread like Keffee. For now I must go back and spend whatever light is left writing. I haven't written in my tablets in many days. He taught me to write so that I might not let his ideas die. She wiped her hands against her sides and started to leave. Then, out of the corner of her eye, she saw two figures on horseback come up over the rise of a hill. They were riding steadily. They were coming towards the path. One of them was a black man. It was Nidde.

She leaped down from one rock to the other, twisting her ankle, and then she was at the entrance and through the guards and running across the field and Meion was riding toward her.

He was home. As soon as they had taken the horses to be cared for and as soon as he had hugged Kleis and met the twins and spoken to Leucippius and Penelaiaa, they went up the mountain to a place above the lake, to a moss-covered bower beside a spring of cold blue water, and there they made love with great fierceness and held onto each other crying and laughing and both talking at once. Later, Meion got out the pouch of gold coins and showed them to her and told her about Olynthia and how Olynthia had taken Nidde into her bed and made him so crazy he had climbed up on a horse and ridden it all the way home as if he had been doing it every day of his life. "And this is the power of the goddess whose eyes are always changing color," he said. "The one whose voice is said to relieve pain. The one who rules the others, even Zeus."



~

Later that night, when Meion and Auria went back to her tent, the twins began to draw near to Meion and to Nidde. At first they would only look at the men from behind the painted chest by the door, then they came within a few feet and stood holding hands and examining them. Then they moved in very close and began to breathe as one. "They always do that until they get used to someone," Auria said. "Once they decide you're safe you can't get rid of them. Ask to see their pigeons, Meion. If they show you their pigeons you know they trust you."

“I have trained hawks to let pigeons fly upon their backs,” Nidde began. “In my country the pigeons are so fat they can no longer fly.”

“I saw a hawk this morning,” Meion added. “Perhaps I will snare it and ask these pigeons if they wish a steed.”

“Vultures also make good steeds for pigeons,” Nidde added. “But they lose all races to hawks and won’t fly in the rain.”



“If I knew where some pigeons were being kept I might go try to catch that hawk,” Meion added. “Remind me in the morning to go look for pigeons.”

“We have them,” the twins spoke as one. They had brought themselves almost into Meion’s lap. “Ours are fat.”

“Fat pigeons!” Meion exclaimed. “Just what I was thinking of.” Then the twins sat down crosslegged upon the floor and began to chatter about pigeons and the river that ran by their home and how they were going back there very soon. A melancholy overcame Nidde at that and he pulled Philippus into his arms while Meion kept Theodorus by his side. “I had thought of moving to another tent,” Meion said. “Because there were no young men in this one to help haul water and tend a pigeon nest. Now I will be content to stay in this one. You must not go back to your village soon as I need you here.”

“It is the same with me,” Nidde added. “I have much work that needs doing for my fine new horse. Every morning it must be brushed and groomed and cared for. The leather of the bridle must be oiled. There must be boys around a tent or I won’t eat there. These two are a good start but we should find a few more boys soon. When it is time to hunt we will want beaters for the ground birds.”

“We’ll help.” Philippus and Theodorus cuddled nearer to the men. “We will do everything. You won’t need more boys.”

"Feed them honey cakes," Meion said. "Fatten them up. These boys are a gift from Apollo. He saw our needs and met them as a god will sometimes do. Praise to Apollo, Nidde. Now we are complete."

"Now we will drink goat milk and honey cakes and sing one song to the gods who treat us so lightly and then we will bank the fires and sleep." This from Auria, who had stood up to survey her little band, feeling fiercely proud and content and wanting Meion to herself again. "It will be a long day tomorrow training hawks to carry pigeons and praying we have been forgotton in the cities on the plains." She went over to the locker where Kefallinia had stored the honey cakes they had made the day before and took out ten of them and distributed them among the people in the tent. Then she went to a water-cooled locker and brought out goat's milk and poured it into stone cups and passed them around.



Little Aeo got out his lyre from behind a stack of rugs and began to play softly on it, looking up into the starlit sky outside the door to the tent.

Paris held in his hand the golden apple
"To the fairest" carved upon it. A fierce wind
Came calling, *discord is the fruit of this.*
Still the young man held the apple. Such power
He dreamed of, holding it. Surely the goddess
Now would love him, surely now a bride was his.

Behind the boy was his father's city, Troy, the golden
Bride of man, behind its gates women were weaving.
In its streets children played. On its benches
Old men were talking, telling of traitorous wars.

The golden sun shone down upon them. Choose, the god
said to Paris. Why do you hesitate?
I see a girl in a white himation,
Sprigs of laurel in her hair
She steps from the palace
And walks down into a field of yellow flowers
In her wake the flowers close
In her wake all things are sleeping.
*Choose,* the god is now insisting
*Choose the goddess who shall rule us.*

By the time the song was over the golden twins were sleeping, Kefallinia nodded with Kleis in her arms and Meion and Auria banked the fires and tucked in their little brood and then went far out into the woods and slept upon the ground until the morning.

# Chapter XXIX

"Brasidas will accept your offer," Hyperbolus said. He was in Cleon's bedchamber, reporting on a meeting of the morning. "He will rout out the mountain camps and bring you Leucippius and Clarius. But Elen Alkmeionadae is not with him. He can't guarantee he can find her. I hear she flew the coop." He waited to see if Cleon was in a mood for joking, then went on. "I guess he did too many boys in his youth to be any good with a woman. Anyway, she's gone and he doesn't know where."

"He'll bring in Leucippius and Clarius and clean out that nest up there?"

"He said he would, in exchange for his little hop-hops."

"That will do then. Tell him the day he delivers Leucippius and Clarius or proof of their deaths he can have his hoplites and put them on boats or walk them home. They are no good at building anyway. They are driving everyone crazy down there and fighting among themselves. We've had to kill a dozen of them as warnings to the others. Well, this should keep Brasidas busy until it's time to sail home. My astronomers say it will be an early winter with hard rains. Yes, this whole undertaking is good, Hyperbolus, I have to give you credit for convincing me to make the offer."

"It won't be that easy. I had in mind that we could put Brasidas in touch with one of the other commanders up there. Those little outposts are not united. My spies tell me they fight among themselves. After Leucippius the most powerful chief is one named Braseus. Shall I try to bribe him? Or mention it to Brasidas and let him try?"

"How much would it cost?"

"Not much. He's a barbarian from Macedonia or Thrace. He would probably turn on Leucippius for twenty horses."



"Then do it yourself. Tell him to cooperate with Brasidas and I will guarantee his payment."

"You are good to work with, Cleon. I think we are going to work well together. There is room in Athens for both of us, don't you agree?"

"So far," Cleon said. "So far it seems to be working out. Send your heralds then. Let's do all we can to help."

A few days after Meion returned, Clarius was at the pass talking to the shepherds about moving the sheep to a winter pasture beyond the lake.

"They must not be taken until the winter solstice," the oldest shepherd was saying. "When the yellow star lines up with the seven children. Not before. If you take them too soon there will not be enough food to last all winter and the ewes will bring forth sickly lambs. Once my father's brother took them too soon. . . ." The old man pulled his beard, remembering that bad decision. A boy took the old man's hand. He was the old man's grandson. "We have to keep everything we value behind the walls," Clarius was saying. "It is unlikely, but soldiers could come here. We have to be prepared for anything that could happen. Like knowing that wolves are there who can take the lambs."

"They never take our lambs," the old man was irritated now. "Our dogs are very fierce. Look, here comes a soldier now." He pointed way off into the distance. A rider was appearing and disappearing through the trees on the hill. "It is as busy as a city around here. This is three riders in two days."

A boy in a brown cloak, Clarius was thinking. No, it is Elen. No one else in the world rides like that. "That is not a soldier," he said to the old man. "That is a woman I have desired for many years to my sadness. A woman I did not wed." The old man shook his head. These people from Athens were very strange. There was no way of comprehending the sadness they caused themselves or their fascination with it. "How is it you did not wed her?" he asked, to be polite. "Was she diseased?"



"No, there was too high a price on her," Clarius answered. He followed her with his eyes until she recognized him. She stopped twenty yards away and dismounted and walked toward him, holding the horse by the reins. She had not changed.

"I have grown old," he said, when she was near enough to hear. "And you have remained the same."

"I am old also," she answered. "And come with bad news. Where is my son?"

"He is here."

"Come along then and I will tell you what I know." She handed the reins to the old man and allowed Clarius to embrace her. "I have missed thee and thy goodness," she said to him in the soft Ionian accent the Athenians used for speaking to children. "Cleon has sent Brasidas to kill us," she added. "He has traded our lives for Brasidas's hoplites. We will not have much time. Take me to see the others now." They left her horse with the shepherds and walked up the hill. Clarius held her hand in his and every step he took seemed to be filled with all the light in the world although she had come to give him the worst news anyone could have brought to him. He held her hand and walked beside her believing he was the most fortunate man in all of Hellas.

That night Auria sat with Meion and his mother and talked long into the night. I could not love her, Auria decided, but neither will I dislike her. I will honor her for bringing my husband into the world. "I will leave the two of you alone," she said, getting up from the circle in which they sat. "I am honored you are here. I have waited and hoped to know you."

"And I you," Elen answered. "She is a strong girl," she said to Meion when Auria was gone. "I could not have imagined her."

"So it has been said of you." Meion laughed. "The gods are busy, even in times of war."

# Chapter XXX

It was several days later. Auria lay on a flat rock above the lake watching the men at work. The rock was warm from the sun. Here and there in the crevices moss grew. It was a moss called *fumaria* that Philokrates had loved to roll between his fingers as he talked. Auria reached out and picked some of it. He is always with me, she reminded herself. As long as I live and as long as Kleis lives. The little girl was playing nearby, in a grove beneath beech trees. Behind her the men were bent over maps. Meion was standing by Leucippius's chair, pointing to the map and talking. Clarius was with them, listening.

It will not be long, Auria thought. It will soon be over and we will know our fates. The gods will favor us or they will destroy us, or there are no gods anyway. I am the only one who does not pray to them. Even Meion calls on them and makes obeisances. Even Leucippius and Penelaiaa observe the holy days. She rolled the moss between her fingers, then raised it to her nose. Its smell was said to drive away melancholy. She closed her eyes. The quick clean smell was like the earth at morning. Auria stretched out and laid her hands flat against the rock to soak up its warmth. She had made love to Meion many times in the night. The closer the Spartans came the more intense everything became. "Auria." Kleis was headed her way dragging a branch behind her. "It won't stay on top."

"Your roof is falling off. Well then, I shall repair it for you. We are

Hellenes and make the world do what we wish it to." Auria got up and took the branch and set it carefully down on top of the disorderly pile of branches and twigs; then she knelt and kissed the little girl. "How big you have grown. How long your legs have become and how fierce your little brow." A ray of sunlight was falling across the child's face and down her shoulder and arm. "You want to go to Meion?"



"No. I'm making my house."

"Then stay. I'll be back in a moment." Auria left the child beneath the trees and walked over to where the men were intent on their plans.

"If they want us badly enough they will rout us out," Clarius was saying.

"They can't take the pass against javelins and archers."

"There are at least a thousand of them. If they are willing to lose men they can do whatever they like."

"How many more days will it take before they arrive?"

"Not more than two, unless it rains. It will slow them down if it rains. They have to ford the river and there are pack animals."

"They could leave the baggage on the other side. If it were me I would leave the baggage there and send raiding parties."

"Then we are doomed." Meion began. He looked up and saw Auria. "Except that I refuse to be doomed in the face of an illiterate horde of Spartans. Where is Nidde, Auria? Have you seen him this afternoon?"

"He said he was going to scout down into the meadows. He took a bow." Now the sun that had blessed Kleis's face was across the face of Meion. His lips seemed to Auria to be the softest thing in the world, a secret she knew like the moss she rolled in her palm. "There is a stew making beside the ovens," she said. "Penelaiaa and Keffee are making a feast. Well, if the Spartans come they will have a gift from me. I know how to make a poison that will make them lose the feeling in their legs if even a small cut is made with an arrow dipped in it. I will go and find the plants today."

"Do it then," Leucippius said. "Do it now."

Auria left Kleis with Leiakes, and went to her house and pulled on her boots and tied a sack around her waist. As she was leaving Meion was coming up the path. "Stop here," he said. "Stay with me while I have my noon meal."



"I am going to the river to search for a plant to make poison. I have seen it there." She lowered her eyes, then raised them again. "I do not like to use the things of the earth for evil uses. Still, they are attacking us. We must defend ourselves."

"What is this poison?"

"It is called *atropa.* When it is distilled it causes men's limbs to fall asleep. I am not certain it will work on arrows but we will try. Will you go with me to gather this nightblooming plant?"

"I have to go back to Leucippius. Come inside for a moment. Come inside with me." Then he led her inside and began to make love to her. In the daylight, with people not a hundred yards away.

"I have to go to the river."

"The river will wait. The river will not go away."

It was an hour later when Meion went back to his work and Auria ran down the old path to the river. She ran along with Metis beside her, thinking that she must take Kleis and the twins to the woods to teach them about plants as Philokrates had taught her. "I leave them with the barren women too much," she told the dog. "I will be a better mother when this battle is over. When we have fought and won. When the world is safe again I will stop spending all my time at the lyceum and talking to Clarius and lying around with Meion like a hetaera. Yes, I will take them the next time I go and teach them where to find mint and roots and fine herbs for cooking." She stopped and watched a row



of migratory cranes stretching their wide wings against the sky. Then, walking more slowly, she began to search for the deadly dark red blossoms of the *atropa.*

Later, with the arrows all around her and *atropa* drying on their tips, she began to think of a story Philokrates had told her about Prometheus, the half-god who had given the gift of fire to man. He had been punished by the gods for doing it.

"But how could fire be bad?" she had asked. "Why would the gods deny fire to man? Why would they want us to be ignorant and cold? How can they be cruel and selfish if they are gods? You make me mad telling me this story."

"They bound him to a rock forever to be torn apart by birds. Think deeply about it, Auria. What could that mean, to be torn apart over and over again?"

"Like not knowing what to do. Wanting two things at once. That's the answer, isn't it? Knowledge brings confusion. You told me that before. Like I want to make you a new cloak but I don't like to weave and besides you're happy with your old cloak and wear it summer and winter. I am bad not to like to weave."

"Everyone doesn't have to weave. Let the weavers weave. It is enough for me if you do your lessons and learn what I teach you. Someone must know the medical arts to tend the people here when I am gone.

What if I died and Keffalinia broke her arm and there was no one who knew the position of the bones to mend it? So, we will get out our bones in the morning and work with them again."

"I hate that old skeleton. It makes me think of people being dead."

"See, you are being torn apart, about the bones. You wish the knowledge of them, but you do not like the things they make you know. We were talking of Prometheus."



"You didn't answer my questions. Why did the gods punish him for giving warmth and fire to men?"

"It is not fire the story is about. Think of it, Auria. What is fire to us? What does fire mean?"

"I already know. You have told me before."

"And what did I tell you?" He stretched his legs out until he felt the warmth on the bottom of his feet.

"You told me fire was power over the earth, over the natural order of the earth. Man comes into the order and is subject to it and then he turns on that order and makes it obey different laws. Turn into fire, he says to wood. Turn into swords, he says to bronze and steel. Turn into cloth, he says to the flax. Turn into houses, he says to wood and stone."

"What else?"

"Turn into soldiers, he says to people. Turn into slaves."

"Yes, that is true also."

"Then what must I do? I do not like to think of terrible things like this Prometheus when it is dark. Then I will dream of him tied to the mountain and try to find ways to get him down."

"He could ask Zeus to forgive him and take fire back from man."

"No, it can not be taken back. Too many people know about it now."

"Come here to me. Come sit by me and warm my old bones and I will tell you about Esappho when she would come to see us on Kos and how she made us all laugh with her impiety and madness. You can dream of her dancing with her maidens instead of gods fighting among themselves in the clouds." Then Auria would go to him and sit in the crook of his arm until it was time to go to bed.



Later that day Auria sought out Clarius and spoke to him about it. "Yes," he said. "I have also pondered this Prometheus question. Aeschylus wrote a play about it. I wish you could have seen it with me. It was very controversial and the audience booed it at first as being too philosophical, with not enough action. There was a great passage in it that I have remembered. Prometheus has saved man by his gift of fire and he is defending that action to the chorus. 'I stopped man from foreseeing doom,' Prometheus said." He quoted further:

*Chorus:* What cure did you provide them with against that sickness?
*Prometheus:* I placed in them blind hopes.
*Chorus:* That was a great gift.

"You are worse then Philokrates," Auria said. "You make the story more hopeless than he did."

"Perhaps our story is hopeless."

"I have made a poison for the arrows. You must get some of it and keep it in a vial. There is enough for many arrows. Be careful not to let anyone drink it or get it into a cut, even an insect bite. It will deaden the skin around any place it enters. Well, I must go and see to the children now."

"Auria."

"Yes."

"Do not let old myths cloud your days. I feel your fate will be a happy one."

"It is happy today. To talk with you is a happy fate, however long it lasts." They embraced and Auria went to see about the children and Clarius went about his work, remembering his own wisdom, which she had the power to call up.

# Chapter XXXI

Brasidas was not coming himself. He had been ordered to bring the fleet back to safer waters before the rains of late October made it impossible. He left the besieging of Leucippius's camp to Ionius, the only one of his generals crazy enough for such an undertaking. He gave him a thousand men and one hundred cavalry and supplies to last for three months and wagons to carry the baggage. Also, he promised him a victory in the streets of Sparta if he succeeded in capturing the exiles. He turned over everything necessary to Ionius, left a small guard on the fortress, and sailed around the Peloponnese to Halieis. Word of all this reached the camp soon after it happened, driving everyone to work even harder on the walls. In the daytime everyone worked from sunup to sundown moving rocks and mixing mortar and building towers or making weapons. At night they gathered around the gallery of Leucippius's house, talking and drinking wine or hot drinks made from boiling the small yellow fruit of the lemon trees and mixing the juice with honey.

"We built a wall around my grandfather's house when I was a boy," Clarius was saying. "I would go every morning and watch it being built. He was a great man, one of the ones who overthrew the Persians at Salamis. He never forgot that and taught me that a man only has to be a hero once in his life, after that he will always know who he is and what he is capable of. The great battles of Marathon and Salamis. I listened to those stories every night of my life. Fifty years ago we won those victories and the great age of Hellas began. Now, we destroy ourselves. Forgetting the Spartans were our allies in our greatest moments. Still, they did not come to our aid at Marathon. They were in a religious festival and believed they could not fight until the next full moon. And yet, they made up for it at Salamis and saved the day. Do you like to hear all this history?"



"Oh, yes," Auria said. A man coughed, a dog barked, a dove called in the meadow. The men and women settled down to listen. Clarius was a great storyteller when he was in the mood.

"How did it begin?" Auria said. "Why did the Spartans attack Attica?"

"Hellas sees the Peloponnesians as liberators. Men look for war, Auria. As soon as there is grain stored for the winter, men will find something to resent. Some days I think we should not have made farms but only roamed as they do in Arcadia, taking what we need from the land and living in half-built shelters. Well, I am no philosopher. I must tell you of a play I saw in Athens last year."

"But who started it? Who attacked what city? Someone must have begun it."

"First there were rumors everywhere and suspicions. Then the Thebans, thinking war was going to start, made a surprise attack on Plataea, an ally of Athens, part of the Delian League. The Plataeans fought back, surrounding them inside the walls with wagons and carts and raining down stones and tiles upon them from the roofs. A heavy rain began to fall, adding to everyone's misery. At last the Plataeans expelled the Thebans but soon the Spartans invaded, laying waste like mad children. Meanwhile, Pericles had called all the Athenians into the city. Everyone was miserable, crowded together inside the walls. Then plague broke out. I saw all I ever wish to see of human misery in those months.

"For three summers now the Spartans have invaded, laying waste the crops. In return Athens has sent ships to invade the Peloponnese. Now Pericles is dead and we do not know what will happen next. Well, enough of that. I will tell you of a play I saw last summer, by Euripides, who is the best of the playwrights, except for Aeschylus."



"I have not seen a play," Auria answered. "Although I have longed to see one. I have seen mimes. Are they like mimes and farces?"

"Plays are about gods and men. How men do certain things and the gods or fate intervene. This play was about a stepmother who falls in love with her stepson. She was in the service of Aphrodite. The young man was pledged to Diana, and was so pure as to be quite prissy and unattractive. The audience was booing him all through the play. His name was Hippolytus. He turns down his stepmother's attentions and she causes his father to murder him."

"How did he kill him?" someone called out. "What means did he use?"

"A great bull came from the sea and drove his chariot off the cliffs. There are many godly jealousies woven into the human stories."

"I like poets better than playwrights," Auria said. "Poets are simpler and tell how they feel and you can understand and remember their poems. Like the great Esappho. Philokrates used to sing me her poems. I know one by heart. Shall I sing it?" Oh, yes, everyone murmured, so Auria sang her favorite Sapphic poem:

Some say infantry
And some say cavalry

But I say, the face of the boy you love
Is the most beautiful sight on the green earth.

"When all this is over I will send for my books and give you the poems of Esappho for a wedding gift," Clarius said. "There are nine books of Esappho's poems all bound together. 'The Wedding Songs,' they are called. I will give them to you. They are on parchment with decorations on the letters at the beginning of each poem. Very Persian. I would like to read them again myself, now that you remind me of them."



"The moon is three quarters full," a woman answered. "My father said he thought the rains would be early this year."

"Pray for us all as we learn to meet our deaths," said a third, and then Penelaiaa called on the musicians to play and the men and women moved out into the clearing and danced until the moon had reached its zenith and begun to swing far to the east in the sky.

In the morning a runner arrived saying the Spartans were camped a day's march away. Then the people stopped work at noon and bathed and washed their hair and put on their finest clothes and gathered beside Auria's lyceum to hear Leucippius and Clarius speak to them about how the defenses would be manned. Men with signal torches were stationed along the route to the river where the Spartans were camped. Every move the Spartans made would be watched and reported.

Leucippius was carried up onto the lyceum stage in his chair. He was wearing a stark white himation fastened at the shoulder with a beautiful brooch in the shape of an eagle. His hair was smooth and combed back from his forehead. He held a spear across his lap. When the people were gathered around him he raised the spear with both hands, then brought it down, then raised it, then brought it down. A stillness fell over the people and he began to speak.



"Count yourselves," Leucippius said, raising his arms again. "Call out your names and the names of your children." The people began to call their names, "Leucas, Daasias, Mnemo, Mnynia, Hippius, Phillia, Donna, Galaxia, Big Leta, Little Leta, Petrui, Eumene, Paesti, Lucus, Cinc, Doxi, Nat, Hanna, Linda, Sirope, Bithia," and on and on until the count was finished. Penelaiaa added her name to the list, then told the number to Leucippius and he nodded his head and began to speak.

"We are two hundred and fifty-three men and women and sixty-five children. We hold a position that is impenetrable. Work on the walls will be completed by sundown tomorrow. Our flocks are above us in a valley no one but the shepherds could find. We have two springs that will give water as long as the world shall last. Even if they should poison our lake we will have water. Even if they destroy the fields and cut us off for a year we will have food. It is October. The rains will come soon and after the rains will come snow. Traveling will not be easy. No reinforcements will come to aid these Spartans. To be on the safe side we will send the children higher in the mountain, to the caves that are sacred to the old shepherds who painted them with bright colors against the elements and wild lions that plagued the first men to live in the highlands. All of these good things, things that bode well for us, I can tell you. All that is left of me is a sword to secure your lives. Clarius, whose mind darts like lightning across the sky, protects and leads you with his sword. Penelaiaa, daughter of Phidias, devises her own plans to keep you safe. The noble Meion is here, who has labored in the mines of Laurium and escaped to live among us. Many more of great strength and courage, many quick-witted, we have among us. On the other hand this invasion is led by a drunkard and pederast, a man who the lady Elen Alkmeionadae says is mocked by his own troops. They put on embroidered shoes and belts and have gawdy skits mocking their own leader. He is the only Spartan stupid enough to lead men up an unknown mountain to wage battle with winter only weeks away. 

"Also, there have been white cranes on the wing, a good omen for me always. My arm is healed and I can shoot a bow as I could when I was a youth. The teacher and physician, Auria of Thisbe, has made us a poison so potent that I killed a bird with an arrow which only grazed its wing. We have sentries and warning fires and, in short, have done all that could be done to protect ourselves.

"Still, some of you may wish to leave. It will not be held against you if you do. If you wish to leave, take whatever you need for your journey, excepting the livestock, and no man will hold it against you. Come forward and say what you believe is best for you. Speak up and tell us how you feel."

There was much rustling about and whispering, and finally a man named Menoeceus, who was a harness maker, came forward and stood before Leucippius's chair and spoke in a low voice. "Some of us will leave then, good friend and good leader. Not because we are cowards, or fear to fight these Spartans, but because this is not our battle. The ones in Athens wish the blood of the Alkmeionadae but I and others are only simple people and have lived many years away from the city. I have a skill that is welcome in any village and six children to protect, so I will take them and any that wish to join me and leave by the back passes. I will leave in the late afternoon of this day, before the Spartans come any closer." He paused. "We would like to take with us part of the goats and sheep, so we do not go away empty-handed after building your wall."

"In good faith," Leucippius said. Then he turned to the crowd. "How many of you will follow Menoeceus?" There was more whispering and stirring and talking among themselves. The voices became louder and families began to argue among themselves. "Stand to the right, all who would stay," Leucippius called out. "And to the left, those who think they must leave. None of this name-calling. We have no time to fight among ourselves. Come, make your decisions and stick by them. The gods are never far away. They are weaving our destinies right now for all we know." Auria turned to Clarius and heaved a sigh at that.

"Why does he bring in superstition at a time like this?" she whispered. "He doesn't believe the fates weave our lives."

"It is no time to talk philosophy." Clarius squeezed her arm and Meion frowned at her.

Penelaiaa walked up on the dais and stood beside her husband. "May I speak?" she said. The crowd hushed its jostling and turned to her to listen. There was hardly a man or woman there who had not come to Penelaiaa a dozen times for advice. "Do not stay here unless you have a true desire to fight with us," she said. "Five passionate men who believe in what they are doing are worth a hundred who are half-hearted for good or ignorant reasons. As for me, I fight for my freedom every day of my life, in one way or the other. I have stood by the pond's edge and watched the newly hatched ducklings pulled down into the water by turtles while a foot away the parents lifted their yellow beaks in helpless appeal to the skies. In seven years the population of ducks on our lake is diminished and the turtles are so numerous they nip at our toes when we swim there. So it is with good and evil. I do not mean that it is evil to leave or wise to stay. Make your decisions now, however, and let us help the ones who would leave be on their way." She stepped down and the decision-making speeded up and in the end all but a hundred men and women decided to leave. They packed up and embraced the ones who were going to remain, and, waving and crying, they began to wind their way out of the camp by the back path. The younger men had gone ahead to get the flocks. Auria and Meion stood on the top of the hill watching them leave.



"How many are left to us?" she asked, when the last man was gone.

"About a hundred, with twenty children." He paused and stood up very straight, looking away, then he continued. "I had not thought so many would leave. Well, I'll spend the afternoon with the builders helping finish that last piece of wall. Then we should go and practice with bows. I haven't used one in so long I may have lost my touch."

"Leucippius says our bows will do no good against their armor, even with poison tips."

"Then we must be even better archers. There are always places an arrow can enter." He turned to her and took her hands. "How strange that we should be always in danger. It seems as though the times you are in my arms are only islands in a great ocean of days in which I must worry that you will die."

"I will go and find the twins and Kleis and tell them what is happening. Think how they must find all this if it bothers you and me."

"They were running around all morning pretending to be at war and beating each other over the head with sticks."

"I will see to them and then join you at the target tree. Perhaps we are born to fight and die. Philokrates said there was a long time before man had fire and homes and could sleep in shelters without fear of enemies. I feel those old times in me when I imagine soldiers coming over our walls. I wish to kill them by the hundreds." She ran her hand down the long muscle of this arm. "Today is all we have," she said. "Any day is no different from another."

"I will see you when the sun is low," he answered.



That night they sacrificed a lamb and cooked a great pot of black bean soup and Kefallinia baked a special bread with spices and honey. At midnight Clarius left with two lieutenants to go to Braseus's camp to see if he would reconsider and come to their aid. "He could come at their flanks from the woods. He could lend us much help with no danger to himself. Anyway, it's worth a try. We have another day. The Spartans won't come until the moon is full. If they wouldn't come to Marathon until the moon was full, surely they won't be any wiser with a madman leading them on a mad mission."

"It is futile to ask Braseus for help," Leucippius said. "But go ahead. There is time."

"Take Metis if you like," Auria said. "In case of wolves. They are hungry this time of year. Take Metis and the yellow hounds he has taken to sleeping with."

"Tomorrow Auria must take Kefallinia and the children to the caves," Leucippius said. "I want them to leave in the morning."

"I will do it gladly," she answered. "I have been thinking of it all day. I will go now and see which women want to go and which will stay to fight."

"Which will you choose?" Clarius asked. He lowered his eyes and would not look at her.

"I will return and stand by Meion in the battle," she added. "If there is a battle I will join in it. I am good with a bow."

"So be it," Clarius said, and took his leave.

Clarius and his companions walked all night, up winding paths where the trees were sparser. The stars were bright above them. Metis and his yellow companions ran ahead, silent and surefooted. They were following a path that had been made by animals a thousand years before. Wild goats and small prehistoric deer had laid the track that led from Leucippius's camp to the barren upper reaches of the mountain. Clarius and his followers walked swiftly along the path. The stars faded and the sun began to light the earth. At the turning where the path led down to Braseus's pastures, Clarius left the others and went to scout ahead. He walked quickly down the path, thinking of pleas he would make to Braseus. He is trying to ape Leucippius, Clarius told himself. He has this camp up here and he is modeling it on Leucippius's and is wearing his cape fastened at the shoulder in the manner of Leucippius and even had a pin made in the shape of an eagle, like the one Leucippius wears. Yes, that is the answer. I must find a way to make him think that helping us makes him Leucippius's equal.



Clarius came to a place where the path crossed a mountain stream, a waterfall with a narrow wooden bridge across it. A bridge just wide enough for a horse and a man. Below the bridge was a meadow, and there, in a corral, were twenty or thirty of the fat golden horses the Spartans breed from Thessalian stock. Hundreds of them had been driven across the plain near Plataea during the first summer of the war. And here was Braseus with a pasture full of golden Thessalian horses.

He has betrayed us, Clarius thought. He turned and hurried back up the path and across the bridge. When he was on the far side he took his sword and hacked at the supports of the bridge until the main ones were sawed almost in two. Below the bridge was the waterfall and a steep drop of almost a hundred feet. It might be a child, Clarius said to himself when he was done. It could be an old shepherd or a child. He shook his head and gathered his robe around his waist and went back to his companions.

While Clarius was still gone, scouts arrived saying the Spartans had set up a camp and seemed in no hurry to march.

"Let the rains come," Penelaiaa said. "Bring the great storms of the month when leaves turn the color of blood, let the month of gold save us now."

"Why would they set up a permanent camp?" Leucippius wondered. "They can't stay in these mountains this time of year. When it snows we can come at them from ambush like the barbarians wage war."

"That Ionius is a madman, as I have told you," Elen said. "All the Spartans are mad. They appear rational because they hold to the same old ways year after year, but that is their greatest madness. They will do the same thing even when it is wrong. It is their habit to set up a permanent camp before they attack and they will do it even if it goes against good sense and they see the rains are coming. Brasidas is more civilized than the rest and brags on his Athenian grandmother. He says she was of royal Athenian blood, as if we were Egyptians. He has books and art and can read and speak Aeolic. This Ionius, however, is the worst of them. He paces around all day and can not be still. If his father were not an ephor he would not be a general. We are his big chance. If he can bring us in he can have his victory and justify his life. No doubt he is slobbering in his sleep at the thought of it. If we are lucky that will cause him to make mistakes." She looked at Auria, who was following every word she said. "I am talking nonsense, Auria. Pay no attention to my ramblings. It is because I fear for all of us."

"Go on," Leucippius said. "Keep talking. All Greeks love to talk. There is nothing to be ashamed of in talking." 

"There is nothing more. Only that ambition will cause him to make mistakes. If good can come from evil, which they say it sometimes does."

"It is time for me to take the children," Auria said. "I don't like those caves. They are too exposed, but they will have to do for now as they are all we have."

"They were not sent for children," Elen said, to console her. "Spartans do as they are told. They are punished for doing things they think up for themselves. They will not pursue our children."

"So I pray," Auria answered, and took her leave.

At the bakery Kefallinia had the women who were in charge of the children lined up with their packs. Auria spoke to them and they struck off up the path, the big children guiding the little ones by the hand, the women scattered among them. It was not going to be a fast climb and the caves were two hours away for a swift walker. "We will go slow for awhile, then fast, then slow again," Auria said. "And we will sing all the way. Come on, Keffee, there are no men here. Let's sing the kitchen songs. 'Oh, a woman can not spread her legs as if she were a pan of dough. A woman must have leavening before she puffs up and lets go.' " Kefallinia was embarrassed and the little children were hysterical with giggles. So Auria marched in front of the little procession, singing the bawdiest songs she knew and making up lyrics to make them even bawdier. "What's this old thing you bring to me? This won't do to stir the dough. You've pickled all its juice with wine. Take it away. No, no, no. No, no, no. Take it away. No, no, no."



So the little column proceeded up between the plane trees and the evergreens, picking its way around rocks, following a washed-out canyon that was a river in spring. Several times Auria stopped after the children had gone by and started avalanches, practicing to see if it could be done. There were sixteen children now and twelve women and Kefallinia and Little Aeo, who was carrying Kleis and herding the twins in front of him.

Anytime she looked up Auria could see Kleis's yellow curls bobbing along over the shoulder of Little Aeo's weskit. The caves are not high enough, she thought. They are not high enough and they are not hidden. Even with fires at the entrance they wouldn't stop anyone, a man or a wildcat or a vulture coming to steal a child. She reached out her hand and there was Metis beside her. "Who told you to come on this march?" she said. "Old wolf killer. Old snake destroyer. Well, I'm glad of it. I am glad you found me." Metis was still as strong as a lion. He was the strongest dog in the camp and could hold any three of the others at bay. One moment he would be lying under a tree looking like an old toothless man and dribbling all over his chin and the next he would have three sheep dogs whimpering behind a building for trying to take his food. He kept ahead now and Auria was cheered up by his presence and began to sing again, regaling the little pack with her teaching songs. "Alpha is the first of letters, beta is the second one. When you gather twenty letters you can lie as well as statesmen, you can lie as well as poets, you can lie like playwrights do, you can lie like priests and prophets, you can lie like kings and sophists. . . ."

# Chapter XXXII

When Clarius returned he took Leucippius aside and told him what he had found. "Don't tell the others yet," he counseled. "It will only frighten them and make them weak. We must make a plan."

"What part do you think Braseus will play? Would he attack us from the rear?"

"I do not know. Ask Meion. He's Meion's friend." They called Meion and the three men discussed it.

"He would never attack us," Meion said. "For any price or any number of horses. He is a decent man from a race of decent men. I could go to him. Tell me again what you did to the bridge."

"I weakened it so the first man over it will fall to his death. Also, so they can not pursue us."

"What if he did not mean to betray us?"

"If he took the horses he has betrayed us. They are golden Thessalian horses. No one breeds them but the Spartans and the Thebans. He has already betrayed us, Meion."

"Then I will go and talk to him. There are only fifty of us now, Clarius. More left this morning, without telling anyone goodbye, sneaked off in the dawn. There are not enough left to withstand a seige, much less take the chance of Braseus's cutting off the rear. Let me go to him."

"Go then," Clarius said. He walked over to the side of the room and looked out upon the dark foreboding of the cloudy skies. "We meant to be men with new ideas, Leucippius and I. We meant to seek out and find the good for man. To live our lives in the pursuit of goodness. I regret that I weakened that bridge. I am gone back to barbarism. I thought I saw a child fall to its death because of my fear. When we were young we knew there would have to be new forms of courage, new ideals, as Socrates calls them, new ideas brought to life by men with the courage to live and die for them. Go on then, Meion. Run swiftly and save a man or child from my vengeance, which is the Hades of the mind." He turned, but Meion was already gone.

It took almost four hours for Auria and her charges to make the two-hour climb to the caves. The last half hour the children were whining and stopping every ten feet. Whatever fear the grown women were feeling had translated itself into bad behavior among the children. They were pushing each other and holding back.

"Is this any way for the brave warriors of my gymnasium to behave?" Auria had stopped on the path and was talking to them. "Is this what all our practice was for? For you to turn into a lot of frightened hares at the first march we go on?"

"My foot hurts," Theodoris said. "I don't want to go up here. I want to go back home."

"There's a spring right around that boulder," Auria said. "If you will walk that much further without a single cry or whine, then we will stop and bathe our feet. Now come along. Who will walk that far without complaining or having to be carried?"

The children called out a halfhearted agreement and Auria marched off in front of them, singing one last song she had invented:

Men and women, women and men,
We who walk upon the earth
We who conquer everything
Build and conquer
Build and name

They turned a corner of the path and there was the spring, with a small statue of Artemis and a bowl for offerings. The older women removed their shoes and put their feet into the water. The children waded in and held onto the women's knees. Auria took off her sandals and added her feet to the others. She was beside Keffee, who was holding Kleis, and she reached out and put her hands on the woman and then the child. "The mountain has given us this spring and it will give us sanctuary," she said. "You can trust the earth when all else fails, Keffee. He always told me that." One of the twins came up behind her and snuggled down into her side. She turned his face up and saw the errant freckle and knew it was Philippus. Then Theodorus got up from a rock and walked across the pond and joined them. "The sun is not going to last forever today," Auria said. "So we must get on. It's not far now. We could carry any of them that can't walk."

"You'll have to carry me if I step on another stone," Keffee said. "Damn the rocks of this hospitable mountain. How could anyone live forever in such high country? You can kill me if I never see the oceans or the plain again."

"Don't talk like that." Auria leaned back and began to pick the leaves from a plant. "It's lionsroot," she said excitedly. "Keffe, it's lionsroot, wild ginseng. It's all over the place. Help me pick it. You can brew it for the children. It will make them a tea that will give them courage.

The gods are good and I forgive Hera all her injustices for this gift." She turned to the other women, who were sitting in a ring behind Kefallinia. "Look, here is a good omen and a gift from the mountain. This is worth its weight in gold." They had gotten up and were watching her pick it. "It's all over the place. Pull the plants up for the root.



But be gentle. Only take every third plant. Oh, this is the rarest of all the plants I know. To think this has been an hour's walk from me and I never knew it." Then Auria showed them how to chew small pieces of the root and they chewed it and drank water from the spring, and a strange mood settled over everyone, very clear and lighthearted, and they picked up their bundles and walked the rest of the way, thinking they had been blessed. "It makes your head feel wise," Keffee said. "No wonder that old magician always had a cud of it in his mouth."

Auria took Kleis from Little Aeo and carried her the rest of the way herself, telling her how she must be the one in the cave to keep the other children happy and not let them cry or be afraid. "You will only be here until I can send the Spartans crying and bleeding back to their ships," she said. "Meion and Nidde and Penelaiaa and Clarius and all the brave men of our village will send them away. The Spartans will be waving their hands in the air and saying they will never come near our people again because we are so brave." Auria hugged the child in her arms, moving up the last few yards to the cave. "It was in a cave like this that I found you and in two days' time, maybe only one day's time, maybe three days' time, I will find you again. Three times the sun will rise and set and I will be here to find you again. If you become frightened sing my songs and chew the root in your pocket."

"I don't want you to go away."

“I know, my precious baby girl. Golden flower. Kleis of my heart. Well, enough of that. We are warriors now. Today we are warriors.”

“I don’t want to go into a cave.”

“All right,” Auria said. “Then it’s not a cave, after all. It’s a fair at Tanagra and they are giving honey cakes away. The honey cakes are made of the sweetest flour in all of Attica and anyone who eats one will  grow wings and fly anywhere they want to fly. Will you eat these cakes at the fair?”

“Oh, Auria,” Kleis said. “You’re telling me stories again.” She rubbed her little curly head into Auria’s neck and was a dead weight all the rest of the way to the top and Auria carried her like that, pretending there really was a fair at Tanagra and that she was eating the cakes herself until she felt the wings pull out from her shoulder blades and begin to carry her out over the islands of Greece and away to the lands where Philokrates said houses were built on stilts and winter never comes.

The place she was taking them to was well-known in the neighborhood, a series of three caves, where men had lived once during some old time and had painted beautiful paintings on the walls and chiseled out sculptures and seats and benches in the main openings. Auria and Meion had gone there once with directions from Penelaiaa and even spent the night in the largest one. *Always the highest places are the asylums of freedom,* she thought now. So has it always been and now they will protect these that I love. So I hope and pray.

Most of the women had never visited the caves and Auria took time to lead them back to rooms where the walls were painted with scenes of men killing mountain lions. In the light of the dried torches the vivid colors of the paintings came out again and the women marveled at them. "How brave these ancestors were," they said. "How strong they must have been to face such adversaries." There was a scene of men sitting around a fire having a meal. They had plates made of dried mud and a deep stone bowl was before them filled with flowers and nuts and fruits. "They had much civilization," Little Aeo said. "They were



not barbarians. Perhaps they were Hellenes who stopped to live here after they were banished from a city. Perhaps they were on a journey to test themselves and came here to live and look down on the world. It is very high, this promontory."

"Here is a hand," Philippus said, and called his brother. "Look, they left their hands." He fit his small hand into the handprint some painter had fixed to the wall. "Look, he was not larger than me."

"I must go back now," Auria said. "But while you wait you can add your paintings to theirs. Take the black sticks from the fire and paint with them or mix the charcoal with water or the juice of berries. When I return I will see what you have made." She kissed the children and embraced Keffee and Little Aeo and took courteous leave of the others, for Philokrates had taught her that courtesy bred all things, even courage, in the giver and the receiver.

"I'll be back in three days," Auria said. "Get all the firewood you can gather. Get to work on it right now." Then she turned and ran down the path. Don't look back, she told herself. Don't set them an example of that. Go down and finish it. Send the Spartan platoon crying to its mothers or whatever sort of dung I was filling her ears with. Good for her for not believing it. I'm glad she wouldn't believe it. I must find my way back to camp before it's dark. I can't stop for anything now or I'll be lost out here. Thanks to Athena, Metis is with me. She called out to him. He was twenty feet ahead of her. "Come back beside me," she called. “I don’t want you way up there.” Magic dog, she thought. Soon all the magic Philokrates left me will be gone. Metis will die and Phoebe will be gone and there will be nothing left of him but me. Kleis is not him, although when I was young I dreamed his spirit had inhabited her. He is nowhere on the earth but in my head and in the memories of one goat and one dog. When a man dies nothing is left of him but an idea in our minds. Oh, father, be with me now. Guide me down to my home and give me the strength of a thousand men. 

She came to the spring where the lionsroot grew and drank the water and pulled up several roots and tied them into her tunic and took four deep breaths, one for every corner of the earth, north, east, south and west, and then she began to run. With Metis following she ran through the quickening night. There were lights below where the camp lay and fires burning and the sound of metal clashing against metal as men sharpened their swords and practiced with their spears.

## Chapter XXXIII

Braseus had been in a strange mood all day. He had been in a strange mood ever since he had gone down to the plain to collect his golden horses. "Why have they sent us these horses?" the men kept asking him, especially the ones who were related to members of Leucippius's band. "What are these golden horses for? Why do the Athenians suddenly give horses away?"

"They are not from the Athenians. They are a gift from Thebes. To ally us to them." The men were not satisfied with this answer but they liked the horses and Braseus was letting anyone who liked try to break or harness one. These horses are a thorn in my leg, Braseus decided. These horses are of no use to me. I would kill them if they were good to eat. He stretched and pulled his arm out from under a blonde girl who was curled up by his side. He was in a bed of rugs and animal skins, on the floor of his tent, recovering from a party of the night before. "It will storm today," the girl said. "I have been hearing it in the distance."

"What a night. This life is killing me. Move over, let me up. I have to take a piss and then I must go see about those god-cursed golden horses. They are eating everything in sight. The sheep will die because of those horses and when the snow comes the horses will die also and call the wolves to us."

"They are beautiful to watch."

"They are indeed. Now, let me up. I must go and see to this problem I have made for myself." He disentangled himself and stood up. Wineskins were scattered everywhere. He picked up a half-filled one and drank from it. Carrying it in his hand he walked to the entrance of the tent. It was noon. He had wasted another day. What a way to be a leader of men. He drank from the wineskin again, this time more deeply, letting the warm red wine run down his throat until he felt his good nature returning. What legirons these Spartans are, he was thinking. With their buttfucking hoplites and their sour beds. Thinking they can bribe Braseus, son of Agenor, with a handful of useless half-broken horses. I should run these horses off a cliff. Or go to Leucippius and warn him. That's it. I will go this afternoon. He drank again, the idea pleasing him more and more. He finished off the wineskin and threw it on the ground. He had spent five days going for the useless horses and five days bringing them back and now they were eating all the grass in the pasture and no one could think of anything to do with them. Most of them were too wild to be ridden. He walked down to where they were and stood inspecting them. Then he got a rope from a guard and walked out into the meadow and slipped it over the neck of the gentlest one, a three-year-old mare with big soft eyes. She was the only horse anyone had been able to ride. "I'll take this little piece for a ride," he told the guards. "Maybe I'll ride down to Leucippius's camp and offer him some horses."



"Take someone with you," a man said. "Don't go off alone."

"I'll take this head full of poison wine. That will be company enough for me." He laughed and pulled himself up onto the horse's back. He turned the horse in the direction of the path leading to the waterfall. I'll offer our assistance after all, he was thinking. Yes, I have been too independent lately. It is not good to live without allies. There is no one to have meetings with and no swaps to be made of armour or machines of war. Leucippius was a hero in all of Attica once. It is right that he should be allied with me and me with him. I will take him news of these Spartans and their perfidy and offer my help. Braseus rode up the  rocky path toward the waterfall and dismounted and began to lead the horse across the bridge. It sank as he reached the middle. It was so sudden, so amazing. The whole structure gave way and began to slide. So sudden, so amazing. He was swept down into the canyon and left on the rocks below. The horse struggled across to the far bank and threw herself up onto the land and went running blindly down between the trees.

It was dark when Auria arrived back at the camp. The men and women who were left had moved nearer to Leucippius's dwelling. They went from one fire to another, restless, murmuring to each other, sharpening spears, fitting new strings into their bows, trying on pieces of armor. The news from the couriers was not good. There were a thousand Spartans. They had boats and scaling ladders.

"We are surrounded," the men said to one another. "There is nothing to do but fight."

"We could surrender," others answered.

"It may rain," the hopeful added. "A great rain may come and gain us time." They watched the skies. Clouds were gathering.

At midnight the rain began. Everyone was very excited, running around seeking shelter. It might be a real storm, might rain for days, might save them by making the way impassable across the fields.

"Where is Meion?" Auria asked. "What is taking him so long?"

• • •

Meion arrived at the bridge an hour after Braseus fell. He stood a long time looking down over the edge, trying to decide what to do. Finally, he pulled his cloak around his shoulders and very carefully made his way up and around the waterfall by a series of steps cut into the mountain. It was a long climb. He came down finally on the other side and walked into the camp and asked for Braseus. "He has gone to see Leucippius," someone said. "It is funny you did not meet him on the way."



"I have come to ask for help," Meion said. "We are in great danger. The Spartans have sent a whole platoon to invade us. If there are any here who love the mountains and your friends among us, I beg of you to come to our assistance. At least, do nothing to harm us or block our way if we must flee in this direction."

"You have seen the horses," a man said. He was embarrassed.

"Horses are nothing. I know you would not betray us for horses. I know the men of this camp."

"We will come if we can," a second man said. "I will spread the word. When do you think they will attack?"

"Tomorrow night. When the moon is full by their calendar. This rain that is coming might delay them, if it lasts. If it does not they will attack as soon as the meadows are dry enough to stand wagons."

"Some of us will come to aid you," the first man said. "The sons of my brother are in your camp. For his sake I will come. There will be others. Braseus does not rule us. We are free men when we wish to be."

"We will be waiting," Meion said. He clasped the men's arms, then took his leave. When he was half an hour's walk away he heard a loud cry go up in the camp and knew it meant they had discovered the body of their leader. He made a prayer to Athena and walked faster. The storm was coming closer and he wanted to be in the shelter of the trees when it struck.

Auria wandered around from fire to fire until the rain began. Then she went to her empty dwelling and curled up in the bed alone. She was

thinking of the children. I must save them, she told herself. By any means. They must not die and they must not be enslaved. How will I do that, all alone? Where is Meion? Why doesn't he return? How will I face soldiers if they attack us? How will my arrows pierce armor, and if they come over the walls and kill me, who will go to Kleis? She pulled a rug over her legs and curled up into a ball and tried to remember everything Philokrates had taught her of courage. I will set my mind to what I must do, she decided. I will make myself into a wave of the sea, into a beam of light, nothing will keep me from what I must do. If we fail here I will find them and take them to a place of safety. There will be a way. Always a path has opened before. Some god or goddess guides my steps. Or the earth itself. Perhaps it is the earth itself that guides my way. Gaia, knowing everything that moves upon her skin. She ran her hands down the sides of her body. I am too thin. I must eat a great deal tomorrow. I can carry food inside myself like the great beasts of the desert he told me of. Then, however many days it is, I will survive and go to them. Where is Meion? Why did he leave at such a time? I must get up and eat so I can enlarge my body while I sleep.

She got out of the bed and padded across the damp floor to a locker. It was still raining outside, a hard straight rain, a downpour. Let it fill the river and make it hard to cross, she thought. Let it soak their armor and make their spirits damp. Send rain, Poseidon. Hear me, I have called on you at last. She reached the locker where they kept bread and broke off a piece and began to stuff it into her mouth, eating as fast as she could, thinking of Phoebe, how she would find a nice mess of something she liked to eat, honeysuckle or wild wheat or barley, and begin to eat very quickly and methodically, chewing steadily until her little belly was filled up like a pod. So Auria stuffed bread into her mouth, thinking of the intelligence of goats. Meion came in as she had finished the last mouthful and was chewing it. "I am trying to eat for the battle," she said, brushing crumbs off her chlamys. "Where have you been?"



"Braseus is dead," he answered. "Fallen to his death. But it does no good to speak of that. We are in much trouble now, Auria. I am greatly worried about our position here. Still, some of them may come to aid us. They said they would come when the rain stops."

"Take off your wet things and lie down on the bed. It will do no good to suffer tonight. The children are in the high caves. I have not stopped thinking of their faces, which shine at me like beacons. No one will harm them. There may be a thousand Spartans in the fields below but they will never touch Kleis or Philippus or Theodorus or any that I love and have taken to care for. Whatever must be done we will do. Take off your wet things and eat all that you can. We must have food inside of us."

"If the rains continue we will have a respite."

"Here, eat this." She handed him a flat loaf of bread and he broke it in two and sat down on the bed and tried to eat it. He thought she did not understand the danger they were in. "Come and lie down with me," he said. "Let me hold you in my arms while the rain speaks its language. On my way home, I was on a path where the trees are thick overhead, it was very loud and wild and there were great peals of thunder and lightning flashing and I could hear the small animals settling down into their nests all around me. There was not a sound but I could hear them. This is how you make me feel. If I am with you I think of the world as beautiful and useful, full of creatures who live as they should and full of goodness although we know this is not true. Come to me." He laid the bread aside and she curled down into his arms. "Do not think of anything now," he said. "Let us have these hours. Be quiet with me while it rains."



"Tell me a story so I will not see the children and fear for them."

"Once when Nidde and I were gone to search for my mother, we came to the house of the lady of Sounion, who was our benefactor and lent us horses. In the night I dreamed there was a waterfall high in the mountains and you were there and I had to hold you to keep you from being washed away. Today, I have seen the place I dreamed of, with the bridge torn away and the death of Braseus caused by an act of Clarius that will bring retribution to us all, I fear, and all I could think of as I looked down upon his body was joy, that it was not you and my dream had been confused."

"Clarius did what he thought was wise."

"Perhaps it was wise. No one will come that way now without a lot of trouble. The old way around the water takes many hours. That is why I am so late in getting back." She cuddled further down into his arms. "Do not talk more," she said. "I am full of bread, and besides, your stories are not helping. Now I must go tumbling all night over waterfalls to add to my trouble."

"It will go well with the rain."

# Chapter XXXIV

The rain stopped in the night. By dawn the skies were clear. Then morning came and passed with everyone busy at different tasks. Cauldrons of water were set to boiling above the pass. Piles of stones to rain down upon attackers were set in pyramids along the way. Prayers were said. The smoke from oblations was everywhere. So the day passed and the sun traveled across the sky and it was the afternoon of the night of the full moon. The scouts had reported that the Spartans were preparing to move. They had cut down trees and built scaling ladders and flat barges in sections that could be lashed together to cross the lake.

"They will not wait until dawn," Leucippius said. "If they were my troops I would march at midnight and come straight on. They think we are trapped. They think Braseus has cut off our rear and betrayed us."

"Whatever is the most old-fashioned thing, they will do that," Elen Alkmeionadae said. "The more they desire some end the more conservative they grow. They waste more time than old women going over their plans and details. Of course, this Ionius is their madman. Only the gods know what he is thinking."

Auria stepped forward. "Behind the caves is a dry ravine. It becomes a river when it rains but is dry the next day. If we fail to hold off these Spartans and you reach the children before I do, take them that way. It runs into the Phiddii stream that goes all the way to Clarius's sanctuary.

You can not always see the Phiddii but you can hear it and follow it that way. If you will take them there I will join you from wherever I am."

"They have scaling ladders and rafts," Clarius stepped forward now. "They have a thousand men. You must offer them Leucippius and me and get it over with." He looked around. They were seated in a circle, Leucippius, Penelaiaa, Auria, Meion, Elen, and four other leaders of the camp. "No. Hear me out. We must be reasonable. They do not know Elen Alkmeionadae is here, so she could escape with the rest. No, listen to me. We can fight a few days or however long we last or we can give up now. There is no way we can hold this many off. Let us give them what they came for."

"I would welcome a chance to see Athens again," Leucippius added. "There is no guarantee Cleon would kill us. He might wish to ask our advice about how to rule that mob he has taken on. He is a shopkeeper's son. He wears a crown, but what good does it do him if the ones he vanquished can not see him wear it? He used to be quite fond of me. He might wish to keep me for a lapdog. Besides, I have heard the inside of the Parthenon is finished now, painted with outrageous scenes of gods with huge noses and feet. I would like to see the city again before I die. This country life has paled on me."

"They can have me also," Elen stepped forward. She looked very beautiful, with her gold hair plaited down her back in a braid, dressed in a simple brown garment with a rope belt. She went to her son and embraced him. "Any mother would die to save her son. This is no sacrifice. Besides, I agree with Leucippius. They would never kill us. Alcibiades is on his way home with Zenophon and the fleet. They won great victories in the Peloponnese and he will be greeted as a hero. Cleon would not dare kill us with him there."

"There will be no turning over of hostages," Meion said. He held her away. "How could you ask such a thing of me? To bury my honor with your body. Or of Penelaiaa, who has stood by Leucippius all the years of his exile. Who began this talk? The talk of barbarians. Shame on the words from your lips." He handed his mother to Clarius and went to stand by Auria. "We will live as Hellenes while we live. Tell us how we will be placed, Leucippius. Let us go about the business of the day."



"He is right," Auria added. "We aren't going to trade anyone for anything. Stop talking about it. You make us weak to speak of such things. Tell me what time of night or day they will come so I can plan how to put my arrows and, if they take the camp, go for the children. There is nothing else to speak of now."

"I believe they will come in the first hours before dawn," Leucippius said. "They love the moon and will march in its light. Elen, fix mead and wine for us. We will gird for our battle since this is how it will be."

Meion returned to his mother. "I love thee," he said. "I have lived to keep your honor and the honor you taught me." Then he went back to Auria and put his arm on her shoulder. "Come to the pass with me," he said. "We will kill Spartans together." Auria picked up the quiver of arrows. She slung it over her back and kissed Leucippius and Clarius and then turned and went to Elen and embraced her also. She turned again without looking back and took Meion's hand and went to her post.

The sun was almost down the sky.

Below them, in a tent made of the hides of forty deer, the Spartan general Ionius pushed the quivering boy out of the bed and patted him on the leg. "There, now you will be full of me as you fight. Get up now and get my things. I wish to dress." The boy uncurled himself and walked naked across the room to the chest holding Ionius's things. In a corner of his mind he saw the tablets stamped with the head of an owl that his mother had given him in case he should need them and  tried to remember something else, a hand on his face as he was leaving, so long ago. What had that been, that soft hand on his face? He tied his chlamys around his hips, pretending not to notice the blood and semen that ran down his legs. He walked over and opened the tent flap. The moon, which was rising in the west, shone in upon him. I will kill him this time, the boy thought. This is the last time he breathes his nasty breath into my ear. "You promised me a new pair of sandals for the battle," he said out loud. He was mixing wine and water. "Ionius. This wine is no good. Let me get some from Helicon's tent."

"You had new sandals only a month ago. Well, tomorrow when this is over, we will ask the sandler to make you another pair. You are an expensive little piece, Kalithea, and given to tears, but I like you anyway. Run get the wine then. I must dress and get started. I will make my reputation on this little outing. Yes, you have improved my mood and can have new sandals if that's what you want." Kalithea left the tent and found his pack and took out the tablets and tied them into a fold of his tunic and went off to get the wine. "It will not work quickly," his mother had said. "But it will deaden the pain. Think of me at that moment, if it comes to that."

Kalithea returned with the wine and Ionius drank it. Then Ionius went out into the cleared space between the tents and told his lieutenants to gather five hundred men and have them wait for orders. He went back into his tent and drank more wine and ate some bread and cheese and walked out into the moonlight and began to give the men their instructions.

"There is nothing up there but runaway slaves led by a cripple. I do not want to take more than two days to kill them all. Do not take prisoners among the footsoldiers. I want the leaders alive, but not at any cost. Dead will do, as I am tired of this mission. So, who is ready for a harvest of criminals beneath the autumn moon? We will trade these bodies for our comrades who are even now being starved and beaten in the prisons of the Ionian sophists. Who will deliver these Athenian dregs to their cousins for the men of the Peloponnese?"



The men rattled their swords in a halfhearted attempt at enthusiasm and Ionius ordered a triple ration of mead for anyone who was going with him.

"When do we march?" a boy called out.

"As the moon passes its zenith. Two hundred will go over the wall, a hundred will take the boats, and a hundred will take the pass. Secure your helmets with both straps. And keep your heads down. They must shoot from above in those rocks so don't give them a target." Mead was passed in pottery cups and the spirits of the men improved. A second wave of soldiers slept by the fires, dreaming that the morning would find them nothing to do.

It was a cool night for October. A breeze that had traveled all the way from Africa blew across the mountains of the Pindos. Small creatures snuggled down in their nests. The deep roots of the plane trees waited for rain. The planets held their courses, their marvelous elliptical designs. In one design the earth would soon pass between the sun and the moon, casting the shadow of our heroes and their beautiful swirling globe across its dusty wastes. In exactly three hours, as men would later measure time, the shadow of the earth would obliterate the moon. There were men in China and in Egypt who knew this was about to happen. There was a man on Kos, who had known Philokrates, who was waiting for it at that very moment, sitting in a courtyard not a hundred miles from where Auria counted the moments of the strange, cold night and gathered her forces to do battle for her life. The night of the full moon of October the seventeenth, four hundred and twenty-nine years before the birth of Christ, was here.



This is how Leucippius had arranged his troops for the battle. There were left to him now thirty-seven men and sixteen women, including Penelaiaa, Elen, Auria and a wild Katanian woman named Rhea who was a genius with a bow and had given Auria lessons in how to think into the heart of a target and how to turn on your heels after each shot so that the retaliatory arrow would miss its mark.

Leucippius stationed seventeen men at the pass with Auria, Meion, and Nidde. The rest were spread out along the walls and the towers. The walls and towers had been constructed with the expectation that two hundred men would man them. Now there were twenty, with Leucippius and a guard behind them in a break of rocks that commanded the center of the fortified ground. At the last minute a dozen of Braseus's men showed up in full leather armor and took up positions along the wall. They were kinsmen of men who had elected to stay with Leucippius. So the camp made ready for the assault.

"This is madness," Clarius said. "We must give them Leucippius and me and save the rest. The women must leave now and go to the children in the caves. We will not last an hour. They have scaling ladders and rafts and a full platoon of foot soldiers. This is madness to stay here."

"It might rain again," Penelaiaa said.

"You talk like a child. Take the other women and leave now."

"I will not run until we see what happens. If we must run there will be time for it later."



"I will offer myself to Ionius," Elen said.

"No," Penelaiaa was shaking her head from side to side. "I have heard all of this I wish to hear. Honor is still left to us. Do not speak of this again. Either fight with us or leave but there will be no hostages handed over. It might rain. The sky is strange tonight. Or they might turn and run at the first volley of arrows. Our best archers are at the pass. The poison Auria made is very effective. It may frighten them and take the spirit out of them. Anything can happen. It would not be the first time a handful held off a horde."

"Let us take our positions then," Clarius said. "Look at the moon, how marvelous it is tonight. No wonder they honor it." They looked up. It was very bright, a circle of liquid silver. A breeze was blowing. The fragrance of fall leaves was everywhere. "All men die," he added. "We will not be the first." He turned to Elen. "Is this the happy old age you promised me? Is this my hearth and my reward?"

She moved to him and touched his arm. "I always keep my promises," she answered. "It is all as I said it would be. A fire and plenty of excitement and friends around us. Where has Meion gone?"

"To the pass. Nothing will harm him, Elen. He cares too much for life to be a fool." He took her arm and they walked over to the wall and took their places with the others. There was a stone bowl of wine on a trapeza and cups. They dipped their cups into the wine and drank.

Already in the distance they could hear the cheering and the swords of the enemy. Above them the moon was almost to its zenith, arching upwards in its journey to the east.



Across the camp Auria took the arrows she had made and laid them on the stone entry to the pass. She tied and retied her sandals. She opened a pack and took out leather leggings and laced them around her legs. She went over to where Meion was lying beside a fire with his eyes closed.

"I am going to turn Phoebe loose. I tied her in the small pasture. Do I have time?"

"If you hurry."

"Where is Nidde?"

"Right here. On the other side."

"He's been quiet all night."

"He is listening."

"I'm going then."

"Go on." She went down to the pasture where she had left the goat and untied her. "If they breach the pass, run away as far as you can. I have loved thee, old goat of goats, famous goddess of goats, famous for your hard head and fine milk." Auria hit her on the rump and Phoebe moved a few feet away. She lifted her head and stood in the moonlight casting a perfect goat shadow on the dry grass. Auria walked over to her and kissed her on the nose. "You will find me if you wish, I suppose. If not, then there will be one thing less that belongs to me. Unless the idea of you will stay with me, like your shadow." Phoebe bent her head and ate a piece of grass and Auria went back to Meion. The noise of the approaching army was louder. They were visible now, appearing over the hill, starting across the meadow, almost welcome after so much waiting. Auria saw the first rows of them approaching. A sudden great excitement happened inside of her and she lifted the bow and took the first of her arrows and fitted it into the thick twisted gut string.



The Spartans came in phalanxes to the entrance to the pass, four men abreast with their shields raised to present an impenetrable barrier. Still, Leucippius's archers were ready for them and found openings, and the poison tips of the arrows did their work. The first four men fell before they reached the entrance between the rocks. The second four fell across their bodies and for a moment the spirits of the defenders sailed to the skies. They drew their arrows again and more Spartans fell. Still, they kept on coming. The lines of attackers thickened and widened, seeming to stretch out forever across the field. The more of them there were, the harder it was to find a place to put an arrow. As the Spartans came up the pass, the defenders poured the cauldrons of boiling water down over them. The Spartans backed off for a moment, then came forward again, this time with footsoldiers bearing scaling ladders for the boulders where the archers were standing. Nidde pushed off the first ladder with his arms and watched it fall. He turned to push off the second ladder and was pierced by a spear. He fell from the boulders like a bright crazy bird, flailing out into the moonlight. Auria saw him fall and strung another arrow into her bow and shot it into the shoulder of a man on the ground, then another and another. Meion was on top of a boulder fighting off a man with a spear. He used it to push off the second ladder and it fell to the ground with its load of men. Then he turned and ran to Auria. "It's a rout," he said. "We must run now. There is no way."

Auria whirled around on her heels. The night was filled with light. The moon seemed as big as the sun, bigger and brighter than a thousand suns, and the woods were far away and there was no place to run to, no way to escape. She shook off the terrible brightness and moved back against a boulder and fitted another arrow into her bow and took careful aim and hit the first man scaling the third ladder. She took a breath and found another arrow and hit the second one. Meion grabbed her arm to drag her with him down the path. She shook him off and pulled one last arrow out of the quiver and shot a man in the arm. He dropped his spear and threw back his head so that his visor fell back. She reached for an arrow thinking she would shoot him in the eye, thinking she would wound and harm him, blind and kill him, destroy him, leave him torn and send him forever from the world. She was wild with excitement. There was light everywhere, a world of light and arrows flying straight to their mark. Meion dragged her with him down the path. He pulled her along with him. They stumbled and fell down the rocky path and crossed the meadow where Phoebe had been grazing and entered the safety of the woods. "Run," he said. "Don't think of anything."



At the lake the first phalanx of Peloponnesians came over the wall with scaling ladders while rafts of archers made for the shore of the lake. The lake was covered with mist. Cold white milky air rose from the surface of the water and made it impossible to aim at the rowers with any accuracy. A loon called out. He kept calling all during the battle.

Ionius's troops had been halfhearted about this expedition. Now that they were here, however, they broke into wild bursts of enthusiasm. This was going to be an easy way to win a victory and a procession.

Ladder after ladder was brought up and placed against the wall and one by one the soldiers scaled them and dropped down onto the other side looking for someone to engage in battle. Clarius was killed by the first rush of attackers. He was hit by two swords at once, flailing out with his own and laughing hysterically at the insanity of his death.

Leucippius was seated on a raised piece of ground in the middle of the field. He shot arrow after arrow into the men coming over the wall and then at the men coming ashore on the rafts. Auria's poison was effective. When he made a hit it seemed to have a great effect. His guard was falling all around him. Finally there were only two left and a press of attackers were moving towards him with their shields before them in tight formation. He waited until they were only fifty yards away, then took his knife and cut his wrists and laid them on his legs and watched the blood spurt over his robe, twin fountains of blood that would save him a trip to Athens to see the Parthenon. He turned his head and saw the retreating back of Penelaiaa as she took an arrow between the shoulder blades and fell forward across the grass. There was another way to live, he thought. But I have forgotten what it was.



Elen picked up a sword and charged the soldiers. She managed to stick the point into the shoulder of a young man from Tanagra. He killed her with a knife and picked up her body and held it over his head and flung it into the lake. He had no idea she was the trophy he had come to collect. He threw her body far out into the water, then went over and stood in the shadow of a deserted tower to tend his wound. Looking up, he saw the shield of Zeus begin to cover up the moon. He did not know if it was a good sign or a bad one. He had never been taught what to think of such a thing.

. . .

Ionius's boy, Kalithea, climbed up on the barricade. It was very bright. His sword was in his hand and he was dizzy from the mead and shivering from the cold. His cloak was too long and was in his way. He had taken the pills his mother gave him and crushed them into a powder and mixed them into the container of wine in Ionius's tent, thinking he would run away during the battle. Now he was having second thoughts. If he could get back and empty it before the battle ended no one would be the wiser. No one poured Ionius's wine but him. He jumped down on the other side and watched the confusion of men fighting and men arriving by boat. He saw one of Leucippius's arrows strike a man in the neck. The man fell forward and Kalithea ran wildly across the field and up into the woods, dragging his sword behind him.

Meion and Auria had started up the mountain, making for the caves, moving along the path that skirted the camp through the woods. Auria had thrown away everything but a knife she had taken from a body. It was beautifully weighted, bladed on both sides, polished and sharpened to perfection. She held it in her hand and ran in front of Meion. I will know what to do, she told herself. Clarius said the boat was in the harbor at Iphaii and there are people on Lesbos and also Megales who will take us in. Also, we can go back to the hut. I will know what to do. A way will open for me.

"Auria," Meion called to her.

"Don't talk, just climb. Follow me."

~

Kalithea picked his way through the trees. He had always hated and feared the dark. He hated and feared almost everything. He hated his mother who had sent him away and he hated Ionius for desiring him and he hated himself for being an object of desire. He picked his way through the scratchy brush. Behind him were loud shouts of jubilation. The shouts rose, then fell, then rose again. He must go back. If he did not go back he would be nowhere. He felt for his knife and moved it to the front so it would not be in the way of his sword. It was hard to move in the underbrush wearing armor and carrying a sword. Everything was wrong. He stopped and looked up between the high branches of the trees. A shadow was moving across the moon. Everything became very still. The shadow grew. The stillness increased. The sounds of battle stopped. It was the sign to end all signs. The old ones were taking the earth back into their power. The world would end. He would never get home. Kalithea trembled. His butt hurt and his legs were scratched and itching and he didn't know how to get back to where he had been. The shadow completed its journey across the moon. There was no light anywhere. He ran forward and stumbled out onto a path. Someone was running up the path. He lifted his sword to cut the intruder down. It was a child, a girl. He raised his sword again but something kept him from striking the blow. Auria stopped and jumped to the side. "Who are you?" she said. "What are you doing here?"



"I don't know," he said. He turned. A second person was there. Meion charged the boy and ran a spear into his side and Kalithea fell across the path. His sword fell at Auria's feet. She bent to pick it up but she could not bring herself to touch it. "Let's go," Meion said. "There may be others. Do not touch anything. Leave it there." The sky was bright again. Their shadows fell across the body of the boy. "He is only a child," Auria said, and she was weeping. "It is only a boy."

"Go to Kleis," Meion said. "Lead the way. Don't look back. Don't think of anything." Auria turned her face up the mountain. She felt her jaw tighten. She saw the big eyes of Kleis shining up at her and she held her hands out and breathed the universe into her lungs as Philokrates had taught her to do and turned and began to climb.



Far away, in a village near Sparta, the mother of Kalithea woke in her sleep feeling a terrible pain in her legs and got up and went out into the courtyard and looked up at the sky. The brightness of the stars and the brightness of the moon were unbearable and yet she could not stop looking at them. As she watched, a great shadow began to move across the moon and cover it. She ran back into the farmhouse and found one of the smaller children and took him into her bed and curled her body around his. She was thinking of Kalithea, who was her oldest child, of when he was a small thing, before he was taken away for the army. How he would lie in bed with her at night and tell her stories he made up. They were stories about birds that flew down to the olive trees and offered to take him to the heavens to dine with the gods in exchange for being allowed to eat the olives. "I must go and ask permission of my mother," he told the birds. "She does not like me flying off without permission, as I am precious to her."

I will make him a shirt of white cotton, his mother decided. A short cape to cover his shoulders from the sun. Yes, I will buy that thread I saw in the village that Provia makes. If the olive crop is good this year I will buy that and weave him a cape. I will have it sent to the place where he is serving the famous generals of our army. She curled her arms and legs around the small one and tried to sleep, dreaming of weaving a cloak for her child.

In the confusion caused by the disappearance of the moon Nidde pulled the spear point from the muscle beside his ribs and, holding his side together with his hands, he began to roll towards the shelter of the trees. Then, when it was completely dark, he stood up, still holding his side together, and walked into the woods and lay down beneath a great plane tree and began to talk to his body, telling it to knit itself, talking in the soft old language he had known as a child, a language that fell syllable by syllable like water and made more sense than any language he had learned since.

# Epilogue

Now three years had gone by and Auria and Meion had built a house in the valley near Clarius's hut. It was built on a rise overlooking the stream that flowed from the cave. It was a rectangular house of sun-dried brick and wood, four rooms surrounding a courtyard in which Auria had planted persimmon and fig and lemon trees. An arbor for white grapes was along one wall and one for black grapes along the other. On one side of the house was a long central room surrounding a stone hearth. Here there were brightly painted lockers with the names of the children carved on them, Kleis and the twins, the girl Leiakes and four extra children whose parents had been lost in the battle. Across from the lockers was a birchwood loom where Little Aeo had taken to sitting all day, weaving wonderful rugs and pieces of cloth, singing to himself about the high mission of artists as he threw the leaded weights back and forth across the woof. The weights were made of lead he had won in a dice game at the camp and sometimes he would stop his weaving and laugh out loud, remembering the face of his opponent when he had rolled the winning pair.

There was also a baby two years old, a child Auria had given birth to a year after the battle of the camp. His name was Celisius and he was a fat boisterous little boy with bright curls all over his head and a loud voice. He liked to sleep with everyone in the household and would wake in one bed and go and find a spot in another. The Wanderer,

Niddebak called him. Wackewacke. Nidde had found his way to them some months after they came back to the valley, arriving early one morning with a great white scar across his ribs but in no way changed. "How did you heal it?" Auria had asked him a dozen times. "What did you do?"

"I went to a place where deer give birth and held myself together with my hands while it sewed itself back up. The deer came and looked at me and were kind. I have promised not to kill another stag in return for their kindness."



"What did you eat?"

"What was around me."

"You are not telling me all that happened."

"If I told you that spiders wove me back together would you believe that? If I told you a black bear brought me fish or that birds delivered berries from the sky, would you say, this Niddebaknidde is a great liar and believes animals and insects can speak and are watching men with their bright watery eyes?"

"Then I believe it. What else happened?"

"I closed my eyes and my blood came rushing into my side and turned cold at the sight of my poor flesh torn by a spear and built a dam of cold dried blood that grew black, like a great beehive, and then fell to the ground. Then a deer spoke to me and told me snow had buried me in the night and I must wake or die and never see my friends again, so I stood up and with great courage walked to the camp of Braseus and there was cared for. They had buried those of our dead they could find when the Spartans left. They made a great pyre beside the lake and burned the men and women together. Tell me again of how you escaped?"

"When we came to the caves there were other men of our fellowship there and we marched out together, many of us, almost forty, and when we came to the great dividing pass, where the mountains go up and become Thrace and Boetia, most of the people went that way but Meion and Keffee and Little Aeo and the children and I made our way here."



"Well, I will leave you now and go and make plans to go to Ethiopia," Nidde said. It was his way to end all conversations.

Nidde had made a home for himself on the other side of the stream and lived there alone. He was always talking of going to find a wife but he never got around to it, although he disappeared from time to time in the direction of Sounion, always returning with a new horse.

Below them on the plains the Athenians and their allies and the Spartans and their allies continued to fight and lay waste to each other's fields and sink each other's ships. News of the battles and victories found its way to the valley. Men and women came there often to consult with Auria about broken bones and to buy the salves and tonics she made or to talk to Meion about irrigation. He had devised a system of pipes to bring water from the stream to the pastures during the summer droughts, and men came to study his designs.

Outside the house, and joining it by a passageway, was a kitchen over which Kefallinia presided, although she threatened nearly every day to quit and sit in the sun while someone else did the work. There was a beautiful double oven of sundried brick and a square oak table with benches and a stack of cypress bread boards.

At the back of the house was Auria's room, a square room with three windows. In the center of the room was a painted bed, with coverlets from Aeo's loom and pillows made from the linings of ducks' nests. The walls of the room were painted red and blue and violet and ochre. They were painted with scenes from Auria's childhood at the villa of Meldrus Helonai. She had painted portraits of everyone she could remember, with words below the pictures to tell what the people were doing. There were portraits of Philokrates and the Thracians and Kleis's mother and sisters and Metis and Phoebe and other animals.



In the late afternoons Auria would leave the house and follow the path of the stream or wade along its edge where it meandered down to the pasture. It was a stream that came from a source deep within the earth, where the rain of centuries had soaked down through the thin soil of the mountainsides, down through cold gray limestone and back up to become a stream which watered poppies and iris and horsetail and goldenlight and juniper rue, whose power against evil is so strong that it is called, in all languages, the herb of grace. It will ward off plague and is an antidote for everything from toadstool poisoning to snakebite and is believed by some to promote second sight and comfort the heart as well.

When Auria grew tired of the people around her she would take Metis and follow this stream until she was rested and ready to go back home. Then she would stoop down and take part of the stream into her hands and lift it to her mouth. All things are water, she would say to herself. But what of mountains? she would answer, and she would see Philokrates' face shining up at her from each thing that waters, blooms or tears the earth's shell in search of light.

The paper in this book meets the guidelines for permanence and durability of the Committee on Production Guidelines for Book Longevity of the Council on Library Resources.

Designed by John Langston

Library of Congress Cataloging-in-Publication Data

Gilchrist, Ellen, 1935–
Anabasis: a journey to the interior: a novel / by Ellen Gilchrist.
p. cm.
ISBN 0-87805-726-9
I. Title.
PS3557.I34258A78 1994
813′.54—dc20 94-19473
CIP

British Library Cataloging-in-Publication data available